Divi
the Susp
Cristina Sumners

THIEVES BREAK IN

"The setting is seductive, the writing pleasurable, the characters congenial, the atmosphere cozy and the thrills muted." —*Los Angeles Times*

"It is the author's success in cozy knitting—a sufficiently intricate plot, satisfying characters, mildly adventurous picturesque setting—that attracts my admiration. . . . A satisfying who-done-it." —*Mystery News*

"Cristina Sumners' inspired Divine Mystery series may well be the answer to a cozy fan's prayers—a touch of humor combined with a well-conceived plot." —*Peninsula Post*

"This rich, intricate story is one to savor. Sumners' narrative powers are such that everything comes alive. . . . Sumners' second divine mystery is simply divine." —*Romantic Times*

"A real treat . . . literate, fun and filled with pleasantly eccentric characters." —*Booknews* from The Poisoned Pen

"Dazzling . . . Sumners is so skilled. . . . Characterization is really at the service of the plot." —*Drood Review of Mystery*

CROOKED HEART

"A winner . . . [for those who] thrive on Jan Karon's Mitford novels and Adriana Trigiani's Big Stone Gap series."
—*Sante Fe New Mexican*

Yea, mine own familiar friend, in whom I trusted,
which did eat of my bread,
hath lifted up his heel against me.

Psalms 41, verse 9
King James Translation

FAMILIAR FRIEND

CRISTINA SUMNERS

Bantam Books

FAMILIAR FRIEND
A Bantam Book / August 2006

Published by
Bantam Dell
A Division of Random House, Inc.
New York, New York

This is a work of fiction. Names, characters, places, and incidents either
are the product of the author's imagination or are used fictitiously. Any
resemblance to actual persons, living or dead, events, or locales is entirely
coincidental.

Bantam Books and the rooster colophon are registered trademarks of
Random House, Inc.

ISBN-13: 978-0-553-58432-5
ISBN-10: 0-553-58432-4

Printed in the United States of America
Published simultaneously in Canada

www.bantamdell.com

OPM 10 9 8 7 6 5 4 3 2 1

This book is for my son,
who turned twenty-one
the week I finished it.

Tim, always remember three things:
I love you.
I'm proud of you.
The future belongs to you.

ACKNOWLEDGMENTS

The time has come to pay tribute to the splendid town of Princeton, New Jersey. I lived there for two years while I finished up my undergraduate degree at Vassar College by taking courses at Princeton University and transferring the credits to Vassar. The Seven Sister colleges, you see, in the years before they and the Ivy League universities went co-ed, kept losing their students when they upped and married Ivy League guys before they graduated, so the Seven Sisters figured out this transferal-of-credits scheme.

Princeton in the mid-seventies was a great town; I loved it. So much so that I modeled the town of Harton after it as just about everybody knows who is familiar with Princeton and has read my first novel, *Crooked Heart*. This book returns to Harton after taking my two detectives, Tom and Kathryn, to England for the action of novel number two, *Thieves Break In*.

This book also very much involves their parish church, St. Margaret's, which is modeled after Trinity Church in Princeton, where I was confirmed at the ripe old age of twenty-six. I grew up a Presbyterian and still have a great respect for that church: it taught me the value of excellent preaching, to name only one thing. But I fell in love with the Middle Ages when I read Chaucer in college, and I kinda thought I wanted to become a Catholic. But having grown up *terribly* Protestant, I didn't think I could go all the way to Rome, so I settled for becoming a high church Anglican. I was at Princeton at the time, so I took instruction from the University chaplain, was confirmed at Trinity Church, and spent my first two worshipping years as an Episcopalian there, learning those heretofore unfamiliar hymns (and weren't they glorious!) and growing accustomed to the liturgical year (I can still remember the fragrance of the evergreens they used to deck the place in Advent; Trinity Princeton has the best sense of festival of any parish I have ever had the good fortune to live in). As you can tell, I cherish a fondness for that parish to this day, some thirty years later.

Which is why I hope they'll forgive me for planting a dead body in "their" driveway. But that's how I got my start writing murder mysteries. The only blot on my life in Princeton was that I was unhappily married; I went for marriage counseling at the University's Roman Catholic Chaplaincy, Aquinas Institute. That wasn't as crazy as it sounds; one of the priests there, a lovely man named Walter Nolan, had been happily married, but his wife had died, so he had become a Catholic priest. At the time I lived in Princeton he had quite logically become Aquinas Institute's resident marriage counselor. I'll be forever indebted to him because, with his compassionate under-standing, he helped me break free from my dead-end marriage. But I digress.

My appointments at Aquinas were at nine at night, and afterward I took the shortcut home through the Trinity Church driveway. One witchy October night, when the air was fresh and wicked and all the shadows were danc-ing, as I reached the darkest part of the drive, I thought to myself, "This would be a *perfect* place to find a body!"

Well, you see, I'd read Nancy Drew as a child and then switched to Agatha Christie at about ten, and then pro-gressed to Rex Stout and on to Ngaio Marsh and Dorothy Sayers and P. D. James, so what can you expect?

So I went home and started to write a novel about a young woman who was miserably married and was com-ing home from a marriage counseling session and found a body in her church driveway. The story of how this be-came not my first novel but my third to be published is long and complicated, and I won't bore you with it.

But I do want to tell you how it got to be twenty-five years between the beginning of that novel and my first novel getting published. I didn't have faith in myself. I worked on it in bits and pieces of spare time, but I said to myself that I couldn't justify spending *real* time on it because it was just a fantasy. People like *me* don't turn into published novelists. I'm telling you this so that you don't do the same thing to yourself.

If you have an idea for a novel, SIT DOWN AND WRITE IT! Have faith in yourself. Do not cheat yourself out of a quarter of a century of a writing career, as I did.

Oh, and get yourself a great agent. I did. Her name is Linda Roghaar, and she is worth her weight in sapphires.

CHAPTER 1

The destruction of Tom Holder was carefully planned. Joel took months producing a suitable scheme.

He began with the principle that a man should be attacked at his weakest point. Studying Holder, his life, and his activities as best he could from a careful distance, Joel soon decided that Holder's weakest point must surely be Mrs. Holder. Louise.

The woman dressed like a bag lady. Mismatched articles of clothing hung off her dispiritedly, as if they knew they had no business being together. The hems of her skirts were amazingly uneven. Her blouses were so many decades out of date that they could not have been obtained anywhere but thrift shops. Sweaters and jackets were dragged inefficiently over these blouses so that sometimes the arms were fully into the sleeves and sometimes not. Frequently these ensembles were tied together with dreadful knitted scarves that seemed to be of the lady's own making.

It was obvious that her husband earned enough money as Harton's police chief to keep her in proper clothes; for one thing, they lived in a perfectly respectable house. Small, and nothing fancy, but a good, middle-class house, not a slum. And of course the man dressed decently himself. Joel concluded that Mrs. Holder must actually choose to dress the way she did, and therefore she must be seriously touched in the head.

It was necessary, therefore, to observe the wife, even strike acquaintance with the wife, without the husband knowing these overtures were being made, and since the husband was a policeman, some subtlety was called for. One of the first things that occurred to Joel was that he could not possibly stalk Mrs. Holder in his own car.

He had not yet decided whether he would, in the end, reveal himself to Holder as his tormentor or whether he would prefer to remain forever tantalizingly anonymous. If he wanted to leave the latter option open, it was important that Louise not be able to furnish any information that might lead to him. Therefore he could not follow her around, learning her schedule and habits, perhaps ultimately park in front of her house and pay a call, or strike acquaintance in order to work some scam on her, unless he abandoned his own conspicuous car for some more forgettable vehicle.

So it was that early on a crisp autumn morning Joel drove to Newark Airport, parked his red LeBaron convertible in long-term parking, and caught a shuttle bus to the car rental cluster. Guarding against the possibility that at some future point an attempt might be made to trace his movements all the way back to this relatively innocuous beginning, he timed his arrival well. He wanted to go unnoticed, lost in the early morning rush hour, and he hit it exactly on time. Every line at the Avis counter was three deep in drowsy travelers who had arrived on the various red-eye flights from the West Coast.

None of the lines appeared shorter than the others; wanting another criterion for choice, Joel glanced at the clerks behind the counter. He would choose the one least likely to pay any attention to him, the one most likely to be doing the job on autopilot.

Joel had been reared in reasonable affluence. As in most places in America, that meant he had been reared in mostly white neighborhoods, gone to mostly white schools and a mostly white college, and worked in mostly white workplaces. He was afflicted, therefore, with that almost universal American racism, that faint, unacknowledged, embarrassing, never-to-be-admitted assumption that black people are, on average, just a bit less bright than white people are. So he got in the line where the clerk behind the counter was a young black woman. In fairness to him, it should be said that his racism was exacerbated by his conservative taste in hair fashion; the front half of the girl's head was covered in golden cornrows and the back half was an explosion of orange frizz. And she was wearing purple dangling earrings that were at least five inches long, for heaven's sake, and shiny.

What Joel did not realize was that the earrings were shiny because they were made of titanium, which cost a pretty penny indeed, and Loreen Sanchez could afford them because she was not just one of the clerks at the Avis office at Newark Airport, she was the manager, and therefore drew a hefty salary. In fact, at twenty-two,

Loreen was the youngest manager of a major airport Avis office in the country, and she had earned that position because she was as sharp as eight barrels of tacks. Joel had picked the wrong line.

"Good morning, sir! How can I help you?" Loreen beamed at Joel with her "red-eye smile," a nice combination of bracing friendliness and sympathy; she'd been working on it for years and it was very good. It made customers feel she understood how miserable they felt.

They went through the routine: he wanted a midsized sedan, no, he didn't have a reservation; he needed it for two weeks, yes, he'd be bringing it back to Newark, no, he didn't need insurance, he'd be insuring it with his regular insurers in Harton.

All the while these uninspiring transactions were going on, Loreen Sanchez's mind was ticking fast. It was perfectly clear to her that this customer had not been on a plane all night. He had none of the signs, and if anybody knew the signs, Loreen did. People didn't get off the red-eye with trembling hands and eyes ever so slightly wide with excitement. This guy was *wired*, and it wasn't because he'd been drinking coffee all night. This wasn't caffeine; she knew caffeine. This was something else. And it was something wrong.

He lived in Harton; that was about an hour and a half drive from the airport; obviously he owned a car, because he had a car insurer in Harton. If he needed a spare because his own was in the shop, it would have been a hell of a lot easier to rent one in Harton. He'd driven, or taken a taxi, all the way to Newark to rent a car other than his own. That seemed to indicate some need for secrecy. It could be something as relatively innocent as an affair, which would have been none of

Avis's business. But if the guy was going to rent an Avis car and do something illegal with it, it could turn out to be very much their business. Not that they could be held accountable, strictly speaking, but still . . .

Risking the customer's impatience, Loreen gave him a huge smile, begged his pardon, gathered up his papers, and said she'd be back in a moment. Retreating to the office where she couldn't be seen, she made a photocopy of his driver's license and insurance card and then wrote a few terse sentences on the photocopied sheet, a practice she invariably followed when a customer made the hair move on the back of her neck. She then put the piece of paper in a special file.

She returned to the counter with yet another smile, the customer's license and insurance card, Avis's rental papers, and a set of car keys, and handed them over.

The customer took these items from her with an urgent haste that only served to exacerbate her misgivings. He managed, barely, to throw her a breathless "thanks" over his shoulder as he stalked hastily away.

Out in the parking lot, Joel felt as though he'd escaped from something, but he wasn't sure what. The way that black girl had looked at him! As if she suspected him of something! But that was stupid, she couldn't have known anything, he was just renting a car. He gulped in huge lungfuls of the cold, welcome air, and strode along the rows of identical trunks until a number painted on the asphalt told him he had arrived at the beginning of his vengeance.

CHAPTER 2

It was one of those magic nights that October frequently produces in New Jersey. The leaves made speckled golden haloes around the streetlights, and the air was sharp and restless. Mason Blaine marched briskly down the sidewalk that ran along the shadowy street where he lived. He congratulated himself on his habit of walking to and from the campus as long as the weather was good. Some of those lazy young fools on the faculty drove everywhere. Stupid of them. They'd only get fat and unfit. And they missed the pleasure of being alone on a night like this, walking along, crunching the first fallen leaves underfoot, enjoying the rustling dark. It was nights like this that Halloweens were made of. A witchy night. That little breeze, stirring the leaves. Nights like this, you could see why people used to believe in elves. All those movements in the shadows, if you were the fanciful type— Out of the corner of his eye Blaine caught a movement that did not seem to fit into that kind of fancy. He turned to see what it was, but too late.

An annihilating blow struck the back of his head; he actually heard the crunch as his skull buckled like a broken egg, but thanks to the effect of shock, and the fact that he was unconscious if not dead by the time he hit the ground, he felt no pain.

The figure holding the crowbar stood for a moment hoping a wild heartbeat would subside. Deep breathing was supposed to help. Everybody said deep breathing helped. But it was taking too much time, and there was no time to waste. Quick: to the car parked at the curb. Open the trunk. Put the crowbar back in. Close the trunk. Drag the body onto the floor of the backseat. Close the door gently. Get in the car. Drive away discreetly. It was a quiet neighborhood. Keep it quiet.

An intermittent breeze bestirred the leaves to confidential whispers among themselves, and beyond the reach of the streetlights the shadows were alive with the movements that had reminded Mason Blaine of elves.

It was lost on Tracy. She was walking home from her session with Father Edwards, and her brain was too heavy with trouble to notice the mischievous air. Everything was awful. It was so bad, she could hardly believe it. She wondered how long she could endure it. And when she couldn't endure it any longer, what then? Divorce was no more a viable option than murder. You couldn't break a promise you made to God. Or before God. But wasn't every promise made before God? Was marriage that particular? Wasn't— No. Never mind. No good speculating. Divorce was out. There could be no escape that way.

Escape. Wouldn't it be lovely. Just to vanish. Just to slip out on a night like this, and not come back. A night like this, Tracy thought, noticing it for the first time. Yes, if one wanted to vanish, this would be a perfect night for it. There was something fresh and wicked about the air. The trees were doing subtle little dances in the breeze, uttering soft susurrations to one another.

She was walking along Stocker Street from Augustine Institute, and turned to take her usual shortcut on the single-lane driveway that cut through the grounds of her parish church, St. Margaret's. As she got farther from the streetlight behind her on Stocker Street, the night darkened around her. Her impression of the supernatural quality of her surroundings intensified. Yes, this was a night for vanishing. Plenty of shadows to disappear into. No, that wasn't a shadow; that was somebody disappearing into one. No. Yes? Hard to say. Her imagination, probably. And that lump in the driveway ahead was *not* a lump, it was just another shadow.

The leaves rustled, and all the shadows moved, and things that his grandmother would have called leprechauns played just outside the circles of the streetlights. But Sergeant Flannery was deep inside the building, and ample amounts of brick and glass shielded him from the sort of weather that could provoke such fantasies. Not that it mattered. Sergeant Flannery would not be brought to contemplate the existence of leprechauns were an army of them to stomp across his desk. No, Sergeant Flannery's fantasies did not run in that direction. They ran straight home to his wife.

She'd have a fire going, now, and would bring him a hot toddy. And she'd be wearing that new robe, that pink thing. He liked that pink robe. Damn night duty anyway. Especially night duty at the desk. Talk about *dull*. Not that days were that exciting. In a town this size, a traffic fatality was a major event. Oh, God, that last one. No, better to be dull than that. Not the thing to think about. Think about Nancy.

His gaze wandered over the deserted lobby of City Hall. The Police Department was separated from the lobby only by a thick glass wall, and from the desk Sergeant Flannery had an excellent view of lots of modern sofas and potted plants. It was a scene he knew by heart. But suppose Nancy were to come in. Just to say hi. Just to bring him some cookies. Just to give him a kiss. Suppose she came to one of the front doors over there, and pushed it open. She'd walk across the lobby toward him, smiling. She wouldn't say anything, because the glass wall would be between them. But she'd walk across, smiling . . .

She was running.

He shook off his drowsiness and sat up straight, frowning. A girl—no, a young woman—was running across the lobby toward him, and she was plainly terrified. She wrenched open the glass door, stumbled into the room, and clutched at the front edge of the desk for support.

"There's a body," she gasped. "At least I think it's a body. I mean, I think he's dead. He must be dead. In the driveway—the St. Margaret's Church driveway—"

"Now, now," said the sergeant, coming out from behind the desk to pat her on the shoulder. "Calm down. You want a drink of water? It's probably just a drunk, you know, passed out on the ground. We get 'em sometimes like that."

Tracy shook her head emphatically. "No," she said.

The Sergeant smiled tolerantly. "You got a lot of experience with dead bodies?"

"No," Tracy admitted.

"Then what makes you so sure this guy isn't a passed-out wino?"

"There's a knife in his back."

"No shit," said Sergeant Flannery, who never said things like that in front of ladies.

It was only about forty yards from the front door of City Hall back to the church driveway, but Tracy found her legs unsteady, and it seemed like a long walk. She was leading a couple of highly interested policemen back to where she'd seen it. Good Lord, suppose it wasn't there? *Could* she have imagined it? Anything was possible, with this night full of whispering leaves and restless shadows.

The leaves whispered, and the shadows moved, and the sharp air carried hints of fireside tales of creatures that you never glimpse. Kathryn, numb from hours of tension and dizzy with fatigue, stood motionless at her front door, feeling the soft sting of the air against her face.

"Oh, God," she whispered, "Mother of All Beauty, it is too fine a night, too witchy a night, to feel as ragged as I feel." Instead of entering the house immediately, however, she turned her back to the door and leaned against it, savoring the cold, and whispering a fragment of one of the Prayer Book canticles: "O ye stars of heaven, bless ye the Lord, Praise Him and highly exalt Him for ever; O ye dews and frosts, bless ye the Lord—" Suddenly she chuckled and said in a somewhat louder voice, "O ye ghosties and ghoulies and long-legged beasties, bless ye the Lord! O ye things that go bump in the night, praise Him and highly exalt Him for ever!

"O.K., Koerney, that's it for you for the night," she scolded herself, turning and dragging her keys out of her pocket.

She entered the house, shrugged off her coat and hung it on the newel post, then scowled at her reflection in the front hall mirror. "My dear," she said, "for a clergybeing, you are a sorry sight." She fumbled with her collar buttons. "Fie on the Methodists anyway for inventing these damn-fool things," she muttered, tossing the buttons and the stiff white collar into the cut-glass bowl on the table under the mirror. She began to take the bobby pins out of the remains of a braided twist at the back of her neck. She had added three pins to the collection in the bowl when a formidable matron came surging down the stairs.

"Kathryn? My dear, do you know what time it is?"

"No, Warby, but I don't suppose it could be much later than two A.M."

"No, seriously—it's after ten! Have you had anything to eat?"

"I got a sandwich out of a machine at the hospital while the doctor was checking him over."

"How is the boy?"

"O.K. now, I think. They gave him a sedative, and put him in a room without sharp things or cords or anything. I'm mostly worried about what the Seminary will do. Do Presbyterian seminaries keep people who've tried to kill themselves?"

"My dear, I don't know! Ask somebody at the Seminary. But do you think, after this, that he'll want to? Go on with it, I mean?"

"I don't know what he'll want, and frankly, after four hours, I'm too tired to care. I'll pick it up again tomorrow. Meanwhile, what *I* want—"

"Is your supper."

"No, matter of fact, I don't think I could eat. Just something to untie this ferocious knot in my neck. A cuppla fingers of Scotch."

"Of course. Shall I bring it to your room?"

"Oh, thanks. But make it the living room. I think I have need of a bit of Mozart before bed." Kathryn turned toward the living room, but as she did so, the telephone rang. Mrs. Warburton, in the act of scooping Kathryn's paraphernalia out of the cut-glass bowl, saw the look on Kathryn's face.

"Shall I tell whoever it is that you're not here?" she asked. "Or asleep already?"

"Asleep already. I'll call 'em back tomorrow. Thanks."

Mrs. Warburton vanished in the direction of the kitchen, and Kathryn went to the living room to rummage through her CD's. Almost immediately, however, Mrs. Warburton reappeared.

"It's Tracy Newman. I think you'd better talk to her."

Kathryn looked at her housekeeper in surprise, then walked over to the telephone. She sank with a sigh into an overstuffed chair, and picked up the receiver.

"Hello, Tracy?"

"Oh, Kathryn! Oh, thank God you're home—I don't know what—oh, dear."

Kathryn forgot instantly that she was tired. "Tracy, for heaven's sake, what's wrong?"

"Oh, it's—I'm rather shaken. I'm at the police station. I just found a dead body in the St. Margaret's driveway, and they want—"

"You *what*?"

"I just found a dead body in the driveway of the church, yes, I'm serious. They want to talk to me—the police, I mean—and I've called Jamie to tell him I'll be home later, but I—well I'm afraid—he'll—he'll get sort of antsy—and I know I shouldn't ask, but I was just wondering if you could possibly—"

"Of course I could. Glad to. I'll go right over. But Tracy, what sort of a dead body? A heart-attack dead body? A run-over-by-a-car dead body?"

"A knife-in-the-back dead body."

"Tracy! My God! It wasn't somebody from the *parish*, was it?"

"No. No, they made me look at his face, and it wasn't anybody from St. Margaret's."

"Well, thank God for that." Then, as though hearing what she'd just said, Kathryn made a noise that sounded like "Ungh." "*That* was selfish, wasn't it? I suppose I ought to say a prayer for his soul, whoever he is, and obviously we'll all be doing that on Sunday. But still, if I'm perfectly honest I have to admit that I'm glad he's not one of ours. Selfish, as I said. But *anyway*, ye gods, girl! You're walking home and you discover a dead body. That sort of thing isn't supposed to happen to real people."

"Yeah, that's what I keep telling myself, only it doesn't go away. And it's worse because I'm thinking what kind of a mood Jamie is going to be in, sitting around waiting for me to come home."

"Relax. I shall hasten over to your place and pour bourbon down his throat."

"I think we're out of bourbon."

"I'll take my own bottle."

"I can see your halo from here."

"Dazzling, isn't it? I'll be off right away. You take care of the police, I'll take care of Jamie, and we'll see you at home soon, I hope."

"Sure. Thanks, Kathryn."

Kathryn hung up the phone and sat still a moment. Then she emitted a sound that started as a howl of anguish and wound up as a fit of giggles. Mrs. Warburton, who had tactfully retired to fetch the Scotch, returned at this moment. Observing Kathryn's state, she asked hesitantly, "Is everything all right?"

"Oh, yes, yes, Mrs. Warburton, everything's just *lovely*, I can't *believe* what a charming day it's been I simply don't know if I can *endure* any more delightful things happening in my day; Tracy has crowned it all by tripping over a corpse in the St. Margaret's driveway and I'm off to soothe the savage husband"—she plucked the drink from Mrs. Warburton's hand and headed for the hall and up the stairs—"which, as we all know, is a thing that cannot be done in clericals, as Savage Husband gets but savager at sight of Mere Female Dressed Like Priest, ergo we must assume some frillier and less threatening vesture, and while I go up and change would you, please, dig up the fullest bottle of the best bourbon we've got, and stand by the front door with it so I can grab it as I go out?"

Mrs. Warburton blinked, opened her mouth, shut it, blinked again, and said, "Of course, dear."

Kathryn left a few minutes later, dressed in slacks and sweater of a deceptively feminine pink, and carrying a bottle of Jack Daniels. She never drove to the Newmans', as it was only a five-minute walk. But this time when she got to the curb, she actually paused by the car for about ten seconds. She was incredibly tired. But as she reached for her keys she suddenly realized she was also angry, and she decided not to drive. Better to walk it off.

The first two minutes of the walk she spent glaring at the sidewalk and thinking that if Jamie weren't such a bastard, his wife wouldn't have needed to ask a friend to go pacify him while she was delayed by the police, which meant that if Jamie weren't such a bastard Kathryn would be listening to Mozart and getting ready for bed right now. The third minute of the walk she spent pointing out to herself that most of her anger was not righteous wrath at a husband who picked on his wife, but her own irritation at being dragged out of the house when she was bone-tired. The fourth minute she spent reminding herself that it was Tracy who had dragged her out of the house, and it was less than honest to be mad at Jamie just because Tracy lacked the guts to stand up to him and tell him to get off her back. The fifth minute Kathryn spent deciding that it was high time she stopped putting all the blame on the husband just because she was partial to the wife, and also high time she engaged in some serious prayer on the subject of her animosity toward Jamie Newman. By the time she rang their doorbell (one of six desecrating the door-jamb of a nineteenth-century house on Merton Street) she was informing herself that she was overly judgmental, emotionally dishonest, and long overdue to see her spiritual director. As Jamie descended the stairs she scrapped the whole discussion, shoved it to the back of her mind, and braced herself to be civil.

Jamie opened the door, and lit up with real pleasure.

"Hey, I'm glad you're here; big news! I tried to get Cunningham, but he hasn't left the library yet. You'll never guess what's happened."

"You're right, I wouldn't, but I don't have to guess. Tracy called me from the police station, which is why I'm here; you know me and my vulgar curiosity. By the way, I hear the bourbon supply in this house is negligible?" She held up the bottle.

"Negligible? It's nonexistent! And you are a doll." He took the bottle, put an arm around Kathryn and kissed her neck with an exaggerated smack. She repressed a shudder. He swept her up to an apartment on the second floor. "We do have some Scotch, you'll be relieved to hear, though it's nowhere near up to your standards."

"Jamie, you'd be surprised by my standards; bring it on."

"Neat, and water on the side?"

"How well you know me."

As Jamie busied himself in a minuscule kitchen, Kathryn looked around in the cramped living room for a place to sit down, but books and papers seemed to cover every surface. Jamie came back, observed her dilemma, laughed heartily, and said, "I'm hopeless! Once I get going, the papers go everywhere!" He surveyed the scholarly clutter for a minute, then said, "Here, you hold these"—he handed her the two glasses—"and I will tell Garcia Lorca he must yield to a lady."

With these words he scooped a stack of books out of a dilapidated armchair and began to look for another place to put them, making jokes about his untidiness, and talking to the authors of the books about minding their manners. Kathryn watched him playing the amusing host, returned his smiles with a few smiles equally expansive but less sincere, and wondered for the fiftieth time why on earth Jamie Newman couldn't expend some of this overly-deliberate charm on his wife.

When finally both of them had seats and drinks, Jamie inquired brightly, "Well, what do you think of the body in the driveway? You're our murder expert, after all."

Since the last homicide case in which Kathryn had been involved had been the murder of someone she dearly loved, this remark was horrifically tactless, and Kathryn decided to simply wait in silence until Jamie figured this out. It took him about four seconds.

"Oh, Kathryn, I'm so sorry, I shouldn't have reminded you—"

She waved a forgiving hand. "It's all right."

"What I meant was," Jamie continued, trying to cover his embarrassment, "do you think the guy was mugged, or what? I mean, that driveway is pitch black and deserted—I've told Tracy, if I've told her once I've told her a thousand times, I do *not* want her walking around this town after dark—*now* look what happens—if she'd been a few minutes earlier it might have been her."

"Jamie, I really don't think so. This town is actually quite safe after dark, at least in the university area, under normal circumstances. Consider it, how stunned were you to hear about a corpse in the St. Margaret's driveway? This is not a normal event for this neighborhood."

"Well, whether this was a mugging or not, it *could* happen in a place like that, and I don't want Tracy walking around at night this way. She doesn't have to go there at night. She could talk to Father Edwards anytime during the day. Why Thursday nights?"

Kathryn knew as well as Jamie that Father Edwards had set the Thursday night appointment time as being most convenient for himself, and that Tracy had politely accepted it. Kathryn also knew, better than Jamie, that his irritation was really not over the time of the appointments, but over his embarrassment at having his friends know that his wife went for marriage counseling. He himself had refused to go.

Jamie stalked over to the window and peered out. "No sign of her yet. God, she's taking her time."

"I daresay it's the police who are taking her time."

"Well, what am I supposed to do in the meantime? She promised me she'd mend the lining in the sleeve of my corduroy jacket so I could wear it tomorrow, and now she'll probably say she's too tired."

"That's no problem. Give it to me."

"Oh, I couldn't ask you—"

"You didn't ask me. I volunteered. What's the matter? Afraid I'll botch it up?"

Jamie grinned. "I don't know. *Can* you sew? I mean, doesn't that fancy housekeeper of yours do all those menial chores for you?" He went into the bedroom to get the jacket, leaving Kathryn to remind herself not to get angry.

She mended the jacket while he continued to fume about his wife. When she reached the limit of her patience, she abruptly changed the subject.

"You know, Jamie, I don't think this body is the victim of a mugging."

Jamie was an academic, and as such always up for a good argument. "What makes you think so?"

"Well, for one thing," Kathryn mused, "assuming a mugger was stupid or inefficient enough to kill rather than merely disable his victim, why leave the knife behind? Why not take it along to use for his next job? And another thing: There are a dozen places within ten minutes' walk of here that are just as dark and deserted as the St. Margaret's driveway—consider Prosper Gardens for instance—that are *not* directly across the street from the police station. If you were going to set up as a mugger around here, surely you wouldn't do it under the noses of the police?"

"You're saying it's an actual murder?"

Kathryn set another careful stitch in the sleeve of the jacket. "I don't know. I'm just saying that as a mugging, it seems to have a couple of holes in it."

But Jamie's imagination was off and running. "O.K., then, let's look at murder with a capital *M*, by which I take it we mean the deliberate killing of a particular individual. You wouldn't do *that* under the noses of the police either, would you?"

Kathryn considered this rebuttal for a couple more stitches, then looked up at Jamie with a mischievous smile. "Depending on the individual, it might be the best place to do it."

"Oh, I hate it when you go clever on me," Jamie complained.

"Let's say, for instance, somebody wanted, God forbid, to kill Tracy. If they were intimately acquainted with her schedule, they would know she walks from Augustine Institute back to this house shortly after ten P.M. every Thursday night, taking the shortcut through the St. Margaret's driveway. All they'd have to do is hide in the dark there with a suitable weapon. It wouldn't matter that the police station is across the street because the police aren't in the church driveway. Speaking of police."

The sound of a car was heard pulling up outside the house, and as the car door opened they heard the unintelligible rasp of a police radio. They looked out the front window to see Tracy getting out of a patrol car.

"I hope that's just a courtesy," Kathryn said. "I'd hate to think she was so done in that she needed to be given a ride the length of two blocks."

Jamie rushed down the stairs to greet Tracy with husbandly solicitude, while Kathryn went to the kitchen to gather ice, vodka, and Kahlua. She emerged from the kitchen as Jamie was leading Tracy to the sofa.

"Poor baby! Was it awful? Now you just sit right here and calm down, and we'll get you something to— Oh."

Tracy extended a hand to take the black Russian Kathryn was offering, and thanked her. To Jamie's fluttering she held up a hand and said, "I'm all right."

"Then tell us about it. We've been arguing about whether it was a plain old mugging or not. Kathryn says not. She thinks it's a real live murder."

"Well, she's right. No question of mugging. His wallet was still on him, with lots of money in it. Would you like to know the victim's name? I can tell you now."

"I guess so," said Jamie, "but you said it wasn't anybody you recognized."

"I said it wasn't anybody from St. Margaret's. If I said it was somebody we knew, but couldn't tell you who, you'd be worried for fear it would be somebody we'd care about."

"Oh," said Kathryn, "all right, I'll bite. Who is the gentleman with the knife in his back, whom we know, but whom, I gather, we do not care about?"

Tracy announced, giving appropriate weight to every name, "Everett Vergil Mason Blaine."

"Tracy!" Kathryn gasped.

"Jesus!" Jamie exploded.

They both began to talk at once. How did she know? Was she sure? Did the police know who he was—or *what* he was?

Tracy assured them that she was quite sure, and that the police knew.

There was a deep, stunned silence.

Kathryn muttered something unintelligible and crossed herself.

Jamie murmured in a hollow voice, "My God. I was talking to him an hour ago. He's *dead?*"

"Very," said Tracy. "Exceedingly. Most carefully dead. Twice dead."

"Twice dead?" her audience chorused, in perfect unison.

"Yes. I told you he had a knife in his back. Well, he also has a cracked skull."

Again she was besieged with a garble of questions, but Kathryn flung up a hand and commanded, "Wait! Quiet! We are getting nowhere. Tracy, just tell us what happened, the whole thing; begin at the beginning, and tell us every blessed detail, and we will try to be quiet."

Tracy groaned. "I should have made a recording." She took a long swallow on her drink, and began, with dull patience, to recite: "I left Father Edwards at ten-ten. I know, because I looked at my watch as I left, to be sure I wasn't going to be later than usual getting home. I left the grounds of Augustine by the end of the driveway that lets out onto Stocker Street. I began to walk up Stocker toward the church. There was very little traffic. I didn't notice anyone else on the sidewalk. I turned into the St. Margaret's driveway to take the shortcut to Merton Street. It looked the same as it always does: dark. There was a breeze, and so the trees were shifting around a bit making for a lot of moving shadows. As I came to the bend in the drive, about in the middle of the church property, where it's particularly dark because it's farthest from the streetlights at both ends, and there are all those heavy evergreens, I thought I saw something in the driveway ahead of me. I got closer and saw that it was a man stretched out on the ground. I stopped. I was frightened. I didn't know if he was dead or sick or what. I thought it might be someone who'd had too much to drink, and I might find myself in a difficult situation if I woke him. But the longer I looked, the less he looked like a man asleep, and even drunks don't usually pass out in the middle of an asphalt driveway when there's grass handy. So I walked up to him, very quietly, and when I got about five feet away I saw"—she took an audible breath—"I saw that there was the handle of a knife sticking up out of his back. I dropped my purse, turned around, and ran like mad. By the time I got back to the street, I had figured out that the thing to do was keep running, right across the street to the police station. I went tearing in there like a banshee and I'm sure the guy at the desk thought I was crazy. I said, 'There's a dead man on the grounds of St. Margaret's Church, at least I think he's dead,' and the cop said, 'What makes you think he's dead, it's probably a drunk,' and I said, 'He's got a knife in his back.' The cop started yelling and pushing buttons. A couple of other policemen came from somewhere, and they asked me to show them where. I went back across the street with them and showed them. They started looking around, shining flashlights around. One of them asked me to tell him how I found him. I think the other one felt his pulse or something to see if he was dead. Then the cop who was talking to me asked if I knew who the dead man was, and I said no, I hadn't even looked at him, because it never occurred to me it was somebody I knew and besides, I couldn't see in that light. And he held up his flashlight and said would I mind, and I said no, though I wasn't real turned on by the idea, so we went over to the body and he shone the light on the face, and even though he was lying on his face, the head was turned a little in our direction, and it was easy to see that it was Mason Blaine. Of course I couldn't believe it, so I stood there, staring, and finally knelt on the pavement to get closer, but there was no mistake, and I think I just said, 'Good God,' or some such thing. And the policeman said did I know him, and I said, 'This man is the Chairman of the Spanish Department at the University,' and the cop whistled, and said was I sure, and I said I was. Then I got up and went over and sat on the grass and just watched. Lots of people started coming. One of the first, thank God, was Tom Holder. I must say it's nice, when you discover a body, to have the Chief of Police be a member of your church. Anyway, there was an ambulance and photographers and things. Somebody collected me and took me back across the street to the station, where they offered me a chair and a cup of coffee and my purse, which I'd entirely forgotten about, and which one of the police had picked up. Then I told Tom and thirty-two other people about how I found the body, until I was sick and tired of telling it, especially since there's not that much to tell——I mean, what can you say? 'I was walking down the driveway and I saw him lying on the ground.' Period."

"But what about the cracked skull?"

"Oh, right. I overheard that in the police station. The doctor—whatever you call him, medical examiner—said that the knife didn't kill him, that he'd been hit on the head with something first, and that killed him, and by the time the knife was put in him he'd already been dead several minutes. At least."

"Sounds like somebody wanted to make very sure he was dead." Kathryn looked thoughtful.

Jamie disagreed. "I think it sounds like somebody hated him so much, he had to kill him twice because once wasn't enough."

"Granted, given the character of Mason Blaine, that's not at all unlikely, but doesn't it seem to you that if somebody was just indulging in an orgy of hatred, he would have beaten his skull to a pulp with whatever he hit him with in the first place, rather than hit him on the head, and then stab him in the back?"

"Maybe he did beat his skull in, and then stabbed him. Tracy?"

"No, it didn't look like that, and I'm not sure I want to discuss it."

Kathryn allowed as how that was understandable. "What I'd like to know is, what was Mason Blaine doing on the grounds of St. Margaret's Church at this time of night?"

"Yeah, what about your neat theory about somebody walking through there at a regular time every Thursday night, the way Tracy does?" Jamie demanded. "It's a sure thing Mason Blaine didn't do that."

"That's right, you said you were talking to him an hour ago. Where? Where is Mason Blaine on Thursday nights?"

"Goodrich Library, teaching a seminar. I oughta know. I'm in it."

"No, really? And you were there tonight?"

"I certainly was, and so was he, alive and healthy. My God!"

"What's the matter?"

"It just hit me. Tracy, you found him at ten-ten?"

"I left Augustine at ten-ten. I must have found him about ten-fifteen."

"The seminar adjourns at nine-thirty, and a few of us were talking with him afterwards out in front of the library. Then we said good night, and he walked off in the direction of Prosper Street, and we all went over toward the Student Center."

"Jamie," Kathryn said, "you were probably the last people to see him alive. I think you'd better call the police."

Jamie, clearly delighted, fairly leapt at the telephone. Tracy sighed. "I *thought* I was going to get to go to bed."

Jamie was already explaining to the police who he was, and that he'd been talking to the murder victim a half hour before he was found dead, and that furthermore he was well acquainted with the victim, and might be able to tell them lots about who the deceased knew and what he did and so on. When he hung up he looked gratified. "They're sending somebody right over," he announced. He saw Tracy's grimace, and added, "Oh, that's O.K., honey, they've already talked to you. You can go on in to bed, and we'll keep it quiet out here. I think I'll go put on some coffee."

Jamie bustled out to the kitchen, and Tracy smiled ruefully at Kathryn. "You seem to have done a good job," she said quietly. "I'm not getting reamed out about anything, so he must be in a good mood."

"It was touch and go there for a while, but I mended the jacket for him."

"Oh, ye gods, I entirely forgot about that. Thanks. You probably saved my hide."

"I gave him the opportunity to say how astonishing it was that I could sew, considering I had a fancy housekeeper to do menial tasks for me."

Tracy winced. "I don't know how you put up with that sort of thing."

"I don't have to live under the same roof with it. How you put up with it is the bigger wonder. I think I'll shove off now. Try to get some sleep, won't you?"

Kathryn reached the sidewalk at precisely the moment a police car decanted two plainclothesmen and a uniform in front of her. The most senior of the three hailed her with some surprise.

"Kathryn! You're out late."

"Hi, Tom. Tracy asked me to come baby-sit her husband while you kept her at the station." She extended a hand to him. Had they been meeting at church, the handshake would have been accompanied by an affectionate but perfectly proper kiss on the cheek; under the circumstances, however, Kathryn was signaling to Tom with her stiffly extended arm that she wasn't going to approach him with inappropriate gestures. Recognizing what she was doing, he returned the handshake with equal distance and a tiny smile. Kathryn continued, "I hope you don't need her anymore tonight. She's bushed."

"No," Tom replied. "We've got her story. But we need to talk to her husband. Bit of luck, getting right on to that so soon. We'll have to see the whole group of people Blaine was with, but the rest can wait till tomorrow. You know this guy, Jamie Newman. Tell me about him."

Kathryn wrinkled her nose in eloquent distaste.

"That bad, huh?"

"Yes, but not for your purposes. You want a witness. O.K., you've got an intelligent, articulate man who's anxious to talk to you and as far as I know has absolutely nothing to hide. Go to it." She made a sweeping gesture toward the house.

"Why don't you like him?"

"His wife is one of my best friends and I strongly suspect he's not very nice to her."

Tom asked, "So that's why you were baby-sitting? So he'd be in a better mood when she got home."

"Got it in one."

"Any chance we can pin the murder on him?"

Kathryn smiled sourly. "I only wish. But I can't think of any reason he'd want Mason Blaine dead. But come to think of it, he's about the only person who knows Mason Blaine who *wouldn't* have a reason to want him dead."

"Not a popular man?"

"You might say so. You're going to have fun with this one. Mason Blaine was a murder looking for a place to happen. But let Jamie tell you about it. I'm going home."

Tom watched her walk away with mixed feelings. He was always glad to see her. Too glad. Much too glad. It was all right at church, when he was expecting it, he was used to it, he could control it. But he was working now, he hadn't expected it, and he couldn't afford the distraction. Unaware that he was doing so, he shook his head as if to clear his mind of her. Then he glanced at his Sergeant and said, "Well, you heard the lady. Let's let Jamie tell us about it."

CHAPTER 3

Absolutely," said Jamie Newman. "It's a standing joke in the department. Mason thinks it's beneath his dignity as department chairman to have to teach a seminar at night, and he resents the hell out of the fact that the schedulers this semester broke the sacred rules and scheduled his Golden Age seminar at eight P.M. So, it's supposed to end at nine-thirty, and by God it ends at nine-thirty. On the dot. You can set your watch by it. Mason even makes sure that nobody else is talking or asking a question after nine-twenty-five so that he can wrap it up on time. At precisely nine-thirty he stops talking, closes his notebook, puts his books in his brief-case, and stands up, and that takes him about ten seconds, I promise you. Then he heads for the door of the seminar room, and woe betide the student who stands in his way. You can ask him questions if you tag along beside him on the way to the elevator, and he'll answer on his way through the bowels of the library, but once he hits the main entrance and the open air, he finishes his sentence and then he's off. That's it, he's gone. He marches home. So about a half a dozen of us saw him set off from the front entrance of Goodrich Library at nine-thirty-five at the absolute latest."

"You say he was going *east* from Goodrich?" Tom asked.

"Oh, yes, he always walks home by Prosper Street."

"Was he carrying his briefcase?"

Jamie hesitated. "He must have been. He always does."

Tom thought a minute.

"Do you have a map? Of the town, I mean? Mine's in the car."

"Sure, somewhere in my desk, just a second—"

Tom studied the map a minute, then asked Jamie for another cup of coffee. As Newman left the room Tom whipped out his cell phone, punched a number, and muttered, "Flannery? Listen, tell Colczhic to leave four people at the church and hold it tight and I mean tight, I don't want Trenton chewing my ass. Get everybody else over to Blaine's house, 315 Patterson Road. Tell them to start on foot *in the street*, stay off the sidewalk, moving back along Patterson toward Lovell. Then if you haven't found anything, split up." Tom outlined the three possible routes Blaine could have walked from Goodrich Library to his house if he had started on Prosper Street. "What you're looking for is Mason Blaine's briefcase. If you find it, for God's sake don't come within ten feet of it. And don't let anybody else either."

Jamie came back with the coffee and Tom thanked

him for it. Then he asked Jamie if he could remember all the students who had been in the group who had seen Mason Blaine walk away from the library that night. With a little hemming and hawing, Jamie managed to come up with all the names, and Sergeant Pursley wrote them down. Did Jamie know their addresses? Sure, they all lived at the Graduate College. And they would all be at the Spanish Department at 9:00 A.M. the next morning for various classes. Tom remarked silently to himself that certain aspects of this case, at least, seemed to be arranging themselves conveniently.

Then he began to ask more general questions. What kind of person had Blaine been? Did he have any enemies?

"Well! *Enemies*. That's a very strong word. I wouldn't know about *enemies*, precisely. But as for what kind of person he was, well. I suppose this is not the time to get all polite and not speak ill of the dead, right?"

"I'd appreciate it if you'd just tell me the truth."

"Well, the truth is that Mason Blaine is an arrogant bastard. *Was* an arrogant bastard. He was the world's greatest expert on the Golden Age of Spanish Literature, and he's the main reason some people came to study here, but nobody liked him, least of all his own graduate students, the ones he directly supervised, because he treated them like dogs."

"In what way?"

"Made them fetch and carry, made them Xerox stuff, do secretarial work that wasn't properly their work to do. And all the time acting like they ought to consider it an honor, and not even thanking them for it."

Tom scratched his head. "Doesn't sound like much of a motive for murder."

"Oh, God, no!" Jamie exclaimed, horrified. "I wasn't suggesting it was. I was just telling you what sort of person he was. You *did* ask."

"So I did. Well, was there anything else about him, more than being unpleasant to his graduate students, which you can tell us about? Something, I don't know— *bigger?*"

Jamie shrugged his shoulders and looked stumped.

Tom tried again. "In Blaine's wallet it says in case of accident notify somebody in Virginia. Obviously he wasn't married. Didn't he like women?"

Jamie smirked. "I'd say he liked them too well to settle down to one."

Holder's eyebrows went up. "O.K., if he had more than one, how many and who were they?"

"Oh! Well!" The smirk vanished. "I don't mean to give you the wrong impression. I don't really know anything about his private life—well, I guess it's just a matter of a general impression, you understand? Mason *acts* like a ladies' man, so everyone assumes he is one. You know how it is."

Holder knew how it was, all right. Jamie Newman had assumed, quite suddenly, the elaborate nonchalance of the incompetent liar. Tom went after him, politely (at least at first) but thoroughly. Surely he must have heard something said? Even casually? Something, perhaps, he didn't believe? Didn't students always make jokes about their teachers? Had jokes, comments, wisecracks, been made about Blaine's, uh, appreciation of women? Couldn't Jamie remember any of these comments or wisecracks?

He couldn't. He was awfully sorry, but he couldn't. They had all been so general, so patently absurd. "You know, things like, Mason bought a raffle ticket and won a date with Angelina Jolie, but he wasn't interested because she was too old for him. Things like that, just silly jokes. There was never any real *content* to them."

Tom Holder was stymied. He was used to witnesses who lied stupidly, who could be tripped up by cross-questioning. But this young man, though he lied badly—that is, you could tell he was lying—did not lie stupidly. He talked a lot and said nothing, so you couldn't challenge him. And he was quick, quick enough to make up something to say that sounded real, like that Angelina Jolie bit. If it hadn't been for that breezy manner, he would have been very convincing.

It might not be important, this thing Jamie Newman didn't want to tell the police, it might be only that he wasn't sure about it and didn't want to repeat gossip, it might not be anything *guilty*, exactly . . . but then again it might. What if, for instance, Jamie didn't want to say anything about what women Blaine had been fooling around with because one of them had been his own wife?

But as soon as Holder had the thought, he canceled it. No, Mrs. Newman was not the type of woman that men fooled around with. A plain, skinny little thing, with short black hair and scared eyes and a funny mouth. Holder had been surprised to find that her husband was so remarkably good-looking. Yes, an attractive fellow, no doubt, but what was he *hiding*?

When Tom's cell phone rang, it didn't seem to him that anything productive had been interrupted. It was Flannery.

"Sir? Colczhic just called in. They found the briefcase."

"Where?"

"Patterson Road, about twenty yards west of Blaine's house. On the path on the north side of the street."

"Tell Colczhic I'm on my way. And tell him I said good job."

Tom extricated himself from Jamie's hospitality (Didn't they want more coffee?) as rapidly as civility would allow, and went down the stairs with Sergeant Pursley eager in his wake.

As Pursley drove his superior to Patterson Road, he had a question. "Uh, Chief? How did you know where to look for that briefcase?"

The temptation to appear omniscient was strong, but Tom Holder was a modest man and honest to boot. "I didn't know for sure. But Blaine had it when he left the library, and it wasn't with the body at the church, so I figured he dropped it when he got whacked as he was walking home."

"Oh!" Pursley digested this statement, knowing he was being honored with the Chief's confidence. "You think he got whacked walking home and the body was *taken* to the church?"

"Yep."

"But why couldn't Blaine have walked over to the church, or driven his car, or gone in somebody else's car, and then been killed over there right where we found him?"

The car rolled to a halt at the traffic light by the First Presbyterian Church, and Holder restrained himself from telling Pursley to run it. After all, the briefcase wasn't going anywhere. But he was excited. "Well, if you promise not to tell anyone, Purze, I'll let you in on it. It's not my brilliant powers of deduction. I just got a feeling, a strong feeling."

"You mean a hunch?"

Holder meant a conviction, but he knew Pursley wouldn't grasp the distinction. "Yeah, call it a hunch. I just looked at that body and knew that the guy hadn't been killed there, he'd been put there after he was dead. Fifty bucks says the Trenton guys will bear me out once they check over the ground."

The car moved again. "Then what made you think he was killed walking home? I mean, just because he wasn't killed at the church."

"Just because it's simple. If he was taken to the church after he was dead, you're right, it could have happened several ways. He might have been riding in a car when he was killed. He might have been in his house. Or in somebody else's house. Or anywhere. Or he might have been walking home and somebody was lying in wait for him. I decided to try that one first, because from the standpoint of the killer it's the easiest. You don't have to persuade Blaine to get in your car or let you in the house or anything like that. You just hide behind a bush with a baseball bat and wait for him. So I tried the simple theory and I got lucky. Let's just hope my luck holds."

A knot of dark figures stood on the north side of Patterson Road; there were flickers of flashlights among them. Pursley pulled the car up a few feet away, one of the figures hurried forward and became recognizably Colczhic, and Chief Holder was hustled over to look at the prize. This he did from a cautious seven feet, raking the ground with the flashlight he had plucked from the deferential hand of one of Colczhic's underlings. "Have you disturbed the ground around it?"

"No, sir, we spotted it from about ten feet off and none of us have come any closer than we are now."

"O.K.," said Tom, "the chances of anybody else having dropped this briefcase here are about eight million to one, but I'd give a month's salary to be able to prove this is Mason Blaine's before we call Crime Scene."

"If you'll come around here, sir?" Colczhic led his superior by a rather circuitous route to a spot on the opposite side of the path. "You have to get down pretty low, sir," he apologized, telescoping into an easy squat that Holder's middle-aged knees duplicated with more difficulty.

The beam of Colczhic's flashlight insinuated itself between the ground and the top of the briefcase, where the leather curved up toward the clasp. About three inches of the underside of the case was visible in the tiny wedge of light. "E.V.M.B.," Holder pronounced, with immense satisfaction. "Beers all around. Now rope it off."

At this point there was nothing left for the Harton crew to do but wait until the crime scene team arrived from Trenton. Tom left Pursley in charge of the Patterson Road site. He himself returned to the driveway of St. Margaret's Church, where he again gazed down upon the body of Mason Blaine and became, if anything, more convinced that the man had not met his end in the place where he was lying. And it wasn't just because they'd found his briefcase over on Patterson Road. The briefcase was merely corroboration. Tom had been certain before that. *Dead certain*, he said to himself grimly.

CHAPTER 4

Kathryn emerged from fathoms deep, cursed her ringing alarm clock, and repeatedly whacked the snooze bar. Finally she dragged herself out of bed, assembled herself in record time, threw herself down the stairs, and plumped herself down at the breakfast table just in time to avoid the gentle recriminations of Mrs. Warburton. Tea, orange juice, toast, and one egg over easy magically appeared. Mrs. Warburton sat down opposite Kathryn with a bowl of oatmeal and a face full of curiosity, and Kathryn did her best to fill her in on the previous night's adventure between bites, but there wasn't much time. It was one of the mornings Kathryn was scheduled to assist Father Mark at the 8:00 A.M. Eucharist at St. Margaret's before going off to the Seminary to teach her classes.

Kathryn lived only three blocks from the church and they were pretty magnificent blocks. The pre-Revolutionary houses were the element that impressed most people, but Kathryn was more impressed by the maple trees, which at the moment were decked in their gaudiest autumnal finery. It was one of those diamond-bright days when the air is clear and sharp as a knife. Kathryn hugged her coat around her and felt intensely thankful to be alive, and began to talk to God quite specifically about it.

As she neared the church, however, two things intruded upon her happy thoughts. First she became aware, from some distance, that the church grounds—the *entire* church grounds—were marked off by yellow police crime scene tapes. Next, as she got closer, she saw the Rector and Tom Holder and heard their familiar voices in unfamiliar heat. The Rector's voice, in fact, was rapidly rising in volume.

Tom was on the inside of the tape. Father Mark was on the outside, tall, handsome, silver-haired, and incandescent with fury.

Kathryn had never seen him more than mildly cross, and she was shocked. It was like looking at a stranger.

"What the *hell* do you think you're doing?" he was shouting at Tom.

She couldn't hear Tom's reply because it wasn't as loud as the Rector's; it was clear Tom still had some slim hold on his temper, but it was also clear that the hold was tenuous and loosening fast. Tom was gesturing, obviously explaining that the people crawling all over the place on their hands and knees were completely necessary and so were the yellow tapes.

It did him no good.

"It's a sacrilege!" yelled the Rector. "Do you realize my congregation is arriving for Eucharist any minute now? How are they even supposed to get in?"

Kathryn was now close enough to hear Tom reply, "We'll station a man at the Stocker Street end of the driveway to tell people to come around to the Merton Street side. And we'll have a man at the gate there"—he gestured again—"to lift the tape so people can get in."

Father Mark fumed in silence for about three seconds, then pronounced, imperiously, "All right. But I want all of this crap off the premises, and all of these people, by *noon*, do you hear me?"

"Where the *hell* do you get off telling me how to do my effing job?" Tom yelled full in Father Mark's face, while turning an unaccustomed shade of purple. Every single member of the Harton police force, not one of whom had ever heard the Chief raise his voice in anger, stood with mouth wide open. The crime scene team from Trenton all stopped what they were doing as if prepared for a brief sideshow. Kathryn had arrived at the curb across the street from them, close enough to be heard without shouting.

"Tom! Mark!" she cried in a voice like cold water.

Both men whirled to face her. To their credit, both looked embarrassed.

"Tom," she said levelly, striding across the street, "I suggest you return to your work. Mark, you and I have a Eucharist to celebrate."

Tom jerked his head in a nod, turned on his heel, and went to speak to one of the Trenton team.

Kathryn took the Rector by the elbow and forcibly wheeled him to face the gate Tom had indicated. As she marched him up the sidewalk she scolded under her breath, "Mark, for God's sake, what's got into you? If it's a sacrilege, it's not Tom who committed it, it's whoever murdered Mason Blaine. Tom and his gang are just trying to clean it up. And you can't tell the police to vacate a crime scene because you don't like them cluttering up your pretty little garden!"

"Kathryn," the Rector replied frostily, "we are not talking about a pretty little garden, we are talking about a *church*."

"It wouldn't make a particle of difference," Kathryn replied, undaunted by the Rector's hauteur, "if it were the Holy Sepulchre. It's a crime scene. It's going to get treated like one. Don't you want this guy caught, the guy who parked a corpse in our driveway here?"

Father Mark was unlocking the side door to the church. "Of course I do."

"And do you really want one of your parishioners strolling onto the church grounds and accidentally tripping over and destroying forever the only clue that might have caught him?"

Father Mark had arrived at the vestry door and was unlocking it. He sighed. "Why did I ever invite you to be on the staff of this church?" he wondered aloud. "You can be so intensely annoying."

"I can, can't I?" Kathryn agreed placidly. "By the way," she added, slipping off her coat and reaching for her vestments, "you haven't forgotten we've got an appointment this afternoon at four, have you?"

"No, I haven't. What are we talking about?"

"Surprise," said Kathryn, offering further proof of how annoying she could be.

Outside, Chief Holder was listening to one of the crime scene team, who also happened to be one of his poker-playing buddies.

"Not a hope in hell of getting tracks from the tires," Sid was telling him. "The grass is too thick and healthy, as you can see for yourself. You got a pretty place here, you keep it nice. Not like some of the churchyards we see in Trenton."

"Yeah," Tom acknowledged. "It helps to have a lot of millionaires in the congregation to pay the gardeners. Anyway, you're telling me somebody drove off the driveway here, and back on here, right around the place where Blaine's body was lying?"

"Yep."

"Make my day and tell me you can prove they did it last night while the body was lying here."

"No can do."

"Didn't think so, just thought I'd ask. O.K., I'm gonna leave you guys here to get on with it while I get over to the university to talk to people who knew Blaine. If the Rector comes back out and gives you any grief, this is what you do: You talk to him politely, you call him 'Father Randall,' and you make it very clear to him that he owns the inside of the church building but we own the grounds. Until further notice. Period."

"The only thing that's gonna be hard about that is the polite bit. And you weren't so polite yourself, there, a minute ago."

"Well, try to make up for me."

" 'Morning, Tom," a voice sang out behind Tom's back.

"Aw, shit!" Tom muttered under his breath. Sid Garvey tried, not very successfully, to hide a grin. Tom turned. " 'Morning, Nick."

Nick Silverman was the District Attorney.

"How's it going, Tom?"

"Well, we've established that the victim was killed as

he walked home last night from a class he taught at the University library, then his body was moved to here, obviously in a car, though why it was moved we don't know yet. I'm on my way over to the Spanish Department now to talk to the faculty and then to the graduate students he supervised. I've talked to one of those students already, and it seems Blaine was a womanizer, so I'm hoping it's going to turn out to be a woman, you know what I mean, a man behind a woman. That kind of thing usually comes to light pretty fast because everybody knows about it."

"Good. Good. Well, you know I'm always here to help."

"Sure."

"And Tom—"

"Yeah?"

"This one *has* to get cleared up pretty fast. You know why, don't you?"

"Because every newspaper in the state is going to be barking up my ass about it because the victim was the chairman of one of the departments at the University."

"That's one reason. Haven't you noticed the other one?"

"The other one?"

"Tom. That's where your body was dumped, right?" The D.A. pointed to the spot on the asphalt where Mason Blaine had been sprawled. "Now take a tiny little walk with me." He took Tom's elbow; when they got to the end of the church driveway, Silverman pointed to the left, past Augustine Institute, to a huge yellow house, pale in the morning sunshine. It was the Governor's Mansion. Tom swore.

"Exactly," said the District Attorney.

CHAPTER 5

The morning sun picked out the gold lettering on the spine of Professor MacDonald's favorite Cervantes, but he did not notice. He politely thanked the person at the other end of the line, hung up the phone, and stood staring at one of his book-lined walls. He could state, to a volume, how many books there were on those shelves, and he had read every one of them. Any number of them he had taught, and three of them he had written (in addition to some forty-seven articles in sundry learned journals). It was a life's work, a professional passion of thirty-two years, lined up in inventoried rows on three walls of shelves. Ordinarily he derived great pleasure from the sight of those shelves; it was an indulgence he granted himself, to let his eyes wander over his books, while satisfaction welled up inside him like cool wine. But as he stood, his hand still resting on the telephone, it was not satisfaction that showed in his eyes, and for the first time since they had moved into the house, he stood in his study without seeing the books.

After a few minutes he went down the hall to the living room. The living room was large but cozy, furnished in traditional style and in shades of burgundy and hunter green. In a chair at the far end, close to the French doors giving out onto the patio, sat a comfortable-looking lady in a fluffy pink housecoat. She was knitting.

"Henry," said her husband.

"Yes, dear?" She looked up, but her hands continued to make unerring patterns with needles and yarn.

"Henrietta, the most—" He broke off, and made an inconclusive gesture with his hand.

The needles stopped. "John?" She laid aside the knitting. "Come sit down, John." He started toward her, then stopped. She repeated, quietly, "Come sit down, John."

He came and sat down.

He looked at his feet, at his hands, at his wife, at the ceiling, at his wife again. She sat with her hands folded in her lap, an expression on her face of courteous concern. At last he took the plunge.

"Mason is dead," he announced.

Mrs. MacDonald allowed her eyes to widen by a genteel fraction of an inch. "Really? How astonishing. I'd have thought his heart was good for another ten years, at least." Her husband looked at her, tried to make words, and failed. She added helpfully, "Very fortunate for you, of course."

"My God, Henrietta, don't say that!" he cried.

For an instant the eyes widened again, as much in inquiry as in surprise.

He answered her: "He was murdered. Not accidentally killed, not killed by somebody who was trying to rob him." His voice shook. "Deliberately murdered."

Not the faintest trace of emotion disturbed Henrietta MacDonald's face. She looked at her husband without astonishment, without horror, but with great intentness; she favored him with a still, unblinking gaze for perhaps ten seconds, and her silence froze even his nervous hands into temporary immobility. "Not so fortunate for you," she remarked at last.

He couldn't help himself; he laughed. "My dear, you are the most unflappable creature! I suppose it's just as well, it exercises a calming effect on me. But not so fortunate for me, indeed!"

"You have this on good authority?"

"That phone call was from the police. Mason was found dead—ah, stabbed—on the grounds of St. Margaret's Church, last night. Found by Jamie Newman's wife, oddly enough."

"How unpleasant for Tracy."

"Oh. Yes. At any rate, the police have asked me to notify everybody on the faculty, and ask them to be in the Department offices at nine o'clock for—ah, questioning." He smiled weakly. "Sounds ominous, doesn't it?"

"Yes, I suppose it must. It's especially bothersome for you, because Mason's job now falls to you, and everyone must know that you would be glad of that. However, we must hope that the police will soon see, when they meet you, that however much you may have wanted Mason's job, you are not the sort of person who would do anything like that to get it."

His response was enthusiastic, and his gestures became more definite. Of course he wasn't that sort of person! The idea was preposterous, utterly preposterous, of course the police wouldn't suspect him! Such an idea would never occur to them. His wife recognized his lecture voice—or an attempt at it. It wasn't quite right, he stumbled over a word every now and then.

And she wondered that he did not perceive the inconsistency in affirming that a certain idea would never occur to the police, while exhibiting not the slightest hint of surprise that the idea had occurred to his wife. Poor dear. So transparent. He was going to need help.

"But I don't know who on earth could have done it," he was fretting. "It's—it's just incredible. Mason! Who on earth—?"

His wife gazed thoughtfully at a philodendron on the table by his chair. "Mason is not popular," she pointed out.

"Of course not. But you don't murder a man just because you don't like him."

"Well, no, not because you don't like him. But it's not a simple case of dislike, here."

"For God's sake, Henry! People kill people so that they can inherit fortunes from them, and that sort of thing; you don't murder somebody just to become chairman of a department. Hell, there isn't even any money in it. Much."

Really, it was astonishing how obtuse— "I know that, John, and when I said it wasn't a case of simple dislike, I didn't mean you." She abandoned her perusal of the philodendron and looked, carefully, into her husband's face. "You will enjoy being Chairman of the Department, yes. You will get a raise of perhaps seven thousand dollars a year. I'm sure the police will look the matter over and leave you out of it almost at once. You would have become Chairman on Mason's retirement, anyway. And in any case, John"—the placid gaze focused into a long, unblinking stare—"Mason has never been any threat to you."

"Mason's never been any threat to anybody! Pompous old ass, and alcoholic to boot!" He pushed the philodendron aside and reached for the cigarette box on the other side of it. Two of the cigarettes fell to the floor; he made an annoyed sound and picked them up.

Henrietta, who never directly disagreed with her husband, did not do so now; she watched him light one cigarette and restore the other to the box, then endorsed his opinion of the late Chairman, merely adding that it was a pity that someone like that should be in a position where he had so much power.

Professor MacDonald considered this statement for a couple of drags, and was about to reply when his wife transferred her attention to the *Ficus benjamina* in the corner behind him and asked, in a tone too diffident to hold any hint of admonition, if he had indeed notified the people the police had asked him to call.

"Oh, God, what time is it? Eight-fifteen. Forty-five minutes. Yes, I'd better get on it." He moved toward the phone at the other end of the room.

He nearly dropped it in the middle of dialing the first number when Henrietta asked, without looking up from the knitting she had resumed, "Have they asked to see Charles Caldwell?"

In thirty years it had never dawned on John MacDonald that his wife's air of old-fashioned fragility was deceptive. He had chivalrously refrained from sullying Henry's ears with the choicer bits of departmental gossip, and he continued to be unfashionably attracted to what he believed to be her prim naïveté. Henrietta, for her part, would not have dreamed of disillusioning him;

so when he harrumphed and coughed and fumbled with the phone and asked why on earth the police should want to talk to Charles Caldwell, she replied, after a second's hesitation, that she really didn't know, it was a silly question.

She worked her needles, and he stood looking at her for a moment. Then he said calmly, "It's just faculty members they want to talk to, dear, not their husbands or wives. Nothing important, I'm sure. Just to get an idea of who saw him last, that sort of thing."

"Of course, John, that's very reasonable."

"It's all just a matter of routine, you know, this kind of thing."

She agreed with him.

He abandoned the telephone to come back across the room to his wife and pat her on the shoulder. "Everything's going to be all right," he assured her. "There's absolutely nothing to worry about."

She said she was certain he was right, and he was so kind to be concerned about her.

The ring of the kitchen telephone produced something like a snarl from Charles Caldwell. "Oh, damn! Not now!"

"*Very* poor timing," his wife agreed promptly, rising from the breakfast table. "Just when we were settling down to a nice cozy fight."

"We're not fighting!" Charles yelled.

"That's correct. We are not fighting. But you are trying to, and believe me, if you badger me into cooperating with you on that particular venture, you will be sorry indeed!" She effectively silenced any rebuttal by picking up the phone. "Oh, hi, John. What's up?"

Her thwarted spouse glowered at her, but the glower first wrinkled into curiosity, then melted into concern, as Ellen's face went blank with horror, and she began to whisper protests into the phone: "Oh, John, no! *No!* It's—it's impossible!" Then she listened in silence, her head bent, her free hand over her eyes. She had effectively hidden her face from her husband, but her whole posture was eloquent of misery, and he moved over to her and rested a comforting hand on her shoulder. Finally she said, "Yes, sure, John. I'll be there. At nine." She lowered the receiver slowly to its cradle, but she did not raise her head, or lower her hand from her eyes.

"Honey, what is it? What's the matter?" Charles Caldwell turned her to face him, and gripped her shoulders, but she only brought up the other hand to cover her face, and kept her head bowed. "Honey, tell me!" he cried. "Something dreadful's happened—has somebody died? Is it your mother? *Answer* me!" He began to shake her, and with an angry gesture she broke his hold and turned her back on him. Standing behind her, he took her shoulders again, very gently, and whispered, "Someone's died?" She nodded. "Who is it, baby?"

She replied in a small, hard voice: "Mason."

He released her instantly, almost threw her away from him. "Of course I can see that you'd be heartbroken," he sneered. "Pardon me if I don't dry your tears."

"I'm not crying!" She turned on him furiously, as though to exhibit her dry cheeks as proof. "But of course I'm upset. He was— He was a friend of mine." She enunciated the word "friend" perhaps a shade too carefully.

"That much we had established! What has your 'friend'

gone and done to himself? Cardiac arrest while humping his latest mistress?"

"He was *murdered*!" she cried angrily.

"Let me guess," he said, dripping acid. "Your replacement has a husband less tolerant than I am?"

Since she had never struck him, never so much as made a motion to do so, he was caught completely unawares. A ringing slap across his face stunned him, and he barely flung up an arm in time to save himself from the backhand that followed it. He caught her wrists, and in a fury greater than hers, gasped, "Just what do you think you're doing?"

She glared at him a moment; then she saw that the expression on his face was new to her; she had never seen it in any of their fights. He was shocked. No other word for it. He was *shocked*. Then she understood what she had done. She told him. "Getting even. That's what I'm doing. Finally. I've finally done it. For eight years you have used your tongue on me like a club. You have *beaten* me, with words, for your pleasure—"

"You're hysterical! That's the stupidest—" It was his standard response, but this time he didn't get to finish it; she overrode him.

"Yes, damn it, for your pleasure! You *enjoy* yelling. Getting mad for you is like some sort of neurotic recreation. And you will not listen to me when I tell you that I cannot *endure* being verbally *beaten* like that! Well, finally it looks as though I've done something that outrages you as much as your yelling outrages me. Which *hurts* you as much, which *distresses* you as much, as your yelling hurts and distresses me. I think I have just made you hear me for the first time in eight years."

"That's childish," he said, releasing her wrists in a gesture of contempt, and trying to talk through a mouth tightly controlled. The tight mouth was his version of dignity; it made him look petulant. "You're being childish and stupid and I'm not going to talk to you." He turned on his heel and stalked out of the kitchen.

For a minute she stared grimly at the door, which was still swinging, then she followed him to the bedroom. He was putting on his shirt, and he did not look at her when she came in.

"All right, Charles," she said in a voice of ominous quiet, "now you listen."

He turned his back on her, and tucked in his shirttail.

Ellen stood rigid, her arms at her sides and her fists clenched, trying to keep her voice steady. "You abuse me—verbally—any time you damn well want to. You insult me in the grossest way. You choose to think the worst of me in every possible situation. You try your damndest to make me feel as though I'm a terrible wife, and you're the long-suffering perfect husband. And because you're perfect and I'm so terrible, that gives you the right to bawl me out all the time, and now you've gotten to making up absurd and insulting fantasies so you'll have something else to bawl me out *for*, and let me tell you I have had it."

He buckled his belt with shaking hands.

"You yell at me," she continued with suffocated fury, "and bitch at me, and when I apologize for the things that aren't my fault, and confess to sins I haven't committed, and say whatever you want me to say, and try to soothe you, you don't stop yelling."

His face was flushed, and in uncharacteristic silence he examined the tie rack. He still had not looked at her.

"And when I beg you to stop *beating* me like that"—

against her will, her voice was getting louder. "When I say I don't want to fight, why are you *hounding* me, why are you *doing* this to me, you *still* go on yelling and bitching and you're never satisfied till you make me break down and cry, and then you fall all over me and say you're sorry, and you never stop before I cry, because the whole object of a fight as far as you're concerned is to make me cry, you don't care about making a point, you don't care about who's right and who's wrong and what's true and what's not, the whole object of the exercise is to break me down into a whimpering lump so you can play big strong man and comfort me." The tears were streaming down her face, but she had never been further from whimpering; she felt filled with an omnipotent rage, and she berated him in a tone as vicious as any he had ever used on her. "And you won't allow me to stop these—these *hideous* one-sided arguments the only way I can which is by physically *leaving* them, you have literally stood in the door to keep me from leaving the room, you will not *permit* me to simply exit one of these bloody scenes—"

Charles chose a tie he couldn't see, draped it around his neck, and began to work it under the collar of his shirt.

"—And now when *I* at last have made *you* so mad that you feel the way I have felt all those times, so mad you can't *endure* it, now you try to run away from the fight!" She wrenched the tie out of his grasp and mangled it in her hands, and he fought her for it. "Well you're not *going* to get out of it!" she gasped as they struggled. "You're going to know how I felt all these years, you're going to know what it's like to have somebody's anger beating you over the head all the time like a sledgehammer, and you can't escape, it just keeps *coming* and *coming*—"

In a burst of angry power he flung her up against the wall and pinned her there. "Shut up!" he bellowed in her face. His own face was scarlet, and he was trembling. They glared at each other for a minute, both too furious to speak. Then she took stock of his speechless rage, and saw to her astonishment that she had won. She had never won before, but now she had done it, she had turned the tables, she had made *him* powerless. She had done it by presenting him with a fury that was greater than anything he could do to express it, a fury in the grip of which he was helpless. And as she looked at her husband, made baffled and impotent by his own rage, Ellen Caldwell began to smile. Charles colored more deeply; his mouth twisted; she achieved a small, quiet laugh.

Suddenly his hands were on her throat. "Stop it!" he cried, trembling so violently, he could hardly tighten his grip. "*Stop* it!"

Her look of smug triumph vanished; her face began to darken, and she fought for breath, clawing at the iron fingers on her neck. At first anger and breathlessness together contorted her face, but after a few seconds the anger flickered and turned to astonishment, and then, suddenly, to unmistakable terror.

Seeing it, he froze, then willed his hands to relax their grip. Making an effort to control his breathing, he took a step back from her, dropped his hands to his sides, and folded them into careful fists. She remained backed against the wall, her eyes wide with fear. "Oh, come on," he said contemptuously. "Don't pretend you thought I was going to hurt you."

She whispered, "You killed him."

He stared at her for a long minute. The color entirely faded from his face. "You're crazy," he said. It was an observation. Then he said it again, and it was a command: "Ellen, you're crazy."

She swallowed. "Yes," she said. "Yes, of course." She waved a hand before her eyes, as though to clear away an entire scene. "Sorry. I'm upset." She started to move around him, toward the bathroom. "I've got to fix my hair, I've got to be at the department at—"

He grabbed her arm as she passed. "Ellen, you can't think I had anything to do— My God, that's *absurd.*"

"Yes, of course, I said so, I was upset, now *please* Charles, I've got to pull myself together and get over to—"

He took her shoulders in his hands and gripped hard. "Look at me! Just because you were for some stupid reason acting like a goddamn shrew and attacking me physically and I had to stop you, doesn't mean I would do anything to Mason Blaine and you know it, and it's *stupid* and *childish"*—he shook her on each word—"of you to say things like that, and if you go around saying things like that—"

She ought to have been able to fight back. She had been a tower of strength only minutes previously. But the unprecedented physical attack had frightened her, and she was emotionally exhausted. So instead she bowed her head, and flung her hands up to ward off the vicious words as if they were blows. "Oh, stop!" she cried, as the tears started coming again, and her breath began to catch.

"—then what the hell do you think is gonna happen, huh? Yeah? Do you ever think before you say anything? No, Bigmouth of the Year, you do *not*, you just blurt out whatever *childish*, *stupid*, *spiteful* thing comes into your head, it never occurs to you to give a thought to other people for a change, no, you just say whatever you damn well want to—"

A sob broke from her. "Oh, please! *Please!* I'm sorry, I didn't mean it!"

"—because you just have to get your kicks out of making other people feel bad, don't you? Have you ever tried a little thoughtfulness?"

"Oh, please, st-stop!" She sank to her knees, and huddled in a defeated heap on the floor.

He had done it again. Her golden, unprecedented victory was shattered, and there was no reclaiming it. She gave in to great, wracking sobs.

He was on the floor beside her, bundling her into his arms, rocking her back and forth. "There, there, baby, it's all right," he crooned. "Don't cry, honey, I'm sorry, I didn't mean to make you cry; it's all right, baby, it's all right . . ."

He had done it to her again.

In the Drews' house the time between 8:00 and 8:30 in the morning was a period of maximum chaos. Debbie had been hustled off to the bus stop at 8:15, and at 8:30 the carpool would take Meg to the day-care center—provided she was ready. If she wasn't ready, the carpool would leave without her, and her mother would have to take her later, on her way to work.

That extra trip had already been necessary once that week, when, on Monday, Meg's right shoe had not been found before 8:37, at which point it had been discovered behind the toilet, hiding under a damp bath towel.

Consequently Meg's mother, one eye on the clock and one eye on the tuna fish, was putting together a lunch box with dazzling rapidity, while Meg's father mopped up a small pond of milk on the breakfast table.

"Whoops, darling, we've got to be a bit more careful how we pour that, don't we? There you go, all clean, here's another napkin—"

"Meg, honey, you better eat a little faster, it's almost time—"

"Mommy, don't pack those icky cookies, I want the good kind."

"Use your napkin, darling—"

"Which are the good kind, honey? Don't you like these? You ate them last week—"

"No, I didn't, I traded them to Jimmy Richards for a peanut butter and banana sandwich, but his mother won't let him trade anymore, so don't put 'em in, 'cause everybody else hates 'em—"

"Yes, honey, I'll look for the others, but I don't know if we— Oh, my God, Edward, if that's one of your students, tell them the next time they call at this hour I'll personally throttle them."

"Yes, sure, sweetie— Hello? 'Scuse me—You dropped it on the floor, darling, it's right under your chair. Sorry. Oh, hi, John— Well, a bit hectic, you know, trying to get the girls off to school— But John, I teach a class at nine o'clock— The *police?* What on earth—"

Caroline bagged a sandwich, snapped the lid of the lunch box closed, observed that her husband gave all the appearances of a man turned to stone, and swept her younger daughter off to find her coat.

Four-year-old Margaret Drew, breakfasted, lunch-boxed, coated, and shod, was thrust onto the front porch to wait for her ride, and her mother went looking for her father.

He was sitting over his half-eaten breakfast, his elbows on the table, his chin resting in his clasped hands.

Caroline pulled out the chair opposite him and sat down. "You're trying to figure out a way to tell me so it will be most dramatic," she informed him. "Don't."

He looked up with a quick smile. "Touché! Well, then, in the most simple and undramatic form possible: That was John MacDonald. He wishes me to show up at the Department at nine o'clock to be interviewed, along with everyone else on the faculty, by the police, who are investigating the murder of Mason Blaine."

The effect of this speech was entirely satisfactory. Caroline sat bolt upright, gaped, and stammered, "You don't—you don't mean it! The *murder* of— He's actually dead?" Edward nodded. "And somebody *killed* him? I mean, *intentionally*?"

"Looks that way. Not just mugging and robbery. Wallet and credit cards still on him."

"Well!" Caroline said. Then she emitted a little half-breath of a laugh. "Somebody beat me to it!"

"Yes." Edward nodded. "I had a bet with myself that you would say that."

"I've always been curious about these bets you make with yourself. What do you win?"

"The added self-esteem that comes from having figured out my incomprehensible wife!"

She laughed, slipped off her house-shoe, and felt for his foot under the table. "I'm actually such a *simple* creature," she said soulfully, her toes tickling his ankle, and beginning to move up his leg.

"If you're trying to seduce me, forget it. I don't seduce at the breakfast table."

"Why not?" she wondered, with the air of one asking an academic question.

He considered a moment. "I think it has to do with my sense of order, and how my ego is dependent on order. But we're off the subject," he said firmly. "Mason has been murdered."

Caroline tucked both her feet primly under her chair and regarded him with an almost businesslike earnestness. "How do you feel about it?" she asked.

Edward bent his mind to the examination of this entirely relevant question. "Hmmm. Well, stunned. Incredulous, even. Relieved, I think. Yes, relieved. It sounds terrible to say it, but kind of glad; kind of—a little bit—pleased. How about you?"

"Stunned, yes. Very pleased. No 'little bit' about it. Also very worried."

"Worried?"

"Sure. Aren't you?"

"What about? There's nothing to worry about—now. I'll get tenure now for the asking. Hell, I won't even have to ask."

"That's exactly why I'm worried." Her husband looked more puzzled than ever, and she made an exasperated gesture. "Dummy! Don't you see? He was murdered! Naturally you don't know anything about it, but the police are bound to be a pain, at least at first."

Understanding dawned in Edward's eyes, to be rapidly replaced by skepticism. He shook his head. "No. Too far-fetched. Tenure is no kind of a motive."

"Name me somebody who's got a better one."

There was a pause. Then he answered, reluctantly, "John MacDonald."

It was Caroline's turn to shake her head. "He only had a few years to wait."

"But John said himself that the Department wouldn't *survive* for another five years of Mason quote 'pickling our reputation in Scotch,' unquote."

"*Murder* to save the Department's reputation?"

"O.K., O.K."

"I repeat," Caroline persisted. "Name me somebody who's got a better motive than that they were afraid Mason was going to ruin their career."

"It wouldn't ruin my career if I didn't get tenure here!"

"No, but can you convince the police you don't think so?" There was an uncomfortable silence. Suddenly Edward looked up with the light of triumph in his eye. "Charles Caldwell," he pronounced. Caroline's eyes widened a bit. "Of course," she said, and nodded her approval. "Of course."

"Naturally," he replied briskly. "Stupid of us not to have thought of it earlier." He got up. "Anyhow, I gotta run. They want me in—" he looked at his watch, "ye gods, twenty minutes, and I've got to shave."

He bolted for the bathroom and went excavating for his electric shaver among the detritus his daughters had left behind. He found it cunningly hidden under Debbie's bathrobe. He stood in front of the mirror running the shaver over his jaw; Caroline stood behind him, her arms around his waist, her face nuzzled against the back of his neck.

"Are you trying to distract me?"

"Mmmmm. Yes. I don't want you to worry about this—this mess."

"I'm not worried. You know, you were doing this the other day, and it occurred to me that maybe you get some sort of satisfaction out of making me late."

She looked up, an arrested expression in her eyes. "I wonder if you're right? I know I do feel sexy and desirable and all that when I can distract you, but I never thought about it being a matter of trying to make you late."

"Well, I think that's it. It's a kind of control, you know. I know I wanted to make *you* late to that damn meeting last night. I hope I didn't succeed?"

"Oh no."

"Good thing you went, as it turns out. You've got an alibi."

"Alibi?"

"Sure. More than I can say for myself, unfortunately. John said Mason was killed last night as he walked home after his seminar, which would mean nine-thirty or ten. You didn't get home until ten-thirty."

"But Edward," Caroline laughed, "this is ridiculous! Why on earth should I need an alibi?"

"Well, my love, you have been pretty public about how nice it would be if something fatal happened to Mason."

"Silly! Nobody would take that seriously."

"I don't know, Caro," he said slyly. "You're such a tiger, you know; people might well think you *would* kill to protect your cubs!"

"That is the most *ridiculous* thing I have ever—"

"Hey, Caro, I'm only joking!" He put down the razor and turned to give her a playful shake. "Besides, what difference does it make? You were at—"

"It does make a difference! I don't like you saying

things like that. I know you mean it as a joke, but I mean, people might think—"

"So who cares what people think? As long as you were at that meeting between nine and ten it doesn't matter." He looked doubtfully at her a moment. "You were there, weren't you? I mean, between nine and ten?"

She shrugged. "Of course. Forget it."

He started to ask her something else, but she bent her head, leaning her forehead for an instant on his shoulder, then ran her hands slowly up his chest, and looked up at him with a smile that sent ripples down his spine. "You know," she murmured, "maybe I *would* kill for my cubs and you're one of them, of course . . ." She brushed his mouth with a warm, dry kiss, and then chuckled. "That excites you, doesn't it?"

"You excite me, you witch!" he mumbled into her hair, pressing her hard against him.

She gave a soft laugh. "Mmmm. First I'm a tiger," she purred, "then I'm a witch." Her fingernails were doing something on the small of his back. "That's a lot to handle."

"I can handle it," he said thickly, reaching for the sash that tied her bathrobe.

"Edward!" she mocked. "Twenty minutes!"

"They can wait," he said.

CHAPTER 6

Kathryn walked into the vestibule of the Student Center and smiled at the ID checker. "Hi, Mr. Wyble! How are you today?"

"Just fine, Miss Koerney, and how are you?"

"Enjoying the weather, thanks. Is the gang here yet?"

"Yes, ma'am, they're all in there." He waved in the direction of the old dining room. "Mr. and Mrs. Newman, and the Spanish gentlemen, all of 'em!"

Kathryn thanked him, and stepped into the noisy hall. She scanned the crowd for a second, then began to thread her way through the small tables to an alcove at the far corner of the room where the Spanish Department was accustomed to gather. A tall young man with quantities of uncooperative hair emerged from the alcove, and headed for the cafeteria line.

"Patrick! Hey, Patrick!"

He turned and saw her, and flashed a smile that transformed a set of odd features into something unusually attractive. "Father Koerney! What a pleasure!"

"Stow it, Cunningham," she said, extending a hand, which he proceeded to kiss with elaborate grace. Kathryn watched this operation with mild interest, and commented, "You're in a good mood, aren't you?"

"My dear, the sight of you always puts me in a good mood. I hear you went over last night and poured syrup over Jamie until Tracy got home from the police station."

"That's right. I mended a jacket for him, which is what he wanted her home doing."

"With the result that he forgot to chew her out when she got home. You're a good soul, and I shall light a candle for you."

"The next time you happen to be saying your rosary in front of a statue of Our Lady."

"Which will be late in 2024, right. Are you eating? Shall I go through the line with you? I was just going back for some yogurt."

"I don't want to keep you from your lunch—"

"I've already eaten." He took her elbow and firmly turned her in the direction of the line. "Besides, it's a bit of a zoo back there anyway. Tracy's there, her marshmallow of a boss sent her home when he found out what she'd been through last night. The entire Spanish Department, most of French and Italian, half of every other language, and smatterings of a few odd things like math and physics, are all back there crowding around her, wanting to know everything she knows, which isn't much, and wanting to hear—again—all about how she found the body. I think she's told it fifty times."

"How's Jamie taking it?"

"Pretty well. He was feeling a little left out at first, but when twice as many people were sitting at that table as could fit, he moved off to another table and the overflow started coming to him. He got to tell Tracy's story second-hand, and his own talk with—what's his name, the cop—"

"Tom Holder."

"Holder. He got to tell his own story about talking to Holder, so he's O.K. now."

"Patrick, you know what I like about you? You never try to pretend that the people you love don't have any faults."

"It would be pretty stupid to pretend that anybody didn't have faults. And I've known Jamie long enough to have a good idea of what his are."

"You certainly deal with them placidly. How about the rest of them back there? What's being said?"

"Well, needless to say, nobody's precisely grief-stricken. They're all having a grand time trying to guess who did it. Carlos has caused something of an uproar by making it pretty obvious that he thinks the likeliest suspect is Caroline Drew."

"What? You're joking! Even if she were, how could Carlos be such an idiot? To go around accusing faculty wives of murder! Doesn't he want to come back next year?"

"He didn't precisely accuse her. All he did was remind us all—as if we needed reminding—that Caroline said last spring that it would benefit the world in general if Blaine fell under a truck."

"Oh, fun. What happened then?"

"José said that what Carlos was forgetting was that when she said it, all of us heartily agreed with her, including Carlos."

"Bully for José!"

"So Carlos isn't saying much more than that, but he does maintain that Edward won't show up at lunch today."

"Marvelous. I gather he thinks Edward and Caroline did it together."

"As for what Carlos thinks, I've held the opinion for quite a while that Carlos doesn't think at all, but at any rate, he isn't explaining himself anymore. He just sits there looking knowing and hostile."

"Oh, now, that is very good. 'Knowing and hostile' precisely describes how Carlos looks all the time. Shall I go sit next to Jamie and butter him up?" she asked. "Just in case his satisfaction with playing second fiddle wears thin?"

"That won't be necessary. Valerie's there."

"*Damn*. Patrick, what are we going to do? Don't tell me, I know. Nothing."

"Except wait till it blows over."

Kathryn looked bitter. "Does he do this often?" She spoke quietly because they were inching their way through the cafeteria line and there were people all around them.

"He's never done it before. I think the problem is his ego. Jamie's used to being with gorgeous women and then he went and fell in love with Tracy's offbeat wit or something and married her before she knew what he was doing. I couldn't believe it when he brought back this poor little dab of a thing from Vassar and told me he was engaged to her. Then after they were married Valerie flapped her eyelashes at him, and she's much more what he's used to."

Patrick paid for his yogurt and Kathryn for her salad

plate and they began to make their way back across the crowded room.

"I wonder if we could pin this murder on Valerie," Kathryn speculated. "What do you think?"

"I think that's the most brilliant idea I've heard in decades."

As they entered the alcove, a few of the crowd detached themselves from homicide speculations long enough to greet Kathryn and invite her to pull up a chair.

"Thanks, but I think it would be the better part of valor to start a new table at this point, don't you? Hi, Jamie! Hello, Valerie. Thank you, José," she said, sitting in the chair he drew up for her, and waving to Tracy over the heads of her rapt audience.

José asked her if she had heard about their big news; Kathryn assured him she had, and they fell to discussing it.

Patrick looked worried. "We can all think of about half a dozen people who would just love to have Mason Blaine out of the way. They're all friends of ours. Or acquaintances, at least. I for one can't imagine anybody in this Department bumping Mason off, but try to tell the cops that."

"Ah, that is right!" José exclaimed. "To them, we are just some people who don't like Blaine, some people who want him to be dead. We are all—ah, *como se dice sospechosos?*"

"Suspects," said Kathryn, whose south Texas childhood enabled her to catch most of the Spanish that decorated her friends' conversation.

"*Sospechosos* is right." Patrick nodded. "I have a strong feeling that this is going to get grim. That is, unless people like John MacDonald and Edward Drew can produce alibis."

"Can they?" Kathryn asked. "Does anybody know? Who's seen them this morning?"

"Nobody except the police. MacDonald canceled his seminar this morning, and Edward canceled his 301 section. Carlos was up in the Department office around ten, and the secretary said that the police had cornered every faculty member in the place, and talked to them all about an hour apiece; MacDonald, Edward, and Ellen Caldwell seemed to be the favorites, and one can see why. Though Ellen's husband might be more to the point."

"Exactamente!" cried José. "I hope that he did it, and that the police find out *muy de prisa.* Before they come to start asking bad questions to all the students."

"I'm afraid your hopes are doomed to disappointment," Patrick said dryly, nodding toward the door, "because if those aren't cops, I'm a pumpkin." Sure enough, Tom Holder and Sergeant Pursley were making their way across the dining room to the alcove, their passage marked by a slight diminution in the conversational roar as students turned to look at the conspicuously unstudent-like pair. The people in the alcove became aware of the approaching presences and likewise stared.

Kathryn, from mixed motives of curiosity and hospitality, went to meet them. She smiled at both of them, and extended a hand to Tom. "Arresting somebody?"

"Ha! Don't I wish! No, we're just getting started, just asking a lot of routine questions." He studied her a minute. "You know these people, huh?" Kathryn allowed as how she did, and Holder gave a nod of satisfaction.

"Then you can tell me who some of them are. Carlos Barreda?"

"Carlos is the scruffy-looking one, sitting at the table with Jamie Newman. The one in the faded blue sweatshirt."

"Valerie Powers."

"The blonde next to Jamie." Holder looked, and raised his eyebrows.

"Yes, exactly," Kathryn said. "Do me a huge favor, won't you, and pin the crime on her?"

"Not very charitable, Reverend."

"I've got reason. Sometimes I think I could slit her throat and play in the blood. Don't bother to give me that look. I assure you, I have long talks with my confessor about it."

"Yeah, I believe you would. Stephen Stanworth?"

"Stephen? He's not here and I don't imagine he'll come. He's probably home crying. Why do you want him? Stephen's the only person in the whole wretched department who actually liked Mason Blaine."

"This isn't a list of suspects, it's just all the people who were in that group outside the library last night, talking to Blaine before he started walking home."

"Oh. Good."

"Why good? I thought you wanted to see the blonde get nailed."

"Well, I wouldn't cry if I found out Valerie was the guilty one, but Carlos is a different matter."

"Friend?"

"No, I don't really know him very well. But I—I guess I never noticed it before, but I kinda like him. Carlos is so vulnerable, under all that aggression."

"Well, I don't care if anybody's vulnerable or aggressive

or what. I just wanna know where they were last night from nine-thirty to ten-twenty. And right now I want to know who was absolutely the last person to see Blaine. And the exact time they saw him. I need Barreda, Powers, Stanworth, Jamie Newman again just to check it over, and José—ah . . ."

Kathryn chuckled. *"Espronceda y Montalbán!* Marvelous, isn't it? And he's got about five more names in there that he doesn't use. He's the beautiful one, sitting over there next to the guy with the frizzy hair. C'mon, I'll introduce you. I just hope it doesn't cost me any friends."

"I'll be as nice as I know how to be," vowed Tom meekly. He was rewarded with a wink.

She led him and his companion over to the expectant group in the alcove, and performed introductions, unwittingly impressing Sergeant Pursley by remembering his name and introducing him as though he mattered.

Chief Holder began to explain to Carlos, José, Valerie, and Jamie that he needed to talk to all of them, but separately, that he would start with Jamie, that he would take him up to the Spanish Department, and would the others please come along in twenty-minute intervals. While he was speaking, Kathryn returned to her table, sat down, and turned her chair to listen to Holder's speech. Just as she turned, however, she caught sight of an elegant young man moving carefully through the crowded tables, like a duchess picking her way through garbage. The newcomer did not look pleased with his surroundings, but neither did he look particularly unhappy. Kathryn clutched Patrick's wrist and said, in an urgent undertone, "Is it at all possible that Stephen doesn't know yet?"

Patrick, following the direction of her look, saw Stephen stop to exchange greetings with a friend and laugh at something the boy said. "My God. It must be possible. Come to think of it, what is this, Friday? Sure, he sleeps late on Fridays because he doesn't take MacDonald's seminar. Nobody ever sees him before lunch."

"Patrick, we can't just let him walk into this."

Patrick shrugged his shoulders. "What choice do we have?"

Kathryn gave him an impatient look, shot a glance at Tom, whose attention was on the small group he was talking to, then rose and moved decisively to intercept Stephen.

The elegant Mr. Stanworth was wearing (on a weekday, for Heaven's sake) the three-piece white suit that had earned him his departmental nickname, Colonel Sanders. He had been wearing it the first time Kathryn had met him, at a party in the Newmans' cramped apartment the previous fall, when his reaction to her had determined once and for all her opinion of him.

"Stephen!" Jamie had cried with enthusiasm. "You must meet Kathryn. Kathryn, this is Stephen Malcolm Havering Stanworth, of the *Atlanta* Stanworths, my dear! Stephen, *the Reverend* Kathryn Koerney!"

Stephen struggled for a moment between a desire to cast modest protestations across the social prestige he'd just been credited with and sudden curiosity. Curiosity won.

"The *Reverend*?" he asked, with lifted brows.

"Yes, I'm an Episcopal priest."

The brows lifted further. "But haven't I seen you at Wednesday Mass at the University Chapel?"

In fact the Episcopalians and Roman Catholics at Harton University did a lot of intercommunicating and their chaplains turned a blind eye; the ecumenical movement was alive and well in Harton.

Kathryn, always one to favor the direct response, replied to Stephen, "Yes. Does that offend you?"

Instantly the Colonel was all deference; both hands were flung up and the fingers were made to flutter gracefully. "Oh, no! Not at all!" He favored her with a smile as wide as it was insincere. "No, no offense taken. If you wish to communicate with us," here he spread his arms wide and made a condescending little bow, *"The Church* is happy to welcome you!"

Kathryn resolutely thrust this episode to the back of her mind as she approached him in the Student Center.

"Why, it's the lovely and delightful and *Reverend* Miss Koerney!" Stephen exclaimed in a magnolia-laden drawl. "And how are you this splendid day?"

Kathryn hardly broke stride. Taking his arm, she turned him around and began to walk him back toward the entrance, telling him in exaggerated tones that she was so *glad* to see him, he was *just* the person she needed, and it was most urgent that she talk to him *immediately*, and it would only take a minute. He protested, and tried to slow their progress toward the door, but Kathryn hit on the happy notion of saying that she was sure she could count on his *chivalry* to come to her *rescue*. He went like a lamb. He would do whatever was in his poor power to assist her, but what ever was the problem? Kathryn, murmuring that they needed to be private, steered him out of the Student Center and across to the chapel.

They entered the lofty dimness of the nave, walked up the aisle until they were out of earshot of the guide sitting by the door, and sat down in one of the pews.

Stephen started to ask again what the problem was, but the woman next to him was no longer acting like a flustered damsel in distress, and he stopped, puzzled.

"Stephen," Kathryn said quietly, "I apologize for kidnapping you like that under false pretenses, but I felt I had to get you out of that mob, in case you hadn't— Stephen, you haven't heard about last night, have you?"

"Last night? What about last night?"

"Mason Blaine was killed."

He stared at her, openmouthed. Slowly the astonishment in his face turned to distress, and his lips moved in a silent No. He began to shake his head, and this time it wasn't silent: *"No!"*

"I'm sorry, Stephen. I know you cared for him."

He turned from her, and sat rigidly in the pew, gazing at the front of the chapel as though the deep blues of the east window might offer some soft escape. Finally he said, without turning to look at her, and in a voice barely audible, "How did it happen?"

Kathryn took a long, slow breath, and let it out again. "He was murdered."

Stephen whirled and stared at her. "He was *what?*"

"He was murdered. Hit over the head, and stabbed. On his way home last night from the library. It happened shortly after you were talking to him at nine-thirty. Tracy Newman found his body in the driveway of St. Margaret's Church just before ten-thirty. Stephen: It was quick. If he was hit from behind, he wouldn't even have had time to be frightened, much less to feel pain."

Stephen gaped at her, mute for a few moments. Then he leaned forward slowly, clutching his sides; he bowed his head, and began to moan. Kathryn wrapped her arms around him in a firm embrace and laid her head across his shoulders, holding him so closely that she found herself breathing gently into his dark curly hair.

José had gone at his appointed time to speak with Chief Holder; the rest of the Spanish Department was beginning to trickle out, headed back to the library or to class. Patrick sat alone at his table, and Tracy moved to join him.

"Lingering over lunch? Not your style."

"Lingering over Kathryn's lunch," he corrected, with a wave of his hand in the direction of Kathryn's half-eaten salad. "Stephen came waltzing in here, obviously not having heard the news, so Kathryn headed him off before he reached this den of Blaine haters, and took him off somewhere to break it to him gently. I thought I'd better stick around and guard her food from the cleanup crew, in case she comes looking for it."

Tracy smiled at him. "Breaking your one-hour lunch rule, aren't you?"

"It won't kill me, as long as I don't make a habit of it. As long as you're here, how would you like to tell me about how you found the body?"

Tracy clutched her head, made noises in the back of her throat, and looked around for something suitable to throw at him.

"No, love, do not chuck Kathryn's salad in my face. You wouldn't want her to have to go pay for another one."

"She could pay for the whole Student Center without noticing it. But O.K., I won't throw it at you. I think I remember hearing that salad throwing is frowned upon in polite circles."

"Really? How long has it been since you saw a polite circle? I've about forgotten what they look like, living around this place. How much sleep did you get last night?"

"Oh. Uh. Not a lot. I was more or less tied in a knot."

"You should have had Jamie fetch you a glass of hot milk and give you a back rub."

"Hardly. I think hot milk would make me throw up, and Jamie doesn't give back rubs. I give them to him."

"Selfish bastard." He gave her a puckish smile. "Next time you could use a back rub, come over to my place. I'll give you one."

"Sure!" she laughed. Then she fell silent, and he watched the suffering gather in her eyes. When Tracy was in spirits, she bubbled like champagne; Patrick had long ago assigned to her, in his mind, the adjective "taking." People who had known her for a while tended to forget she was plain. But there was no forgetting it now. The light gone from her eyes, they became unremarkable; unsmiling, her mouth was too small for her face. Tracy looked tired, and five years older than she was.

"Patrick," she said, "do you think I'm—I mean— Oh, damn it, Patrick, am I *that* unattractive?"

"You are forty times more attractive than that platinum-headed slut, and if Jamie had the brains God gave a louse, he would know it."

"Stupid flattery's no good. I've got a mirror."

"I didn't say you were prettier than she is. You're not. I said you were more attractive. You've got wit and originality and intelligence."

"She's not precisely dumb. Dumb people don't get into this place."

"So she can read a novel and write a good paper on it.

She's still got a stunted mind. And the soul of a street-walker. You, on the other hand . . ." He stopped.

"I on the other hand what?"

Patrick adjusted the position of Kathryn's salad plate, found it dissatisfactory, and adjusted it again. "You have the soul of something like a saint. God knows you've got the patience of one. I don't know how you put up with it."

"I've got no choice. I can't leave."

"Yes, I understand that."

"And I can't get him to—to change. I've tried."

"I know you have."

They were silent for a bit. Then Patrick warned, "Heads up. Company's coming."

Tracy looked, and saw Kathryn coming toward them.

"I didn't know if you'd still be here," she said.

"We wanted to save your lunch," Patrick replied, pushing a chair out for her with his foot. "How'd he take it?"

"Thank you. Badly. He quite literally doubled over in pain."

"What did you do?"

"The only thing you can do in a situation like that: I held him. Just held him. As tight as I could, for as long as he needed to be held."

"Did you take him up to the Department to talk to the police?"

"No, I didn't even tell him they wanted him. I sent him home; Tom Holder will find him if he needs him."

Patrick looked at Kathryn's impassive face. "You don't like Stephen," he said. It was an implied question.

She shrugged. "He needed help. I was the only one around to give it to him. Pass the salt, please?"

Tracy gave her the salt, and in doing so showed her more of her face than she intended to. Kathryn took a bite of tomato, frowned, announced that she had lost her appetite and needed to get home anyway, and left them.

They were silent, Patrick looking at Tracy, and Tracy looking at the floor.

"You really ought to go home and take a nap, if you didn't sleep well last night," he said.

"I haven't got time. I ought to go to the grocery store, and there's some housework needs doing."

"Will you stop punishing yourself?"

Tracy lifted her head, and looked at him. Finally she sighed, nodded, and stood up.

He walked her home, poured her a glass of wine, and insisted that she drink it.

"Thank you, Daddy!" she said.

He put a hand on her head and tousled her hair almost as if she were a dog. "Now get some rest," he ordered.

Patrick left, and Tracy crawled into bed and cried herself to sleep.

CHAPTER 7

Kathryn had called him "the beautiful one." Tom Holder, to whom "beautiful" suggested "homosexual" when applied to a man, disagreed with her. The boy wasn't beautiful. Nothing pretty or prissy about him. Just a good-looking boy with a nice friendly smile. (There were twenty-eight female students at the University who had something perilously approaching palpitations at the sight of that smile.) He dressed decently, too, which was more than you could say for the rest of these kids. (José's hand-knit pullover was Irish, and had cost his mother one hundred and thirty pounds on her last trip to London—not that she had looked at the price tag.) Polite, too. As though he had nothing better to do than talk with the cops about a homicide he probably knew nothing about. Or might have committed, Holder reminded himself sternly. Just because the guy didn't look like your average murder suspect, that was no reason to assume things. The thought flickered briefly across the Chief's mind that he had no idea what the average murder suspect would look like. Or the average murderer, for that matter.

"So it's just a matter of routine, that's all," Tom explained as José settled into the leather chair Professor Witherspoon kindly provided for the students who came to see him. Witherspoon was on sabbatical, and Holder was using his office to conduct interviews.

"Oh, yes, of course! I do not mind. I will answer your questions as well as I can." The smile flashed, and spread to include Sergeant Pursley, sitting correctly in the corner with his notebook on his knee. "You must do your work, and I must help, if I can."

"Well, thank you, Mr. Ezpro—" Holder frowned at his notebook, and José laughed.

"It is easier if you call me José, no?"

"Thanks, I appreciate it. Now, if you'll just tell me whatever you can about last night, beginning when the class adjourned."

"Yes. The seminar, it goes from eight to nine-thirty, and when it is over we all go upstairs together. Last night—"

"Hang on. You all go *upstairs*?"

"Yes, the seminar, it is in one of the downstairs rooms of the library, next to where are all the study carrels of the graduate students. So we go upstairs together when the seminar is over at nine-thirty."

"Excuse me. I take it you mean the seminar usually ends at nine-thirty. Do you know the exact time it ended last night?"

"Oh, yes, of course! Even without a watch I would know that! This Professor Blaine, he does not like the night classes. He does not believe that he—the chairman, you know!—should have to teach a seminar at night. So always, always we are finished at nine-thirty exactly, because Professor Blaine will not stay one minute more."

"But he might leave a little early?"

"Oh, no, he would not. You see, he hates the night classes, but he has his duty. He believes only a bad teacher will leave a class early. He says it. He tells the younger faculty members."

"He prided himself on being a good teacher?"

For the first time José hesitated. Then he spread his hands and smiled apologetically. "You know they say, 'Of the dead speak nothing but good.' But perhaps at a time like this that is not wise, no?"

"At a time like this it might even be pretty stupid."

Again the smile. "Yes, I think you are right. Well, then, I try to tell you the truth. But it is necessary for you to remember that me, I do not like Professor Blaine. So maybe I say things, well, maybe if I say a bad thing because I think it is true, who knows? Maybe it is not so bad, truly, with Blaine; maybe I think only it is so bad because I do not like him. You understand?"

"You mean you're warning me that you may be prejudiced."

"Ah, yes! Exactly. So. You ask me, he is proud because he is a good teacher? I say, no. He is proud—oh, for many reasons. He is proud because he has a family that is old and important. I think you say in this country, 'First Families of Virginia'? Well, Professor Blaine is one of those. And he is proud because he has money, more money than a teacher is paid. And he is proud because he is a man who can, how do you say, a man who has women if he wants them. For these reasons he is proud. But he is not a good teacher. He *was*. Many years ago. But not now, now he drinks, he goes on vacations, he is lazy. The work he did twenty years ago, it was important. It was great. That work, that made him chairman here. He is very famous, you know that? People came from everywhere to this university to study the *Siglo de Oro* with the great Mason Blaine. Pardon. The Golden Age, it means. The great time of the literature of Spain. Even from Spain they come—as you see! But no. It is a disappointment. Now Professor Blaine is not great. He is a lazy old man, who gives orders: here, do this! do that! Like we are servants. I forget that he is dead, and I still talk in the present. He *was* a lazy old man. But I talk too much. This you do not need to know. You want to know what happened last night."

"No, no, that's O.K. I need to know all I can about Blaine, not just about last night, but about what he was like. All that's very helpful. You, ah, you say he was a man that women found attractive?"

"Yes, you are surprised. He is—he *was*—what, sixty years old? And yet he was like fifty, maybe forty-five. And a face like Cardinal Newman, you have seen pictures of him? All that white hair, the nose like this, the chin square and proud. And he was careful with himself. I mean, he did exercise a lot. He was strong like a young man."

Holder waited, but José merely looked at him politely, and Holder saw that he would have to ask for it. "Can you tell me what women found him attractive?"

"Oh, many women. I think, almost all who knew him, except, I think, the women who are students. He was so bad as a teacher, so—so unpleasant."

Holder became pointed. "I mean, in particular, *which* women. Name them, José. What women that you know liked Blaine especially? Flirted with him? Had affairs with him?"

José became vague. He was most terribly sorry, he would very much like to help, but you know, he was only a student, and he would not know if Blaine had a date, or if a woman came to his house, or such things. Tom pressed him: Hadn't he heard rumors in the Department? Oh, but one did not listen to things like that, they were so foolish, one of course forgot what one heard.

There was no getting any more out of him, at least not without getting unpleasantly persistent about it. And Holder found he did not want to be unpleasant to this thoroughly pleasant boy. He sighed, and went back to the events of the previous evening.

Yes, the seminar had adjourned at 9:30 precisely. Some people had left the seminar room and gone to their carrels. A few people had stayed in the room, talking—some first-year students: Savenor, Pritchart, Haskell, a redheaded girl whose name José could never remember. Some of the second-year students went up the stairs with Blaine, and walked with him across the lobby and out the main door. There the professor had left them, heading off-campus toward Prosper Street. Professor Blaine always walked home after the seminar, except when the weather was very bad. He had seemed perfectly at ease, just the same as usual. He had mentioned nothing about planning to meet anybody. Blaine had taken exactly the same route he always took, at least as far as they could see him: a minute after leaving them he was blocked from their view by the wall of the chapel. José could not imagine how he came to be at St. Margaret's Church, clear on the other side of the campus. He certainly had said nothing about going there.

Holder could have enlightened him, but didn't. The group that had walked out with Blaine? Jamie Newman,

Carlos Barreda, Valerie Powers, Stephen Stanworth, and himself, José. What had they done then? They'd talked a bit. Stephen Stanworth had suggested they all go over to the Student Center for a beer. Valerie Powers said that was a good idea, and Jamie Newman agreed. Carlos Barreda had seemed undecided. José had not yet made up his mind whether to join them or not, when a man came up and asked Valerie where Cletus Hall was. Valerie said she would show him, and the two had walked off together. Jamie said he was tired and didn't want a beer and left. José had not wanted to sit between Stephen and Carlos ("They are very different, you see, and I do not think they like each other much"), so he started to walk back to the Graduate College. He left Stephen and Carlos standing and talking, halfway between the library and the Student Center. He did not know if they went to the Student Center or not.

If the class had adjourned at 9:30, they would have reached the library door at about 9:35. Mason Blaine had left them right away; he always did. José guessed that Valerie had left them at about 9:45, and Jamie almost at the same time. He himself had left only a minute or so later. No, he hadn't caught up with Jamie or Valerie. Wasn't that strange? No, because Jamie had gone home to his apartment by way of Main Street, whereas Valerie had gone out of her way to show that man to Cletus Hall. José had gone by the shortest route, the one everyone took—straight through the campus, over to Alexander Street, down the road by the Seminary and up the hill to the Graduate College. He hadn't seen Valerie. Of course, she'd gone out of her way, toward Cletus Hall, and might have taken a different route.

Holder thanked José for all his help, and asked him to

go by the Department lounge on his way out and send in Miss Powers.

As the door closed behind him, Holder sighed and turned a defeated gaze on his Sergeant. "Apart from people agreeing on the victim's nasty personality and the time he left the library, we're getting nowhere fast."

"Yes, sir," said Pursley agreeably.

"Don't sound so damn cheerful about it."

"No, sir."

Holder grunted. "It's bound to be a woman. He was plenty rich, but the money goes to the sister in Virginia, who was at home answering the phone when we called her at eleven, so it's a cinch she wasn't in central Jersey spreading a corpse across a church driveway at ten. Gotta be a woman. The trouble is, what woman? What a bunch of clams these people are. MacDonald says Blaine is a bit of a ladies' man, then chokes when I ask him which ladies. Ask Drew if Blaine is a ladies' man, he just looks embarrassed. Ask the Caldwell woman, and she pooh-poohs the idea. Not *that* attractive, she says. Something about that woman. She was sitting on something, you could tell. Anyway. Jamie Newman says oh, yes, Blaine was a womanizer, everybody says so, but ask him the big question and he comes out with jokes about Angelina Jolie. Same as our Spanish friend, here, but kinda defensive about it, didn't you think?"

"Uh, I'm not sure, sir. Uh, sir?"

"Yeah?"

"Uh, couldn't it be something else? I mean, women and money aren't the *only* things."

"No, but hell, they're the only reasonable things in this case. Look at the alternatives. Vengeance, for instance? Maybe he cut some kid's scholarship off last year and the kid killed him for it? Sure. What else is there? He's not the type for a blackmailer. More like the kind of person who gets blackmailed himself. Ladies' man. That's *got* to be it. You don't look convinced."

"Well, sir, I'm sure you're right, and maybe it's a stupid idea, but money isn't the only thing that goes to somebody else when somebody gets killed." Under the skeptical look of his superior, the Sergeant hesitated, then offered, in a small voice, "I mean, there's the job, isn't there?"

"You mean John MacDonald killed Mason Blaine because he wanted to be chairman of the Spanish Department?"

"Well," the Sergeant faltered, "it's possible, isn't it?"

Holder was about to ask Pursley, in a blighting tone, if that little pudding MacDonald looked like the sort who'd stab somebody to get a job not so much different from the one he already had. He got no farther than opening his mouth, however, before it came to him that none of the people he had seen in connection with the murder of Mason Blaine looked like the sort who'd kill anybody for any reason. They were all so damn civilized, these University people. Well, not so civilized that they were above suspicion. Blaine had been killed by somebody who knew him, of that Tom was certain.

He just wished he were certain about something else. Why the hell had the body been moved, for one thing? It didn't make sense. And the way it was found . . . Tom wondered how long it would have taken to perform that maneuver.

"Pursley."

"Sir?"

"Get Colczhic and Halliday and Rossi. Tell them to find a stopwatch. I want them to walk, one at a time, not together, from the front doors of Goodrich Library down the various routes we figured Blaine might have walked home last night. I want them to walk right up to the place we found the briefcase, at full stride, then stop dead. I want it timed to the second. Whatever else they're doing, pull them off it. One at a time, at least a half hour apart. I don't want the whole damn police force strolling down Prosper Street within five minutes of each other. Taxpayers wouldn't like it. Here, take my phone but go somewhere else to make the calls. I've got to do some figuring."

"Uh, yes, sir, but isn't that girl supposed to be coming?"

"Yes, by God, she is!" Holder looked at his watch. "And where the hell is she? It's been five minutes and she was supposed to be out there waiting. The hell with it. Go make phone calls; if she comes before you get back, we'll just let *her* wait a bit."

Pursley obediently left, and Tom began to scribble on a piece of paper in front of him. It was probably pointless—there was no reason to suspect any of the students, what motive could they have?—but he might as well have the satisfaction of eliminating somebody. If he could. Let's see. Blaine set off from Goodrich at 9:35. Valerie Powers and Jamie Newman had parted from the group, in opposite directions, at 9:45. Jamie had gone home to an empty apartment. No alibi there. As for the Powers girl—how long did it take to show somebody to Cletus Hall? José was without alibi from 9:46 or so. Stanworth and Barreda might be eliminated right off the bat, if they had in fact gone into the Student Center for a beer. That would take them half an hour at least, and by that time Mason Blaine was dead. Come to think of it, you could probably write off the others in that group, too; no matter what time they went off alone, Blaine had a good head start on them; they'd have had to catch up with him, even get ahead of him from the looks of things, clonk him on the head as he passed that big cypress, load his body into the car—there would have to be a car—drive over to St. Margaret's Church, unload the body in the driveway, and get lost, all before 10:15 when Tracy Newman found the body. Actually, getting the body over there in time wouldn't have been the hard part; Blaine was almost certainly dead by about ten o'clock, and that left fifteen minutes—he would know more exactly when the results of his three-man walkathon came in. No, the problem would be getting over to Patterson Road ahead of Blaine to set up the ambush. He had a five- or ten-minute head start on every one of those kids, at least— No! Holder struck the desk with his open palm and swore at his own stupidity. Five- or ten-minute head start, hell. It didn't make any difference. Not if the car had been parked close to the library, and the kid had driven over to Patterson. Easy to catch up to a guy who's walking, if you're driving! Damn. He couldn't even eliminate one of those stupid students, unless Barreda and Stanworth had kept each other company. Or maybe if the Powers girl had run into somebody she knew.

And where *was* that girl?

There was a soft knock, and the door opened a couple of inches. A voice softer than the knock said, "Chief Holder?"

"Come in, Miss Powers."

The door came open. Valerie entered, in no hurry, shut the door behind her, and leaned against it. "I'm so sorry I kept you waiting. I lost track of the time."

The voice was like whipped cream.

CHAPTER 8

Holder found himself saying it was quite all right, then kicking himself for being such a pushover. He had fully intended to be stern, but while there might be men in the world—somewhere—who could be stern in the gaze of those wide hazel eyes, Tom Holder was discovering, to his intense irritation, that he wasn't one of them. Trying for a businesslike tone, he told Valerie Powers to sit down.

The apologetic look changed instantly to one of appreciation, and although the "thank you" was not effusive, something in the small smile that accompanied it suggested that Holder had done her a signal favor, and she would always love him for it. She sat down, crossed a magnificent pair of legs, and looked inquiringly at him.

"Ah, we can't really begin yet, Miss Powers, because

my Sergeant has to be here taking notes, and he's out making a phone call. He'll be back in a minute."

"How intimidating," she murmured, "to have somebody taking notes on what you say." It was clear that she planned to be very brave in the face of this ordeal, and it would be a shame if she weren't handled with all the gentleness that chivalry could muster.

"Oh, it's just a matter of routine, you know, get as many facts as possible from as many people as possible, then try to sort them all out." Tom grinned at her, told himself he was an idiot, and thanked God for the sudden appearance of Sergeant Pursley.

Pursley closed the door, nodded to his Chief and said, "All set," and took his chair. The Sergeant found that Valerie had turned to give him a welcoming smile, and he returned it before he knew what he was doing. He shot a hasty glance at Holder, reddened, and fixed his attention on his notebook.

Holder cleared his throat. "Now, then, Miss Powers. First we'd like to get straight just how things happened last night, from the time the seminar adjourned, until you left your friends outside. A couple of people have been pretty definite about when that seminar ended. How about you?"

She gave a tiny chuckle. "Oh, yes, it's one of the standing jokes of the Department. Mason had a thing about it. Nine-thirty exactly, not one minute sooner, not one minute later. You could set your watch by it. In fact some people do, to emphasize the joke."

Holder had sat up a little straighter in his chair, but he tried to keep his voice casual. "Did you know Professor Blaine very well? I mean, on a personal basis, not just as a student?"

"No, not really, Of course I spoke to him when I saw him on campus, and he had departmental parties at his house sometimes, and we all went, and naturally I talked to him at those. But I don't suppose I knew him better than any other student."

"You just called him Mason."

"Oh, that!" Another chuckle. "We all did that, behind his back. When we weren't calling him Evey."

"Evey?"

"For all those pretentious initials. E. V. Mason Blaine, B.A., M.A., Ph.D., Chairman by the Grace of God of the Spanish Department."

"You didn't like Mason Blaine?"

"Oh, no, I don't mean to imply I didn't like Mason. We all make fun of the peculiarities of the teachers here. It's part of the game. And Evey, poor thing, was a bit of a snob."

"You say, 'poor thing.' You don't think he was a bit of a—well, a bossy old man? Unpleasant to students?"

"People keep saying that, everyone says it. But he was never unpleasant to me. Sort of charming. A bit Old World, you know?" Her look implied that Holder did indeed know, that in fact he knew everything about her, and she didn't mind at all.

Holder gave himself a mental shake and got back to the original topic. "What happened after the seminar let out?"

Her account tallied in all respects with those of José and Jamie, although she couldn't remember the names of the first-year students who had stayed in the seminar room, and she couldn't be quite sure who had gone off to their carrels. There was nothing new; Holder made only one major discovery, and it had nothing to do with the events of the previous night.

At one point Valerie slewed around in her chair, exposing another six inches of leg to Holder's bemused gaze, and confided in a near-whisper to Sergeant Pursley that she bet he wanted all those names for the record, and she felt so stupid, but she was very bad with names. The Sergeant stammered that that was O.K., they could get them from somewhere else, and was rewarded with a devastating smile.

And the scales fell from Holder's eyes. I'll be damned, he thought; she's doing it on purpose. When she had first come in, he had stared hard at that pale, brilliant hair and had concluded, in some awe, that it was natural. And she wore no makeup, and her sweater was no tighter than any other woman's these days. Her appearance, however stunning, was unaffected. But her manners were all for effect. The way she moved, the way she talked, that confiding smile—dammit all, Valerie Powers was sitting there deliberately trying to seduce both of them.

Holder had been angry at himself for being distracted by a pretty girl, but now his anger turned and focused on that shining head.

Valerie, dimly aware that she had lost him, tried to get him back. She leaned forward in her chair each time he asked a question, and wrinkled her flawless brow in earnest concentration before she produced an answer. Holder began to be amused.

"I was going to join them," she was saying, "but as soon as I said it I regretted it, because Jamie and José are nice guys, but Stephen is kind of a bore, and Carlos, whenever he has two beers, always starts talking about the blood of the common people on the soil of Spain that cries for revenge."

The word "blood" flicked a switch in Holder's mind; suddenly he heard again a cold voice: "I could slit her throat and play in the blood." He had forgotten that, somehow, in the intervening time, and he hadn't remembered it when Valerie walked into the room and smiled at him. But he remembered it now, and his amusement faded. It had shocked him, that statement. Of course, Kathryn tended to talk in wild exaggeration; she had once told him that hyperbole was her native tongue, and after he had gone home and looked up "hyperbole" he had been forced to agree. When Kathryn was with people she liked, she expressed herself with unhesitating candor. She had told him once that the head of the Altar Guild drove her up the wall screaming, and he had been present when she had called one of her Presbyterian professors at the Seminary—to the man's face—an impenitent heretic. But there was neither malice nor contempt in either of those remarks; she was unfailingly polite to the head of the Altar Guild, and the professor had merely laughed and said he'd rather be an impenitent heretic than a crypto-papist (another one Holder had looked up when he got home). Tom had never heard her say anything that sounded like hate. But the remark about Valerie Powers had sounded like hate. And it had been said without flourish and without humor. Holder was roused to an urgent curiosity; more than anything else about this bothersomely beautiful girl, he wanted to know why Kathryn Koerney hated her.

He became aware that she had stopped speaking. He had been staring at her, an odd expression in his eyes, through at least thirty seconds of silence. She was looking

right back at him with perhaps the faintest trace of satisfaction, and Sergeant Pursley was beginning to get embarrassed. Holder yanked himself out of his reverie. He
had hardly heard the last several sentences, but "Cletus
Hall" had registered.

"So you went to show this boy to Cletus Hall?"

"Yes."

"And after you showed him where Cletus Hall was,
what did you do?"

There was a barely perceptible pause. "I went home."

"Home being—?"

"The Graduate College."

"Did you see José Ez—whatever his name is—on your
way there?"

"No, I'm afraid not."

"Did you see anybody who knew you and can vouch
for your presence at the Graduate College or on the
road to it between nine-forty-five and ten-fifteen?"

Valerie was half-incredulous, half-amused. "Are you
asking me for an alibi?"

"Well, they come in handy," Holder retorted dryly,
"when it's a question of murder."

Valerie immediately looked somber and cooperative.
"Yes, I suppose you have to check out everybody who
knew him, no matter how slightly. I'm sorry I can't help
you with your process of elimination, Chief, but I'm
afraid no one saw me, so I can't prove I went home and
went to bed. But that's what I did."

"All right, Miss Powers. It's probably no big deal, but
we do have to ask, you know. One more thing." Holder
looked at her appraisingly; he decided he would stoop to
a little flattery. "You strike me as a person who knows
people, who understands them. And you're obviously ex-

tremely bright. Do you think you'd be aware of—uh, *undercurrents*, so to speak? Things that were going on in the people around you that weren't obvious to everyone?"

Valerie appeared to consider this a moment, then replied with a graceful touch of modesty that that was very nice of Chief Holder, and she thought she might just possibly be able to help him on something like that.

"Yes, I'm sure you can. Well, it's like this: Just about everybody agrees that Mason Blaine was a ladies' man, but nobody can tell me anything specific. Is there any woman—or women—that you know of who might have been involved with Blaine? Even casually, I mean, even just a flirtation?"

"Well, I hate to say anything that would just be repeating gossip . . ."

Holder made all the right encouraging noises.

"Well . . ." Valerie said with a fine show of reluctance, "I've *heard*, though I don't know if there's a thing in it, that Ellen Caldwell was, uh, friendly with Mason. And then—this may be nothing—in the library the other day I saw Mason go and sit on the edge of the table where, oh, what's-her-name, she's a first-year student, where she was studying, and he talked to her and they laughed a lot, quietly, and the way she looked a bit self-conscious, you know, I thought at the time that, well, there might be something going on there."

"You can't tell me her name?"

"No, but somebody else probably can. Just ask who the girl is with the flaming red hair and all the freckles."

"Oh, yes, the one that's in the seminar that met last night?"

"Yes, that's the one."

Holder asked if she knew anything else that might be

useful to them; she did not. He thanked her, and asked her to speak to Carlos Barreda on her way out, and tell him they would ask him to come in in about five minutes. As she rose, Sergeant Pursley stood up too, and Holder, looking at his face, thought, *I'll be damned if he isn't going to open the door for her.* He did.

When he closed it, Holder told him, "Pursley, you're a fool." Pursley blushed, but offered no defense, and his superior magnanimously changed the subject. "So! Ellen Caldwell. That's got promise, she's married."

"Yes, sir. Maybe we should see her again?"

"Of course. And, what's probably more to the point," he added in unwitting agreement with Patrick's observation at lunch, "let's see her husband."

"Yes, sir. Ah, sir?"

"What?"

"I was just noticing, I mean, I guess it doesn't matter, but, uh, I was wondering why you pressed her so hard about an alibi when you didn't even ask the Spanish guy if he had one at all."

Holder made a face. "Because *I'm* a fool," he admitted. "I should have asked him, of course, but I just wasn't taking it very seriously. The possibility that one of that group might have done it, I mean."

"But you took it seriously with Miss Powers, and uh, maybe I'm stupid, but I can't figure out what made you suspicious of her."

"Well, to tell you the truth, it was just that I remembered what my friend Kathryn Koerney said to me over in the Student Center. You weren't standing close enough to hear, were you?"

"What was that, sir?"

It suddenly occurred to Holder that Kathryn might not want that remark repeated, so he said, "Never mind, it's too complicated to explain. Probably doesn't matter anyway." He sighed. "I'd like to see something that *does* matter." He looked at the short pile of papers under his hand. Nothing. Reports from Campanola and Wilson on the residents of Patterson Road. Had they seen anything suspicious or in any way unusual last night between nine and ten? Had they seen Professor Blaine—or anybody— walking along the street? Had they seen a parked car they didn't recognize as belonging to a resident of the street? And a long list of negatives for answers. Well, that wasn't really surprising. The houses were all set back a good way from the street; most of them had plenty of trees and bushes in their yards, some had high hedges in front; there were street lights only at either end of the block, and the middle of the block was dark as a tomb. It was a residential street that led nowhere in particular, so there wasn't any traffic to speak of. Holder reflected bitterly that you could probably kill a half a dozen people in the middle of Patterson Road at that hour of the night, and as long as you were reasonably quiet about it, you could get away without a single witness.

This person had certainly done so. There were no witnesses at either end. If only the Newman girl had been just a *little* bit earlier . . . Of course, if Tracy had walked right into the fellow, he probably would have killed her, too, so maybe it was just as well.

But what had the murderer been doing over there where the Newman girl might have seen him anyway?

Or in other words, back to the big question: *Why had the body been moved?*

And what about this car that had apparently driven around the body? Tom did not believe for a minute that a car had swerved in a curve off the church driveway at some other time, perhaps the day before, for no particular reason, and then by wild coincidence somebody had come along and put a dead body just in the spot the car had driven around. Apparently Tracy Newman had not been the first to see the body in the driveway. Somebody else had taken the shortcut before her, but in a car. Seeing the dead man, that somebody had chosen to drive around him and go on, rather than stop and notify the authorities. It probably had no meaning, Tom reflected, other than that there was an irresponsible citizen out there. Well, that was hardly news.

He sighed, and told Pursley to call in that other Spanish guy.

CHAPTER 9

After the honest charm of José Whatshisname and the silky allurements of Valerie Powers, Carlos Barreda came as something of a shock.

He burst into the room with a vulgar Spanish exclamation, and waved his hands at Holder. *"You!* You think I have nothing to do today? You say, come at ten minutes to two, and I come, I leave the library where I am doing important work, *ay por Dios!*—and I sit here not working and they say no, I cannot see you, you are talking to Valerie. *Esta puta, ella vale mas que yo, si? Son cabrones, la policia!"* He flopped into the leather chair and glared at Holder. *"Pues vamanos!"* he demanded, making hurry-up flutters with both hands. "Then do it! Ask me questions!"

Holder took a deep breath. He knew no Spanish, but it was obvious that he had been soundly cursed. It would be foolish to get mad. Besides, it might be the best thing that had happened to him all day. If this guy was half as nasty about his friends as he was to total strangers, he might be a gold mine. Not that it was gold Holder wanted. A little dirt would do. So he asked his graceless subject for an account of the events of the previous evening, and within sixty seconds he knew that he was not going to be disappointed. He hardly had to ask questions. Carlos just spouted.

"So the (untranslatable Spanish word) left and went home, and we said we would get beer, but then everyone said no, the (untranslatable Spanish phrase) all left, and me, I do not drink with that *maricón*, that Stanworth. It is O.K. if there are other people, but no, I don't sit with that kind of man alone, it is bad for the reputation! So when *la putisima* goes off with her man and *el estupido* Jamie Newman, he thinks he will not go without her, there is only *el Conde-Duque, Espronceda y Montalban*, who is rich on the blood of the peasants, and that other, who is probably rich on the blood of American peasants, and I think, maybe I don't go, then the *Conde-Duque* he goes, and I say, no! Señor Stanworth, he thinks to make me come, but I tell him to go chase *Mucho-Nombre* if he looks for fun, and he gets very mad—"

Holder judged it time to interrupt. Ignorant of Spanish though he was, there was nothing wrong with his brain, and he had kept up with most of it. He could tell by the context what Carlos's objection to Stephen Stanworth was, though he did not know the word he had called him, and he guessed that what Carlos had called Valerie was equally insulting, though it implied no sexual abnormality—not precisely, anyway. Carlos's tone had told him that the prefix to José's name was an honorable description used sarcastically, but *Mucho-Nombre* was beyond him. He now reminded Carlos that he did not understand Spanish.

In a manner that clearly informed Holder that anyone who did not comprehend Spanish was an utter idiot, Carlos translated. *"Mucho-Nombre*, many names. Everett! Vergil! Mason! Blaine! *Ay que* (totally unprintable Spanish) *es ese hombre!"*

By the exercise of superhuman self-control, Holder managed not to look startled, or even very interested. "You suggested to Stephen Stanworth that he go after Professor Blaine if he was, uh, looking for action."

"Si si si, Stephen will have much more luck with him than with me."

"Professor Blaine was a homosexual?"

"Quién sabe?" Carlos shrugged. "But Stephen is his pet, Stephen curls up by Blaine and makes the noise of a fat cat, and Blaine he loves it, and he smiles at Stephen like they share a secret joke. And maybe yes, maybe Blaine he gets bored with Valerie, and Ellen, and maybe the little girl with red hair, she will not go to bed, so maybe he takes Stephen how do you say for kicks. He is evil, he is a very bad man. I am glad he is dead."

Holder ignored both the main thrust of this speech and its conclusion, and jumped on the one item that tickled his current prejudice. "Was Valerie Powers having an affair with Blaine? At some point?"

"Ay la putisima." Carlos made an exaggerated feminine gesture, then kissed his fingertips in sarcastic homage. "She likes the men so much, she has to have them all, so she starts at the top, what she thinks is the top, I think it is the bottom, she has Blaine. And when she is through with Blaine, or maybe Blaine is through with her, he takes

Ellen Caldwell and she takes Jamie Newman. It is not nice, what she does there," Carlos added, in an unexpected flicker of human concern. "It is bad for the little Tracy, she is injured, and she is a nice girl."

Holder's head was whirling. Mason Blaine had seduced Valerie Powers, or vice versa, or maybe it was mutual, then Blaine got tired of Valerie, or vice versa, or maybe it was mutual, then Blaine took up with a married woman, and Valerie took up with a married man, whose wife it was who had found Blaine's body. He had wanted dirt, but he was beginning to think he was getting more than he could sift. And Carlos was still shoveling.

"—because he is like a poor little dog when he looks at her, and I think she gets bored a little, it is so stupid, to be like that for a woman, he is a smart man, Jamie, but he goes without brains when he goes to Valerie. So I say, she is bored I think, and she will not take him long, and then maybe he will go back to his wife, who is a woman very nice, not like Valerie."

"You think Valerie might have wanted to go back to Blaine?"

"Oh, no, that is over, *punto final*. Blaine he does not know that she is there, he goes and smiles at Ellen and the girl with the red hair." He smirked. "Maybe Valerie will go to the man who wanted to go to Cletus Hall."

"I assume that's a joke," said Holder unenthusiastically. "Now, about Ellen Caldwell—"

"But no! It is not a joke! I mean it! You should see the way she looked at him! But to be fair," Carlos admitted, with another brief lapse into humanity, "he looked at her the same way. Me, I don't think he needed to go to Cletus Hall, he just wanted to talk to that girl with the hair. And he is fortunate. He is good-looking, more than Jamie, and taller, and when he smiled at her like that she forgot the beer with Jamie and went with him. Jamie, he looked like a man who is held by the *cojones* and can do nothing. But the fire in his eyes was like murder."

"But the guy who got murdered was Mason Blaine, so maybe we should get back to that. What time did the seminar get out last night?"

"You waste my time! You talk already with the others, you know already Mason, he always ends the seminar at nine-thirty." More hurry-up movements with the hands.

Carlos, like all the others, verified that Professor Blaine had set off in the direction of Prosper Street by 9:35 at the latest. He then launched into a series of speculations concerning the time each member of the group had subsequently parted from the others. These reflections were fleshed out by enthusiastic, if negative, descriptions of Carlos's companions, from which Chief Holder and Sergeant Pursley were at liberty to conclude that Valerie Powers was a cheap whore, Jamie Newman a fool, and José and Stephen insufferable snobs—and Stephen was a *maricón* to boot. Mason Blaine was simply unspeakable: "So bad there are no words to say it." This fact, of course, did not discourage Carlos from employing such words as were at his meager command. Holder, no prude, began to be thankful he couldn't understand most of them.

One fraction of his brain caught Carlos's time estimates as they flew past, checking them against the ones he'd already heard. The major portion of Holder's thinking processes was dedicated to keeping up with

Carlos's bilingual slanders, and trying to decide how many of them were going to be useful. Having met the supposedly insufferable José, Holder was taking most of Carlos's opinions with a grain of salt. But even salted down, might there be something left over worth looking at?

"So then everybody was gone except you and Mr. Stanworth—"

"*Si si si*, and he said come drink beer, and I say no, I do not want to, and he keeps talking, and I say it is late and I start to go, and he says, no, it is still early, and he looks at his watch, and he says, see, it is not even ten o'clock, and he puts a hand on my arm. I throw his arm off, and I tell him to go after Blaine if he wants that kind of company. He is very angry, and he turns to go away."

"Did you see the watch yourself? Do you remember exactly what time it said?"

"Yes, he waved it in my face. It was just after nine forty-five."

"Then he went away. In which direction?"

"Through Cedar Hall, you know how you can walk through under the arches, well, that is the way you go back to the Graduate College."

"Did you see him go back there? Were you walking behind him?"

"No, what do I care where Stephen went, the (unprintable)! He went through Cedar Hall, and I went the other way."

"Where were you going?"

"Nowhere. What difference does it make? I walked."

"Where did you walk?"

"(Unprintable), anywhere! Who cares? There is nowhere to go, if I go to the Graduate College I catch up with that *maricón*, so I go somewhere else. I walk down to Prosper Gardens, then I go back to the Student Center to see if there is anyone there I want to talk to, and there is no one, and you want to know, did anybody see me so they can say I was there at that time, and not running over to that church to meet *Mucho-Nombre* and kill him, and the answer is no. I did not kill that (untranslatable), and I cannot prove it, and I am glad, because if you think I killed him it is an honor! I wanted to kill him, oh, many times! Now somebody else has killed him, and I am glad!"

"You wouldn't have any idea who that somebody else might be?"

"Que question! Yo no se! Who can know? And I am glad he is dead, so why should I tell you, even if I know, who killed him? But I tell you this: there are many many people who do not like Blaine, you see that already, this you know. There are all the women, *claro*, and maybe there are men because of the women, you understand? And probably you think it is like that, but me, I think it is not for that, not the women, that Blaine is killed. I think it is because of what he does in his job. He is important, you see, and he has power, and other people they do not have that power." Carlos looked knowing, and Sergeant Pursley threw Chief Holder a glance that was nothing less than smug.

"So you think Blaine was killed by Jo—by somebody who was jealous of his power?"

"No, not jealous, no, more like afraid. I see that you do not know about Edward Drew, if you did you would know *immediatamente* what I say. Edward Drew, he is good, he is very good. He writes books, two of them are published, and he is only thirty-three. But Blaine, he is jealous. He was good, too, when he was young, now he drinks and does nothing but look for pleasures. So he sees the young man rising, the young man who comes to take the fame and the reputation of Mason Blaine, and Blaine hates him. *Entonces, que pasa?* Blaine talks to people, he uses his power, and *mira!* Edward Drew will not get tenure. Everybody knows it. And Edward, he is afraid. He is intelligent, yes, he is a good scholar, he will be a great scholar, but he has no courage. He cannot go out into the world and make another place for himself, if he loses his place here. And also there are no other places as good. This department, it is the best in the country, maybe the world. If he is fired here, it will be bad for him."

"You're saying you think Edward Drew killed Blaine in the hopes that with Blaine out of the way he could get tenure?"

"But no, you do not listen! I say he has no courage, that one! He is afraid because of his job, he would be afraid to kill. No, it is his wife, she is a lady tiger, that one. She has said it would be good if Blaine is hit by a truck. You have talked to her?"

"No, not yet."

"Ha! You will see!" Carlos laughed, flung up his left hand in mock terror, and crossed himself hastily with his right. "And pray God to deliver you from such a woman!"

Holder thought it was time God delivered him from Carlos Barreda, but he managed to get rid of Carlos without succumbing to the temptation to say so. When he had gone, Holder put his elbows on the desk, propped his chin in his hands, and stared at his notes in unabated gloom. "Pursley," he said.

"Yes, sir?"

"This is going to be a mess."

"Yes sir, it, uh, does seem to get worse as it goes along."

"Umph. God, I can't believe it. You wanta start listing possibilities? Get a *large* sheet of paper. On the woman angle. Valerie Powers killed him because he jilted her. Ellen Caldwell killed him—oh, because he was about to jilt her. Or they had a lovers' quarrel. Or Ellen was afraid her husband would find out. Lots of good motives for murdering your lover. Or Ellen Caldwell's husband killed him, for obvious reasons. Or there might be a man behind Valerie Powers, the man she dumped to take up with Blaine. Or maybe Jamie Newman killed him because he was afraid Valerie would go back to him. Or Blaine seduced the redheaded girl and she was a virgin and she got her revenge by sticking a knife in him. I'm getting sarcastic, cancel that last one. No, don't, with sex anything's possible. Or he was about to seduce the redheaded girl and some other man killed him to keep him from making the conquest. That one's not sarcastic at all, God help us.

"Then there's the professional angle, which I for one don't believe in for a minute. I mean, my God, who would commit murder to keep a lousy job teaching school, or to get a better one? But just to make you happy we'll take it seriously, and we'll even list your theory first: John MacDonald killed Blaine because he wanted his job. Then Barreda's theory, Mrs. Drew killed Blaine so her husband could keep the job he's got. And if we're going to take *that* seriously, we ought to consider the idea that Edward Drew is not the coward Barreda thinks he is, and he killed Blaine himself. It's the biggest pile of—"

"Sir?"

"Yeah?"

"About the other stuff, other than the professional angle. Do we have to take all that seriously? I mean, everything this guy said? I mean, he kinda looked like the sort of guy who hated everybody, or, well, no, not hated them, just liked to say bad things about everybody."

Holder stretched and leaned back in his chair. "Well, it's a point, I grant you. I'm not saying I swallowed everything he was trying to feed me. But some of it made sense. Ellen Caldwell and the redheaded girl, for instance. Valerie Powers said the same thing. So at least that's what people are saying and thinking, whether it's true or not."

Pursley saw again in his mind the smile that had annihilated his wits, and said manfully, "But all that stuff about Miss Powers, sir, we have no proof that that's not a bunch of, well, just being nasty, not true at all."

Holder grinned. "Sergeant, you shouldn't pick favorites among the suspects. I grant you we haven't got any proof, but I for one believe what Barreda said about Valerie Powers, because it explains the thing about her that I was most curious about." The Sergeant opting to sit in offended silence, the Chief continued for his own satisfaction, deciding he could repeat Kathryn's remark now that it appeared to be justified. "Barreda not only said Valerie was having an affair with Jamie Newman, but he made a point of saying how much it was hurting Newman's wife. Well, Newman's wife is a good friend of my friend Kathryn Koerney. And Kathryn Koerney is not only a priest but a pretty tolerant human being in general, even toward people she can't stand, but she gets downright vicious on the subject of Valerie Powers. Even said she'd like to kill her, and asked me to pin this murder on her. Now if the Powers girl is really leading Jamie Newman around by the nose, and his wife is hurting over it, then that all fits together and makes sense. Don't you agree?"

He got a reluctant "yessir."

Holder pondered a minute, then made a disgusted sound. "Maybe we ought to make a list of the people who *don't* have a motive for murdering Blaine, it'd be a shorter list. Seriously, who is there? José with the impossible long name, and our nice friend Carlos here, and maybe Stephen Stanworth, wherever he is, only if it's true what Barreda said, even that might be some kind of motive."

"Uh, sir?"

"Yeah?"

"Maybe Barreda does have a motive, and we just don't know about it. I mean, look at what he said at the end there: He's glad Blaine is dead, and he doesn't want to help us find out who did it. Then he goes right on and tells us all that about Drew and his wife! Seems to me he was trying just a little too hard to make us suspicious of everybody but him. I mean, think about it—we've talked to most of those people, and they're nice folks. It doesn't make any sense for Barreda to hate them. But why would he say those things about them when he's got no reason to hate them? Easy: He just wants us to be suspicious of them."

Holder gathered up his notes and rose laboriously to his feet. "Nice try, Pursley, but you're wrong. Your problem is that *you're* 'nice folks' yourself. So you can't imagine anybody hating nice folks. Especially hating them *because* they're nice folks."

"*Because* they're nice—?" Pursley stared in bewilderment at his superior.

"Carlos is jealous, my boy. I think Carlos is just so jealous, he can hardly stand it."

CHAPTER 10

Kathryn stepped out of the small stone building where her afternoon seminar had just concluded. She hadn't been happy with it. She acknowledged the farewells of her students, all of whom were setting off down Merton Street back toward the main campus of the Seminary, but she did so rather absently. She was distracted.

She herself turned toward town. The golden weather was holding; they'd had a week of it now, a singular blessing. But Mason Blaine's murder was drawing a cloud across it. No, it wasn't that, she realized. She didn't give a fig for Mason Blaine or his murder. It was that argument between Tom and Father Mark. That was what was troubling her, rattling her, keeping her mind from where it should have been in her seminar.

Well, she was going to see Mark now, and although the topic of their meeting was something else entirely, she would take a few minutes at the beginning of the conversation to speak to him about this morning's scene with Tom.

Kathryn went to the little side gate of St. Margaret's, and told the officer guarding it, "I have an appointment with the Rector."

As she was dressed like a priest, she expected to be admitted without argument, and she was. She walked up to the side door of the church and entered. Given the events of the previous night, she thought it possible that there might be a few more people than usual at the church, drawn there by morbid curiosity. She was wrong. There weren't a few more. There was a mob.

They were milling around the corridor she had just entered, talking nineteen to the dozen, with the unmistakable intensity of people who have just gotten out of a meeting. Kathryn recognized immediately that she was looking not at the idle housewives of the parish who had dropped in to gossip, but at the parish leaders.

A handsome middle-aged woman caught sight of Kathryn in the crowd and hailed her. "Hey! You should have been here. Father Mark called an emergency vestry meeting."

Kathryn kissed the tall fortyish redhead on the cheek and said, "Hey, Tildy. What on earth for?"

Tildy twinkled. "To defend our sacred ground against the onslaught of sacrilegious violation."

Kathryn was not amused. "Tildy, seriously, what's he on about?"

"Well, he seems to think that it's bad for the church, all this murder stuff, and that we have to actively fight it, not just sit here."

"Actively fight it how?"

"Well, for one thing, constant prayer vigil in the

church, nonstop, till the police tapes go down and the cops clear off."

"*Not* constant prayer vigil in the church until the murderer is found?"

"Now *that*, my dear Kathryn, is very interesting."

"What do you mean?"

"Come over here."

Tildy pulled Kathryn gently down the hall and around a corner until they were well out of earshot of the rest of the crowd. Then she resumed. "You weren't even at the meeting and you put your finger right on it. Our Rector, fine man that he is, and I love Mark, I really do, has gone bananas. His territory has been invaded and he's lost his balance. He can't see straight. All the way through that meeting you'd have thought that the bad guys were the police, and not whoever it was that dumped the body in our driveway in the first place."

"And the police," Kathryn pointed out, "happen to be incarnate in the person of Tom Holder, who just happens to be a member of this congregation. What was the Rector doing with that?"

"He wasn't. He was just saying, 'the police.' "

"Damn."

"I thought you ought to know."

"Thanks, Tildy. You're a peach. You're enough to change my opinion of lawyers."

"I'm a shark with a heart of gold. You'd have been able to steer things a bit, you know," Tildy remarked, as they walked back in the direction of the main corridor and the rest of the vestry, who were now exchanging parting remarks with the Rector and with each other, "if you came to vestry meetings."

"I'd have come to *this* one. If I could have. But I wasn't

asked." Kathryn was just wondering if this had been intentional on Father Mark's part (had he wanted to keep a pro-Holder person away?) or if she was being paranoid, when she caught sight of a short, gray-haired man in a five-thousand-dollar suit who was talking to the Associate Rector. "Holy cow!" Kathryn exclaimed. "How did Mark get Link Massey to leave Manhattan before six P.M.?" Link Massey was the C.E.O. of a Fortune 500 company that occupied three floors of the south tower of the World Trade Center.

Tildy replied, "Can't have a vestry meeting without the Senior Warden."

Kathryn shook her head in wonder. Despite Tildy's blithe response, both of them knew that Mark Randall's power as Rector of the church was exceedingly strong and he had just demonstrated it.

Suddenly Tildy grabbed Kathryn's elbow. "Look!" she whispered. "A little comic relief! Trish O'Malley and Suzy Norton. The uncreated Eve under the arm of God, yes?"

Kathryn looked. Suddenly, despite all her concerns about the church's troubles and the feud between the Rector and Tom Holder, she was hard put not to burst out laughing. Suzy, an anemic-looking blonde, was at that moment encircled by the left arm of her friend Trish, and something vaguely unformed about Suzy's expression did indeed make the arrangement reminiscent of the scene on the ceiling of the Sistine Chapel.

But Kathryn didn't feel like laughing for long.

"Kathryn! Why weren't you at this meeting? I know you don't normally come to vestry meetings, but I would have thought you would have made an exception for this one."

Kathryn didn't appreciate the scolding tone, but she wasn't about to get herself off the hook by saying she hadn't been notified; that might possibly have reflected badly on the Rector, and whatever quarrel she might have with Mark, she sure as hell wasn't going to share it with Crystal Montoya. Crystal was another Manhattanite Mark had managed to fetch early out of the city; she owned a gallery in the Village specializing in overpriced Mexican folk art.

"Hello, Crystal, how nice to see you. I teach a seminar this afternoon; it just adjourned. Since the Seminary pays me and my job at the church is voluntary, I'm sure you understand that I couldn't possibly cancel the seminar." As Kathryn was coming to the end of this honeyed speech, an idea struck her. Crystal was Castilian Spanish, tall, blond, beautiful, and divorced. "Crystal, did you know Mason Blaine?"

"Very slightly. Why do you ask?"

"Oh, just wondering," Kathryn replied airily, turning away and rapidly putting several people between herself and any comeback Crystal might care to make, winking at Tildy Harmon as she did so.

The other members of the vestry had been summoned from local jobs, or at least jobs not so far afield, or from their homes. Father Mark had beckoned, and the vestry had come. They had all come. Or at least, as best Kathryn could judge, scanning the departing faces, the vast majority of them had come. That was amazing. It was incredible. It was a whale of a tribute to Father Mark.

Or perhaps it was a tribute to the guy who had put the body in the driveway.

The Rector spotted her. "Kathryn! We just finished an emergency vestry meeting. Somebody's probably already told you. I thought we'd better address this problem right away."

Kathryn couldn't think of anything to say, a fairly rare

circumstance for her, so she just made a listening noise and nodded. She and the Rector moved against the flow of departing vestry members down the hall and into Father Mark's office.

As she sat down, Kathryn was rapidly reconsidering her intention to talk to Mark about his argument with Tom. It seemed to her that in the few hours that had passed since their row, it had escalated—at least on Father Mark's part—into a war, and she wasn't prepared to talk somebody out of a war. Literally, she wasn't prepared. Because it was obviously going to be a very delicate conversation. She needed time to consider, to pray. Then she would talk to Mark about it. For now, she would stick to the subject she came to discuss.

"Now, then," the Rector said, settling down at his desk with a smile, not having the slightest idea she was thoroughly disenchanted with him, "what's this surprise you want to talk about?"

"You're going to need to take notes. Lots of notes. Biiiig sheet of paper."

Father Mark's eyebrows rose. Obediently, he opened a drawer in his desk and pulled out a large lined notepad, closed the drawer, and picked up a pen. "Ready when you are, C.B." he remarked.

Kathryn couldn't resist. "Do you know where that comes from?"

"No."

"Story goes that Cecil B. DeMille had built a movie set, a Western town, and he was going to burn it down for the great climactic scene. He had three cameras set up to film it. They set the town on fire and it burned to the ground. DeMille gets his megaphone and calls out to the first cameraman. 'Did you get it?' First cameraman calls back, 'Sorry, C.B., the film broke.' De Mille calls to the second cameraman, 'Did you get it?' Second cameraman calls back, 'Sorry, C.B., the camera malfunctioned.' DeMille, desperate, calls, 'Cameraman number three!' and the response comes, 'Ready when you are, C.B.!' "

The Rector laughed uproariously and Kathryn found her irritation toward him melting. She had always liked Mark; it was difficult to remain angry with him. So, restored to good humor, she launched into the business at hand.

"I want to create, or fund, anonymously, a college scholarship for a member of St. Margaret's Church. We will define 'member of St. Margaret's church' "—here she wiggled a finger at Father Mark to indicate that he was to write this down—"as a person who has worshiped here regularly for at least two years. This scholarship is to go to someone whose education was interrupted due to lack of funds and who now has to work rather than go to college." She paused a moment while Father Mark scribbled. "The scholarship will pay tuition, room, board, books, all other expenses including *generous* spending money, *plus* the salary of the job that the person has to leave in order to go back to school."

Father Mark looked up at her, eyes very wide and eyebrows in his hair.

"But don't you *see*?" she explained, as if it were the most reasonable thing in the world. "If you're working on your P.H.T., that is, if you're slaving away at some grim, underpaid job Putting Hubby Through to his Ph.D., then it wouldn't be enough to get the money to put yourself through graduate school, would it? You'd still need to have the income from the job so that you could go *on* Putting Hubby Through while you went through yourself."

"As my friends in England used to say, I am a bear of very little brain, Kathryn. Who is Putting Hubby Through?"

"Tracy Newman."

"Ah! Let me get this straight. You are creating an elaborate plot to give your friend Tracy enough money to quit her job as a secretary and enroll as a graduate student, presumably here at Harton, and you want me to help you by disguising the money as a scholarship offered by St. Margaret's."

"I'll say this for you, Mark, you're not stupid."

The Rector again exploded with laughter. When he recovered, he and Kathryn worked out details. The trick was, of course, to define the parameters of the applicant so narrowly that the only person in the congregation who fit them was Tracy.

"Let's see," said Kathryn. "Absent from formal education for at least two years. College Board scores of 1550. *Nobody's* gonna have that but Tracy, I happen to know her Board scores. The scholarship must be used at an Ivy League University. That ought to do it."

"Don't you think that's a bit *overly* narrow?"

"O.K. Ivy League University or institution of similar quality."

The Rector scribbled.

"And I suppose we could lower those Board scores to 1525."

The Rector made a brief note.

"And we'll need to appoint a committee to look at applications."

The Rector raised an eyebrow.

"For appearances' sake." Kathryn tried to keep a straight face, but failed.

CHAPTER 11

Tom Holder looked at the chart he had created and made a noise something like a growl.

Suspect	Motive	Alibi
Charles Caldwell	Jealousy	Wife
Ellen Caldwell	Lovers' quarrel	Husband
Carlos Barreda	Scholarship loss	None
Edward Drew	Wants tenure	None
Caroline Drew	Wants tenure for her husband	None
John MacDonald	Wants to be dept. chairman	Wife
Valerie Powers	Lover's quarrel	Attempting to trace man she showed to Cletus Hall

Unless an unexpected miracle occurred, his optimistic prognosis to the District Attorney was going to be way off the mark. There were just too damn many people who had reasonable motives and no alibis—or useless alibis, that is: their spouses.

That morning, Saturday, they'd had a second go-round of interviews. As always, the second time through produced more information than the first. You wore people down, you got on their nerves, they started to talk. Carlos Barreda held a university scholarship that was awarded according to rules set down by the Spanish Department. It turned out that Mason Blaine was about to change the rules, and that under the new rules Carlos's chances of getting his scholarship renewed would be slimmer. It was widely agreed in the Department that Blaine was doing it on purpose because he loathed Carlos Barreda.

The other thing that was widely agreed was that either Ellen Caldwell was having an affair with Mason Blaine or that her husband Charles believed that she was. If he believed it, that was a good enough motive for him. And if she really was, that was a good enough motive for her. And they alibi'd each other, which was no alibi at all.

These three were Tom's favorites. The Caldwells because sex is always reason enough for murder, and the Barreda boy simply because he had confessed openly to hating Blaine and had so obviously meant it. Now that Tom knew Carlos had a motive, it smelled like a double-blind.

Caroline Drew was supposed to have been at a meeting, but it turned out she hadn't gone; she'd been "bored with those meetings and decided at the last minute just to take a drive." Her husband Edward had been working at home. So had John MacDonald. But Tom had trouble taking the motives of the Drews and John MacDonald seriously; granted, Edward Drew might not get tenure under Blaine, but everybody agreed Edward was a rising star, a brilliant scholar and teacher, and Harton wasn't the only university in the country. And John MacDonald was fifty-three, and had only five years to wait before inheriting the Department from Blaine; it was common knowledge the University wasn't going to offer the chairmanship to anybody else when Blaine retired, because MacDonald was a scholar of international repute.

Tom had equal trouble taking Valerie Powers seriously as a suspect. He couldn't see a beauty like Valerie in a red rage with a man who'd dumped her; she'd be more likely to shrug her pretty shoulders and move on to her next conquest. Would her ego even permit her to accept that she'd been dumped? And besides, there was no clear consensus in the Department about who had dumped whom; a lot of people thought Valerie's affair with Blaine had simply ended by mutual consent.

Tom stared at his chart, banged the flat of his hand on it, and swore. Absolutely the only element of this case he had to be grateful for was that he hadn't seen Louise since it started. Working past midnight, out of the house before six, his life had been blissfully Louise-free for almost three days. Amazing what a lift that was, not to have to endure that depressing drone of a voice at the breakfast table and in the evenings.

But even the absence of his wife was not enough to keep him buoyant in the stubborn lack of progress in his case. Especially since he'd been right in what he'd predicted to the D.A.: every newspaper in the state was barking up his ass. He looked at his watch; it was five forty-five. He pulled open one of his desk drawers and extracted the St. Margaret's Church Directory. While the phone rang he said a little prayer that she would be home. She was.

As twilight fell and Mrs. Warburton tactfully made herself scarce, Tom sat in Kathryn's comfortable living room and sipped Earl Grey from an oversized mug. The first time he'd come to Kathryn's to ask advice it had also been late afternoon, and he had been served tea formally by Mrs. Warburton in a dazzle of Victorian silver. He had learned later that this had been entirely the housekeeper's idea, who had sprung it on a surprised and embarrassed Kathryn, who thought it was completely over the top for a casual call. But Mrs. Warburton, shrewder than her employer on some matters, had known that the policeman, nervous about having invited himself, needed to be treated like an honored guest.

That was ancient history now. Now they were comfortable together; if he wanted coffee (or beer, for that matter) he asked for it; Kathryn no longer felt she had to abandon whatever she was drinking to keep him company. And she had introduced him to Earl Grey and he had liked it; that made him feel sophisticated. Another thing that made him feel sophisticated was that he was beginning to appreciate that the way her house was furnished, which he had at first thought was so plain and ordinary, was anything but.

When Kathryn had first moved to Harton and joined St. Margaret's as a voluntary part-time member of the staff, everybody in the parish had known within five minutes that she was rich as Croesus because she had bought one of the pre-Revolutionary houses on Alexander Street and had it decorated by Elton Kimbrough Interiors. So when Tom had first gone to see her, he'd expected the inside of her house to look like the lavish homes of the other wealthy people he had visited from time to time, sometimes as Harton's Chief of Police on business, and—rarely—as a guest of a wealthy parishioner at St. Margaret's.

He'd been amazed to find himself in an ordinary-looking living room with mismatched furniture in which nothing at all looked impressive. In fact, the overall feeling was simply one of comfort. It was a room you wanted to settle down and spend time in.

But now he'd spent more time in it, and he had considered the unpainted sideboard with the knotholes, and he had run his hands over the fabrics on the sofa and the big chair, and he had studied the rug, he'd decided that there was probably enough money in the furnishings of that room to pay off the mortgage on his house.

He didn't grudge her the money. Tom didn't grudge anybody their money. He had learned at a fairly young age not to value it.

He had still been a humble flatfoot on the Harton force when he and his partner Frank had been the first to respond to a call to a mansion on Library Place at nine o'clock one night. An armed robber, at that unheard-of early hour, had broken in and held a gun to the head of the terrified wife while demanding that her husband produce the cash and jewelry. When Tom and Frank arrived, the robber had gone and the couple were screaming obscenities at each other. Each blamed the other for not having turned on the burglar alarm earlier, and were deaf to Tom's assurances that most people didn't turn their alarms on until they went to bed and a robbery at that hour was most unusual. The wife actually blamed the husband for giving in to the burglar's demands, and the husband's response to that was such that Tom and Frank had to step in and physically separate the couple and order them to sit down on sofas on opposite sides of their enormous living room. The distance did not prevent them from continuing to shout the most eye-popping terms at each other while the two policemen labored to take their statements.

If that experience had not been enough to determine forever Tom's attitude toward money and happiness, Providence had kindly sent him another lesson not two months later. Again he and Frank were on patrol, but this time the call was later, shortly before eleven, and it couldn't have been farther, economically speaking, from Library Place.

It was on Dawkins Street, in the old black neighborhood. There was a coincidental parallel, in that the man who had broken in to the shabby little house had held a knife to the wife's throat while demanding cash and other valuables from the husband. The pair had had little to offer him—some money, their watches (which were not expensive), their radio, and the only two items they really regretted: their wedding rings.

The couple sat together on their sofa with their arms around each other and tears running quietly down their faces. "We don't expect you to catch him," they said. "We can't give you a description because he wore a mask. Just some stupid hophead lookin' to support his habit, he was high as a kite. We only called you because that's what you're supposed to do, something like this happens. The important thing is, we're all right."

The husband looked at his wife and kissed her on her forehead. *"You're* all right."

The wife said to the well-meaning white men in her living room, "And he never even saw our precious babies, sleeping in their beds. They never saw *him.* So they never even had call to be scared. God blessed us this night."

Tom and Frank walked out of the house shaking their heads in wonder, and Tom had spent every minute of his spare time for the next three weeks harassing every fence in North Jersey and New York City until he found the wedding rings. As they were only nine karat and had been fenced for fifty cents, the sale wasn't precisely memorable to the fence and Tom almost missed it, but God smiles upon the pure of heart. The hophead was caught and convicted on the evidence of the fence and Tom got his first promotion, but nothing matched the satisfaction of driving back to Dawkins Street after the trial and returning those rings.

"Mr. and Mrs. Washington—" he had begun.

But no. It was to be Sherri and Joe and he was to come in and sit down and have a beer. By the time Tom had polished off his second beer and met both children and the dog, any racial awkwardness had pretty much relaxed and everybody was feeling more or less like human beings together. Then Sherri asked Tom if he had any children himself.

He had wondered a thousand times since why he had told Sherri and Joe Washington the full and honest story, when he had never told any of his buddies on the force, never told any of his friends at St. Margaret's. Was it because they were black, and belonged to a different world? So somehow it was easier to say it to them? And of course the secret would be safe with them; even if they decided to tell anybody, it wouldn't be anybody he knew.

Or was it because they had what he so desperately wanted, they were so rich where he was so achingly poor? And something craven in him wanted them to know it?

"No," he'd said. "We don't have any kids. My wife Louise and I, we kind of met at the senior prom. We were both students here at Harton High School. My prom date got sick at the last minute and so did hers, and some friends of ours fixed it up for us to go together. Afterwards we went to one of the parties and got stinking drunk, and how I drove home and got there alive I don't know because I really don't remember anything after about two A.M. Obviously I got Louise home in one piece because she started calling me, wanting to go out again, but I was going out with the girl I'd originally had the prom date with. Then three months later Louise calls to tell me she's pregnant and it happened on prom night when we were drunk, it can't be anybody else, she says, because she hasn't been with anybody else. Now, I can't even remember doing the deed, but if she's pregnant she's pregnant and obviously I have to do the right thing by her so I break up with my girlfriend and I marry Louise. And the months go by and there's no baby."

Joe and Sherri stared at Tom, openmouthed.

Tom nodded. "I came home from work one day, she told me she'd been to the doctor and he'd told her she'd had a hysterical pregnancy. That's when—"

Sherri interrupted, "I know what that is. It's when you

think you're pregnant, but you're not. But Tom, how do you know she wasn't just plain lyin' to you? After all, the girl wanted you, she was callin' you."

"I don't know. I've never known. She just said, 'Sorry, Tom. Guess it's too late to go back now, isn't it? We'll just have to make the best of it.' "

"Did you think about getting a divorce?" Joe asked.

"Yeah, but I couldn't face it."

"Why not?"

"We got married in my church because Louise didn't have one of her own. I grew up in St. Margaret's. I was baptized there, I was confirmed there, then I got married there . . ."

The Washingtons nodded. "Yeah, man," said Joe. "I can see that would be tough to go back on."

"But Tom," Sherri cut in, getting back to the original subject. "That doesn't explain why you don't have any kids now."

"Oh, that's what you call the last laugh," Tom replied bitterly. "Three years ago when Louise and I decided it was time for us to start a family for real, we couldn't do it. After two years of trying we both got checked out. Surprise, surprise. Louise can't have children. There has never been any chance in her entire life, before or after that damn prom, that she could have gotten pregnant, by me or anybody else."

He had never, in all the years since, told that sorry tale to anyone else: only to that young black couple who were wealthy in the only thing that counted, and the only thing Tom desperately coveted.

He wondered sometimes if he would eventually tell Kathryn. Sometimes he thought that the only reason he didn't tell her was that he was pretty sure she would respond by telling him he ought to get a divorce. And he didn't want to hear that just yet, because he was beginning to suspect after thirty-two years of marriage that what was keeping him married was not virtue but cowardice. Besides, what good would divorce do him? It might rid him of the woman he didn't want, but he knew that no power on earth was going to get him the woman he wanted.

The woman he wanted was as always dispensing tea, sympathy, and intelligent feedback.

"It's the church driveway that's bugging you, isn't it?" she asked him now.

"Put it this way. Question number one: Why was Blaine's body moved at all? Question number two: Assuming there was some reason for moving him, was there some reason for moving him to the St. Margaret's driveway rather than somewhere else?"

"How are you doing on the answers?"

"I have no idea what the answer to question number one is, but I'm pretty sure I'm ready to answer question number two."

"Bravo! And?"

"Yes."

"Yes, there was a specific reason to dump Mason Blaine in St. Margaret's? For heaven's sake, why?"

"I can't tell you."

"You *aggravating* man!" she cried in astonishment. "Why the hell not?"

"I'm sorry, Kathryn, but you are a civilian. There's a limit to what I can discuss with you."

Kathryn's mouth hung open in surprise, but after a few seconds she managed to shut it.

"I'm sorry," Tom repeated, looking acutely uncomfortable.

"Nonsense," Kathryn said. "You have nothing to apologize for. Naturally there are things you can't discuss with me. It's just that—before—"

Tom nodded his understanding. "On the Grace Kimbrough thing, and then of course when we were in England, we could say anything we wanted to. I know. But this is different. I can't tell you why. It just is."

"O.K. It's different. There's some kind of St. Margaret's connection you can't talk to me about. So let me drop a malicious idea on you. You told me you were checking out Mason Blaine's women. Crystal Montoya is tall, blond, drop-dead gorgeous, fluent in Spanish, and frankly not a very nice person. That makes her Mason Blaine's type, don't you think? And she admits to knowing him, although she says it's only slightly."

Tom sat up a bit straighter in his chair. "Now, *that* is an idea that had not crossed my mind," he admitted, "and it does put together the church and Blaine and women. Thanks. I'll put somebody onto Crystal, very quietly. I'm not about to waltz up to her and ask her for an alibi. After all, unless she did it, we've all got to live with her for the next umpteen years."

"More's the pity."

"Yeah. But you know who I need more than women? I need the men behind the women. Do you know who's dated Crystal, who would be jealous on account of Crystal?"

"That I can't tell you."

They both sipped tea for a minute in silence. Then Kathryn volunteered, "Tom, I might do a bit of spying for you. Don't know if it would do any good, but I could tell you how the usual suspects are behaving themselves. Who's bitching at whom, who's standing by whom, whatever. The Spanish Department is having a party next Wednesday night and absolutely everybody you're interested in will be there. I can get myself invited as the date of Jamie Newman's best friend."

"The Chairman of the Department has just been murdered and they're having a *party?*"

"They've got to. They have no choice. Alberto Chacón, winner of the Nobel Prize for Literature, is giving a lecture at the University that evening; it's been scheduled for a year. The party in Chacón's honor, which is to take place after the lecture, was originally going to be held in Mason Blaine's house, but for obvious reasons it's now been shifted to the MacDonalds' house. You don't let a Nobel Laureate sit around his hotel room unentertained just because your department chairman has snuffed it. Shall I get myself invited?"

"Go for it," said Tom enthusiastically. "At this point I'll take any help I can get."

Kathryn picked up her cell phone and began a search for Patrick Cunningham.

CHAPTER 12

"How much of that were you actually able to follow?" Tracy shouted into Kathryn's ear.

"Slightly less than half, I'd say," Kathryn yelled back.

The shouting was necessary, as the MacDonalds' living room was crammed full of three times as many people as it was designed to hold comfortably and they were all talking at the top of their lungs.

It was Wednesday night, a week after the murder of Mason Blaine.

The Great Man, Chacón, had delivered the lecture of which Kathryn had understood less than half, and was now holding court at the party being given in his honor. Upon entering the room he had looked about, spotted the largest chair, and made a stately beeline for it. He had thrown off his great black cloak, settled into the chair, crossed his legs, interlaced his fingers, and proceeded to interrogate Professor MacDonald as to the state of the MacDonalds' collection of brandy. Chacón's face left few people in doubt as to what he thought of Professor MacDonald's answers, but he condescended to accept a glass of something that was offered him, and a nonstop supply of glasses after that. A sycophantic crowd of students gathered around his chair, most of them sitting on the floor; a few asked questions, but most had the sense to realize that their role there was to worship, so they silently obliged while Chacón pontificated in his powerful voice.

Over in their corner Tracy was yelling back at Kathryn, "You're lucky. At least you speak some Spanish. Jamie *insisted* I come to the damn lecture even though I don't speak a word of it."

"For heaven's sake, why?"

"Because I'll never have another chance to hear a Nobel Laureate speak, quote unquote."

"What an idiot! Sorry, he's your husband, but really! What good does it do you if you can't understand a word the guy is saying? Besides, Desmond Tutu comes to New York on a fairly regular basis, and he's a Nobel Laureate. You could always go hear him."

"Yeah, well, I didn't think of that, and besides, Jamie doesn't always respond well to reason."

"I have noticed that."

Kathryn's irony was not lost on her friend, but Tracy decided not to rise to the bait, instead taking another sip of her drink and letting her eyes wander over the crowd.

Kathryn, mindful of her reason for being at the party, asked, "What do you think? Surely they're a bit edgier than usual?"

"Christ, Kathryn! What do you expect? Of course

they're edgy! Look how much they're drinking! Normally with somebody like Chacón around they'd be on their best behavior, and this would be like a tea party. Speaking of drinking." Tracy rattled the ice in her empty glass.

Kathryn wasn't quite ready for a refill, but she agreed to accompany Tracy to the dining room, where the MacDonalds had set up the bar. As they threaded their way through the mob in that direction, they heard roars of laughter emanating from the room. Left to Tracy, they might never have gotten close enough to see the source of this amusement, but Kathryn could be pretty aggressive when she was curious, and she 'scuse-me'd through the crowd around the dining table, dragging Tracy in her wake, until they had a good view.

It was Patrick Cunningham, and he was mixing a drink. It was quite a performance.

"Now you see, boys and girls, the fact is that this is a bottle of vodka—this *is* a bottle of vodka. You see that, don't you? You see that? And this item here, yes, here we are, this one here, this is a *glass*, I'm sure you comprehend that—*comprenden ustedes*, as we say! And the fact of the matter, the true crux of the situation, is that this glass, this item here, does indeed contain *none* of the liquid that inhabits this bottle; that is, the quantity it contains is *zero*, because, as you see, the glass is *empty*!" At this, Patrick put down both bottle and glass, shoved both hands in his pockets, rocked back and forth from the balls of his feet to his heels, shook his head violently back and forth so that his frizzy hair flew in all directions, and cleared his throat with a great hacking noise. The laughter of his audience reached a deafening roar. He picked up the bottle and glass again. "Now if we were to, so to speak, introduce some of the liquid into the bottle, as it were—"

Everyone in the dining room continued hooting, clapping, and egging him on.

Kathryn turned to Tracy and asked, "What on earth—?"

Tracy replied, "Professor Witherspoon, better known as 'The Spoon.' I've met him at department parties, and if you think Patrick's imitation is wildly exaggerated, that's because you've never met Witherspoon. If anything, it's underplayed."

Patrick finished off his Witherspooned vodka and tonic—it took a good three minutes—to a round of tumultuous applause; Tracy and Kathryn refilled their own drinks and joined him.

"I didn't know you were so talented," Kathryn remarked as they strolled out of the French doors onto the enormous back porch, glassed in during the winter, and spanning the distance from the dining room to the living room.

"Ah," said Patrick with a puckish smile, and draping an arm around her, "there are so many things you don't know about me." He dropped a kiss on the tip of her nose. "But stick around. You have years to find out."

At the other end of the porch this little scene was witnessed by the Drews and José Espronceda y Montalbán. Edward grinned appreciatively and exclaimed, "¡Ay, bien! ¡El monjo tiene novia!"

"Parece que si," José replied; then, seeing the long-suffering look on Caroline's face, added hastily, "Oh! I am sorry! He said, Look, the monk has a girlfriend, and I said, It seems to be true."

"Really, Caroline," her husband remarked, "I'd think you'd learn Spanish in self-defense."

"I don't want to learn Spanish. What I *do* want to learn is what's with Patrick and Kathryn?"

"I'm not sure. I do know that the Newmans have been trying forever to matchmake between Patrick and Kathryn but that nothing's ever come of it."

"Well, that was a pretty specific bit of flirtation there," Caroline pronounced. "Still, she's a bit old for him, isn't she?"

"I think it is a good thing," declared José, "if Patrick goes with Kathryn. He is too much alone. Never, never, does he have a date in all the time I am here. That is not good for a man!"

"What's not good for a man?"

The three of them turned. Valerie Powers had emerged from the living room onto the porch. The Drews regarded her coolly, but José, ever the gentleman, answered her politely. "We are saying, or at least I am saying, that it is not good for a man to be for a long time without the company of a woman."

"Well," Valerie murmured in her silky voice, "I'd have to say yea to that."

Valerie had been trying to make an impression on José ever since she had first clapped eyes on him and she had failed singularly to do so. This puzzled her greatly, since she knew herself to be much more beautiful than any of the girls that José had dated during that time. She would long ago have written him off as hopeless were it not for the fact that Valerie was constitutionally incapable of writing off a man who looked like José and was attached to so much money. So she was still giving it the old college try, and José, poor man, was far too polite to tell her to take a hike. The next ten minutes, therefore, were spent with Valerie trying to get José to ask her out,

Edward feeling sorry for José and desperately trying to divert Valerie, and Caroline finding the whole thing wickedly entertaining and giving her husband no help at all.

This game was interrupted by the arrival of the so-called monk and his supposed girlfriend, together with Tracy Newman, who had by now drifted to their end of the porch. Greetings were exchanged all around, Patrick introducing Kathryn to the Drews.

"Well, Kathryn, what did you think of our Nobel lecturer?" Edward asked politely.

"The hell with that," his wife interrupted. "Ask her what she thinks about our murder."

"Caro!" Edward admonished.

"Oh come on, Edward. Kathryn's a friend of that cop. When he came into the Student Center she personally introduced him to all the graduate students, remember? They told us. So do you really think she's here for literary reasons?"

Edward, horrendously embarrassed, tried to stammer apologies for his wife, but Kathryn would have none of it.

"Not at all," she said. "I think that's very clever. Tell me, Caroline, what do *you* think of the murder?"

Tracy stood on tiptoe to whisper in Patrick's ear, "Kathryn ten, Caroline five."

Patrick bit back a smile.

Caroline looked sourly at Kathryn. "I think it's up to the police to solve it and the rest of us"—here she tossed off the last inch of her drink—"should keep our traps shut. I'm going back for a refill." And suiting the action to the words, she stalked off in the direction of the dining room. Edward made his excuses and hurried after her.

Valerie looked at Kathryn, whom she had met previously at the Newmans'. "Is it true? Are you here to spy on us?"

Shit, thought Kathryn. So much for undercover. "Sure," she replied casually. "I always go to the most hard-to-get-into parties in Harton in the entire calendar year just so I can spy for the cops. It's my hobby. Pardon me, I need to go tape a conversation in the living room." And summoning a seraphic smile, she fluttered her fingers at the group of them and departed feeling rather foolish.

In the living room the Great Man was still holding court. Professor MacDonald fetched him drinks; Mrs. MacDonald kept his plate restocked from the buffet. Around his rock-like presence the party ebbed and flowed. Kathryn searched the teeming horde and found a familiar face. Weaving through the bodies, she managed to reach him without stepping on too many toes or spilling her scotch.

"Stephen!"

"Kathryn! Lovely, dear, Kathryn!" He kissed her on both cheeks. "What an unexpected pleasure! How do you come to be at the MacDonalds'?"

Meaning, thought Kathryn, *how the hell did I wangle an invitation?*

"Patrick invited me!" she answered guilelessly. "Wasn't that lovely of him? And is this your date?" she asked, knowing damn well it wasn't.

The girl in question was small and cute and had flaming red hair and freckles.

"Oh, no," Stephen drawled, "ah have not the honor of calling Miss Hancock mah date, but ah hope she is mah friend. May ah introduced Jenny Hancock, the *Reverend* Kathryn Koerney!"

Jenny was, of course, one of Kathryn's targets, having been Mason Blaine's last flirt—if flirt was all she was. Kathryn extended a cordial hand, wondering if little Jenny was anywhere near as drunk as Stephen clearly was.

"You're a minister?" Jenny asked.

"Yes," Kathryn replied. "An Episcopal priest. I teach at the seminary."

"I think Christianity is a load of crap," Jenny declared.

Kathryn was used to this sort of thing at parties. People started tediously explaining to her why they no longer went to church the minute they discovered she was a priest; it was an occupational hazard of the clergy, suffered by all wearers of the cloth from Baptists to Catholics. The explanation was not usually expressed, however, with such shattering rudeness.

As Stephen, card-carrying Southern Gentleman and Sunday Go-to-Meetin' Roman Catholic, sputtered in shock, "Wha—what—?" Kathryn reflected that the question about how much Jenny had been drinking had probably been answered.

She offered Jenny a glittering smile and remarked in a thoroughly unoffended voice, "There *are* some really crappy things about Christianity, aren't there? To begin with, historically we have things like the Crusades and the Inquisition, but it's not all historical is it? Today the Church is just chock full of so many *hypocrites*. Is that the sort of thing you meant?"

Jenny gaped at her, her pretty mouth hanging open about an inch and a half. Kathryn could tell Stephen was about to laugh, so she stepped very hard on his toe. He got the point.

Jenny finally shut her mouth and nodded. "Yeah," she said. "Yeah, that's what I meant."

"Well," Kathryn replied cheerfully, "I couldn't agree with you more. But let's not talk about *my* work. Tell me about yours. Are you also in the Spanish Department?"

Thus she dragged the conversation ruthlessly in the direction she wanted it to go, and since neither Stephen nor Jenny was a match for her, she soon had them talking about Mason Blaine, how everybody had felt about him when he was alive, how everybody was feeling now, and what everybody was saying about who they thought had killed him.

Apparently the grad students' favorite candidate was Charles Caldwell, because *"everybody* knew Ellen Caldwell was having an affair with Mason and Charles was *wild* with jealousy about it."

"I don't know the Caldwells; are they here?"

"Oh, yes," Stephen replied. "That's Ellen over there, talking to Henrietta MacDonald." Kathryn turned to look.

There could hardly have been two women more different. Mrs. MacDonald was short, gray-haired, and, it seemed to Kathryn, determinedly feminine according to the most old-fashioned standards. She was wearing a pale pink cocktail dress that would not have looked out of place in the 1950s; it had lace at the neck, ruffly sleeves, and an unfashionably full skirt. The extraordinary thing, though, was that this confection suited her right down to the ground, and Henrietta MacDonald looked not only very pretty but also quite appropriately dressed.

Ellen Caldwell towered over her by a good ten inches, and was dressed in slouchy tailored linen that hung elegantly from her overly thin frame. She had chosen the muted neutrals of her clothes to show off the glory of her auburn hair. The hair, Kathryn noticed, hung straight to the shoulder in an unpretentious cut, but it was clear from the way her hair swung whenever the woman moved her head that she had paid a hell of a lot of money for that understated look. As for Ellen's face, it wasn't beautiful; it was better. It was strong, Kathryn decided, and full of intelligence.

"Well," she said. "I can see the appeal. For Blaine, I mean."

This statement was met with cries of disbelief and even derision. Neither Stephen nor Jenny would allow that Ellen was at all attractive, both maintaining that she was skinny as a rail and had a face like a horse and besides, she wasn't that nice a person. Kathryn encouraged them to elaborate on this last observation, which they were only too happy to do, while Kathryn attempted to sift the wheat of useful information from the chaff of alcohol, nerves, and general spite. After another five minutes she decided she had elicited from them everything she was going to get, and it was time to move on. Graciously conceding that they obviously knew Ellen Caldwell far better than she did, and mendaciously saying that she needed to use the little girl's room, she excused herself and went seeking new prey.

After the debacle with Caroline Drew, she was feeling pretty good about her success with Stephen and Jenny. She had ascertained the state of the nerves of two of the players, i.e., pretty shattered. Stephen's accent was never that broad except when he was absolutely blotto. And nobody had ever suggested that Jenny Hancock was a bitch, so presumably she was drunk, too. And they had heartily confirmed one of the suggestions Tom had wanted her to check out.

Damn! she thought. *I should have asked them to point out Charles Caldwell.* But even as the idea crossed her mind, she wavered about it. She wasn't sure she wanted to meet another killer.

"Hello, gorgeous!"

"Oh, hello, Jamie. You're in an expansive mood."

"Well, how often do you get to hear one of the greatest minds of our generation?" He waved his glass at Chacón. "Tracy didn't want to come, but I made her. Doesn't matter if you don't understand the words, I said. To sit in the presence of greatness is enough. When are you going to get that kind of opportunity again?"

"Well, I suppose that's one way of looking at it."

At this moment Patrick appeared and laid a hand on Jamie's shoulder. "A word in your ear, my friend." He pulled him away so that Kathryn couldn't hear what they were saying.

Kathryn decided she should try for a conversation with Carlos Barreda, and thought she saw him on the porch. With some difficulty she worked her way back through the crowd in the living room, but by the time she got to where she thought she had seen Carlos, he had disappeared. She did, however, find Tracy.

"Hail, fair one! How goes the battle?" she asked.

"Not well," Tracy replied. "Getting to that stage, you know. Maybe one black Russian too many."

"Really? You look perfectly sober to me."

"Do I? Well, looks can be deceiving, she said with vast originality. Oh, look who's coming. Our second-favorite blonde."

Kathryn looked around to see Crystal Montoya sweeping toward them.

Crystal extended a slender arm to Tracy with a drink in her hand, saying, "I believe this is yours."

Tracy looked down at it and said, "Oh, yeah, I guess so." She took it from Crystal, but she held the glass without drinking from it.

"Hello, Crystal," Kathryn said pleasantly. "I didn't know you were here."

Crystal raised her eyebrows in an expression that asked so eloquently what the hell Kathryn was doing there that Kathryn was hard put not to laugh. Had it been anyone but Crystal, Kathryn would have explained how she had acquired her invitation to the party, but the Castilian was left to stew in her own curiosity while Kathryn smiled blandly and instead asked her what she thought of the lecture. Crystal's Spanish was superior to Kathryn's but Kathryn's knowledge of Spanish literature was better than Crystal's, and her intelligence was about twice hers, so that the battle was running about even a minute later when Jamie showed up.

"Tracy," he interrupted rudely, "you've had enough for tonight. Here, give me that. I'll drink it." And he took the drink from her unresisting hand and tossed off a healthy swig from it.

Instantly he drew a rasping breath, dropped the glass, shattering it in pieces on the stone floor, arched his back, went stiff as the proverbial board, and fell among the shards of the glass.

CHAPTER 13

Y ou're sure?"

"Absolutely, Tom. You can carve it in granite. It was Tracy's drink. Jamie got it by mistake, because he told her she'd had enough to drink already so he'd take it. Actually, she'd already decided she'd had enough before he got there, she was standing there holding it—" Kathryn put a hand over her eyes for a moment and took a shaky breath. "It might have been her."

"If she thought she'd had enough, why'd she have a drink?"

"Well, there was this odd thing with Crystal, I didn't really understand it. I was talking to Tracy and she said she'd had enough to drink, then along comes Crystal and she hands Tracy a drink and says, 'I think this must be yours,' or something like that and Tracy says yes. Now, I find it hard to picture Crystal going to fetch a drink for

Tracy, but I suppose somebody might have mixed a drink for Tracy and handed it to Crystal and said would you take this to Tracy."

"Obviously I'll have to talk to Crystal. So Tracy accepted the drink even though she had no intention of drinking any more?"

"Well, it was her glass."

"Her glass?"

"The one she'd been drinking out of all evening. The MacDonalds have a multiple set of terribly tacky highball glasses based on the pink elephant theme. There are green giraffes and orange zebras and purple monkeys and such. Hideous, but I guess it helps people keep from getting their drinks mixed up. I was drinking out of a purple monkey. Tracy was drinking out of an orange zebra. Anyway, it was her glass. It had her drink in it, a black Russian; it had obviously been made for her, so she took it. What else could she do? Then she stood there, not drinking it, till Jamie came along and drank it for her." Kathryn shuddered and to her horror started to cry. *"Shit!"* she exclaimed, digging in her purse for tissues. "I don't even like the man and I'm actually glad he's dead."

"Don't be embarrassed," said Tom comfortingly. "It's just shock. Have some coffee. Or water."

Kathryn opted for water, knowing she needed to rehydrate herself after three Scotches. They were upstairs in the MacDonalds' largest spare bedroom, which fortunately had a table and space for three chairs, one each for Tom, Sergeant Pursley, and whoever was being questioned. Upon discovering that the victim had died eighteen inches from Kathryn's left foot, they had started with her, after telling everyone else at the party to remain downstairs until they were summoned.

Kathryn, with shaking hands, poured a glass of water from a pitcher provided by Mrs. MacDonald, even in catastrophe the perfect hostess; next to the water pitcher there was a large thermos of coffee and it was from this that Tom and Sergeant Pursley were taking comfort.

After gulping down half a glass, Kathryn looked at Tom. "Can we get through the rest of this? I really want to get back to Tracy."

"Sure. Except—well, you realize Tracy is the next person—?"

"Oh. Of course. Well, go ahead."

Bit by bit they extracted from her everything she had observed at the party, paying particular attention to everyone's movements during the twenty minutes prior to Jamie Newman's death. Kathryn made a most dismaying discovery. She was not very observant.

She could remember conversations. She could remember nuances. She could remember psychological observations. But she could not remember who was standing where, talking to whom, when.

"*Damn!*" she cried, pounding the table with the palm of her hand. "I am bloody *useless!* I can't remember *anything!*"

Tom regarded her across the table in a tangle of mixed emotions, the chief of which was surprise: his brilliant friend couldn't do what *he* could do blindfolded and half-asleep. Among the other emotions were disappointment (because he needed every good witness he could get) and unholy glee (there was something he was better at than Kathryn).

He assured her it didn't matter, that the main thing was that she had given them a clear picture of the scene when Jamie had died. Now, would she go downstairs and send Tracy up?

"And in case anybody asks, we're here for how long?" she asked.

"Oh, God," Tom groaned. "Probably the rest of the night. And what I'm gonna do about His Majesty down there I don't know."

"Well, I may not have noticed anything else, but I think you might be able to establish that Chacón never left that chair the whole time, and besides, he doesn't have anything to do with our local scandal, does he, so maybe you could at least cut him loose."

"That's an idea." Tom got to his feet and followed Kathryn downstairs. The living room was a carpet of people; the guests were now sitting on the floor talking in nervous murmurs, instead of standing and shouting as they had been prior to the disaster. Tom's entrance produced a sensation, voices clamoring to know what was happening, when they might be allowed to go home, but no voice was more magnificently demanding than that of the Nobel Laureate.

"*Señor!*" he boomed. "You are the man in charge?"

"I am," Tom replied equably.

"When will it be permitted that I can leave?"

"Maybe we can arrange that now. All of you here," Tom turned his head to address everyone else in the room. "I understand that Mr. Chacón arrived here, went to that chair, sat in it, and never moved from it until Jamie Newman died, right?"

There was a chorus of agreement.

"His drinks and food were brought to him?" Another chorus of agreement. "He never left the chair to go to the bathroom?" A chorus of no's. "Or for any other reason?" Another chorus of no's.

"All right, Mr. Chacón, you can go. In view of your, uh, standing in the, uh, international, uh, community, I'd like to apologize for the inconvenience, and one of our squad cars will take you back to your hotel."

The Great Man arose, Tom swore afterwards, in slow motion. He extended his left hand. An awestruck student delicately placed the collar of his cape in it. There was a slow, smooth movement of hands on velvet and then suddenly, with a practiced flourish, the great black cape swirled through the air and settled onto the shoulders of the Magnificent One. He walked out of the MacDonalds' living room, and the students huddled on the floor parted before him like the Red Sea before the Israelites.

As the front door closed behind him, Tom turned back to the living room. "Right," he said. "Tracy?"

Kathryn had been unable to find Tracy in the crowd. She saw her now, rising, white-faced, from a corner, where Patrick had been guarding her like a baby chick. He was holding her by one arm. It seemed to Kathryn that that was not nearly enough support.

"Tom," she pleaded urgently. "Let me come with her."

"Since when are you a cop? And what do you think I am, a monster?"

Patrick had delivered Tracy to the door of the living room, walking with his left arm around her shoulders and firmly gripping her right hand in his.

Tom reached out and took Tracy's hand in both of his, more as if she were his daughter than a witness. "Tracy? I'm so sorry about this. If you'll just come this way—" He led her into the front hall and up the stairs.

Kathryn had to admit she was impressed by this avuncular performance. "How's she doing?" she asked Patrick as they stood with their back to the living room wall conversing in near whispers.

"As well as can be expected under the circumstances. And the circumstances, as you very well know, are twofold. One, her husband has just dropped dead right in front of her. And two—"

"It was her drink."

"Precisely."

"Somebody poisoned *Tracy's drink*." Kathryn shook her head in disbelief. "But who on earth would want to kill Tracy? It must have got into her drink by mistake."

"It wasn't a mistake," Patrick averred grimly.

Kathryn stared at him. "How do you know?"

"Well, this is kind of embarrassing."

"For God's sake, Patrick, Jamie's dead and you're saying somebody's trying to kill Tracy and you're *embarrassed*?"

"You're right. Well, this is not the sort of thing a gentleman normally discusses with his date, but under the circs, here goes. Today I most inconveniently became afflicted with—how shall I put this delicately? An intestinal disorder." He paused.

"Oh, I see. I do remember you dashed off to the gents after the lecture with rather indecent haste."

"Exactly. Well, back to Tracy's drink. I mixed it myself, but no sooner was I finished with it than I had another of my damn attacks and I really had no choice at all but to plunk her drink down on the sideboard in the dining room and beat a hasty retreat upstairs to the facilities."

"All right, but why didn't you take it to her when you came back down again?"

"When I came back down it was nearly ten minutes later—sorry to afflict you with that unsavory detail—and when I looked on the sideboard her drink was gone. Obviously somebody else had taken it to her, so I went into the living room to have a word with Jamie. You'll remember that, I pulled him away from a conversation with you."

This was precisely the sort of thing Kathryn had just discovered she *didn't* remember, but she took Patrick's word for it. "So, when you mixed Tracy's drink, were you by chance chatting up a tall blonde named Crystal Montoya? Because that's who brought Tracy her drink."

Patrick was looking embarrassed again. "Actually, not chatting up so much as showing off for; the rest of the audience consisted mostly of my regulars, plus a bunch of undergraduates in whom I was singularly uninterested."

Enlightenment dawned on Kathryn. "You were doing Professor What's-his-name?"

"Witherspoon, yes."

Kathryn felt the blood in her veins grow chill. "Patrick, you stood in front of a room full of people making a huge song and dance about mixing a drink, and this time, to ring some changes on it, you introduced the information of *who the drink was for*?"

Patrick hung his head miserably and ran his hands through his frizzy hair. "I did better than that," he confessed. "And you see here, boys and girls, that this glass has on it an *orange zebra*, that is, a *zebra* that is *orange*, which is a *most* peculiar color for a zebra, don't you see, one might almost say a *unique* color for a zebra, but *lo*! Watch what happens when we fill the glass with the preferred drink of Ms. Tracy Newman, that is to say, vodka and Kahlua! The black liquid rises, and behold, the black stripes of the zebra join with it, they *join with it*, boys and girls! Now what might Ms. Tracy Newman make of the odd pattern of floating, meaningless orange stripes, blah blah blah."

Kathryn stared at him, finding no words.

Patrick folded his legs under him and slid down the wall, covering his face with his hands. "Then I put the goddamn glass down and left the room for ten minutes and killed my best friend." His shoulders began to shake.

Kathryn sank down beside him and wrapped her arms around him and held tight. She reflected that she seemed to be doing a lot of this lately. The results, she supposed, of an epidemic of murder. She knew better than to try to reason with the unreasonable guilt of Patrick's last statement. One does not attempt to talk people out of their emotions. So she held him in silence, her heart praying for him, her mind racing.

When she had witnessed the Witherspoon act previously all the people in the dining room had been focused on Patrick's every word and move. It would have been the same when he was mixing Tracy's black Russian; the only question was who had been in the room at the time. Tom would be able to put that together fairly easily; each person there would give a list of everybody else they thought was there. Nobody would get it right, but when Tom put them all together and ironed out the kinks, he would get an accurate list.

Then he would have to figure out who would have had the opportunity to pass by the sideboard and drop something in Tracy's drink before Crystal picked it up to take it out to Tracy on the porch. And of course Crystal herself would have to be considered as one of the people with opportunity.

Kathryn wondered what the poison had been; she wondered if Tom would tell her if she asked. She decided not to ask; she'd already been shut out once when she'd asked about why Blaine's body had been left in the St. Margaret's driveway. She hadn't liked the feeling that gave her. She didn't want to give Tom the opportunity to give her that feeling again.

But while all these musings buzzed in her brain like flies, the one big question flashed like a neon sign: Why, why, *why* would anybody want to kill Tracy?

And the answer came back: Since the person who wanted her dead was at this party, among the people Kathryn had jokingly called the usual suspects, that person was the killer of Mason Blaine. Tracy had seen something that night in the darkness on the grounds of St. Margaret's, something she didn't remember, something of which she did not realize the significance. She had not yet told the police. And the killer was trying desperately to silence her before she did.

Oh, this is rubbish, Kathryn thought. *I've been watching too many TV cop shows.*

She was so lost in her thoughts that she jumped when she heard Tom's voice at the door. "Kathryn?"

She looked up to see Tom standing there beside Tracy, who was still looking quite pale but at least seemed to be able to stand without support. Kathryn released her hold on Patrick and leapt up from the floor; he was only a second behind her.

As Kathryn held Tracy in a crushing embrace, and Patrick stood beside them patting Tracy on the shoulder, Tom said quietly to Kathryn, "We're going to let you

take Tracy home now. Actually, when I say 'home' I suggest you take her to your house. Would that be O.K.?"

Kathryn nodded. "I had already decided on that."

"We're going to send you in a squad car. And Kathryn?"

"Yes?"

"We're going to put a guard on the house. On Tracy.
Do you understand?"

"I absolutely understand."

"You'll help us? Make sure she doesn't do anything
foolish? Like try to go out unescorted or anything?"

"Count on me." The look she gave him as she said this
made it unnecessary for her to say more than those three
words.

He gave her a little smile. "I will." He opened the front
door. "Rossi!" he called. "Take these ladies to Alexander
Street." And he hustled them out the door before they
had a chance to say good-night to Patrick, who stood in
the doorway of the living room looking rather bereft.

Tom stepped past him and pronounced in a clear
voice: "Crystal Montoya."

CHAPTER 14

T here's no mystery about it," Crystal said coolly. "I was in the dining room talking to my hostess. I had gone in there a few minutes previously to get myself a drink and she cornered me. She is a very boring woman and I couldn't get away from her. I had met some of the graduate students during the course of the evening and I understand that it is a standing joke that she can bring any conversation around to the weather within five minutes. Sure enough, five minutes later she was talking about the weather. I was looking around for a way to escape when a young man came in, tall with frizzy hair. I hadn't met him, but from his age I would guess he was one of the graduate students. He began to mix a drink, a black Russian, for Tracy Newman, in the most extraordinary, extravagant style. It was a performance, obviously an imitation of somebody that the others were familiar with, presumably a teacher in the Spanish Department. I wouldn't know. Mrs. MacDonald seemed a bit embarrassed by this, so we moved into the corner of the dining room away from the fuss so she wouldn't have to listen to it. Then, thank God, she decided she needed to check on something in the kitchen, so she went off in that direction. Shortly after that the performance ended, and I started talking to the husband of one of the Spanish faculty. His name was Charles. After a few minutes our conversation came to an end and I decided to go out onto the porch. On my way I passed the sideboard. I looked down and there was Tracy's drink. There was no mistaking it: a black Russian in a glass with an orange zebra on it. That boy with the frizzy hair had made a big production about describing it when he was mixing it, the whole room knew it. I don't know why he'd made it and then not taken it to her, but I was pretty sure I had seen Tracy out on the porch earlier, so I picked up the drink and took it out to her."

Tom stared at Crystal with something like dread. "What do you mean, 'a big production,' and 'the whole room knew it'?"

"Exactly what I said. Everybody in the whole room was watching him while he mixed it, so everybody in the whole room knew it was Tracy's drink. I wasn't the only one."

Oh, shit shit shit shit shit. "O.K., Crystal, who else was in the room? That you can name or describe?"

"Well, Mrs. MacDonald, obviously. And that man Charles. A member of the faculty named Edward, last name Drew, I think. An unkempt young man named Carlos who discovered I spoke Spanish and attempted to talk to me but when he began blathering on about the blood of the peasants I moved on. Very briefly there was a girl with flaming red hair . . ."

Shit shit shit shit, thought Tom again. *Too damn many of them.*

"Also," Crystal continued, "a very beautiful young man who spoke perfect Castilian Spanish; his name was José. He was attempting to calm Carlos down, but without success. I left the two of them together to speak to Charles."

"You said a minute ago you started talking to Charles just after you stopped talking to Mrs. MacDonald."

"Did I?" Crystal shrugged, unconcerned. "You know how it is at this kind of party. You mill around talking to people. You don't remember what order you meet them in."

"O.K. Can you remember anybody else in the dining room when Tracy's drink was being made? Anybody you can name, or who was distinctive enough you can describe them?"

"Well, there was a young woman with long, ash-blond hair. I think you would describe her as fairly pretty. But most of the people here are Spanish Department, so I wouldn't have any reason to know them."

"Yeah, that brings me to my next question. What are you doing here, Crystal? How'd you get invited?"

There was a pause, and Tom saw a faint pink tinge appear on Crystal's neck. "Well, I admit to a little manipulation here. I wanted to come to this party. You know, to be able to say I'd been to a private party for Alberto Chacón. So I called up Mrs. MacDonald and said I was a member of St. Margaret's and I was Castilian and I was a lifelong fan of Chacón and I'd had tickets to the lecture for a year and when the party was going to be at Mason's

I was invited and then I kind of just left it hanging. Basically I was so brazen, I made it impossible for her not to invite me."

The Castilian chin was high and the blue eyes regarded Tom unflinchingly. It was a good story, and it sounded authentically Crystal; he had served with her long enough on the St. Margaret's vestry to know that when she wanted something, she usually got it. But he knew she was lying. This intrigued him no end. Why lie about how you got invited to a party?

"All right, Crystal, just one more thing. When you took Tracy Newman's drink to her, did you stop on the way to talk to anybody, take any detours at all?"

"No. I saw the drink, picked it up, walked out to the porch, walked up to Tracy, and handed it to her. No detours, no conversations."

"Well, then, Crystal. I think that's all. You can go home now."

"Well, thank God for that," she said ungraciously, then rose and left the room.

"Chief?"

"Yeah, Purze."

"I hate to sound really stupid but we're assuming this is the same killer, right? Only this time he was aiming for Mrs. Newman?"

"Yeah."

"Why?"

Tom scratched his nose. "Purze, that's not at all stupid. That's the big, fat, smart question of the week. And when we know why, I think we'll know who. Meanwhile I'm going to have a little chat with Mrs. MacDonald. You stay here."

He found the hostess in the kitchen brewing endless pots of coffee. Her eyes were red.

"Mrs. MacDonald, I need you to help me with something."

"Certainly, Chief Holder."

It was funny. The woman *looked* fluffy but she didn't *act* fluffy. "I need you to tell me the name of a young man, probably a graduate student, with frizzy hair, who was doing an imitation of somebody as he mixed Tracy Newman's drink, with the result that everybody knew it *was* Tracy Newman's drink."

Mrs. MacDonald's *sang froid* deteriorated slightly. "Oh dear. That would be Patrick Cunningham. Such a nice—"

But Tom didn't hear the end of it; he was headed back to the living room. He remembered a head of frizzy hair comforting Tracy Newman. "Patrick Cunningham?" he called. Sure enough, Tall Frizzy-head stood up. The young man looked like hell. "Come upstairs, please," Tom invited, in a cordial but businesslike manner.

Patrick threw himself into the chair Tom indicated and when Tom began, "Please state your name for the—" he exploded savagely, "My name is Patrick O'Reilly Cunningham and I live at the Graduate College and yes, it was me, I'm the stupid goddamn idiot who made it perfectly clear to a whole goddamn room full of people that *here*," he mimed, pointing with his right hand to an invisible glass in his left, "right *here*, is Tracy Newman's glass, so if anybody feels like coming up and putting poison in it you know right where it is."

"Take it easy, Mr. Cunningham," Tom said placidly. "I can understand how you'd be upset, but there's no point in blaming yourself. You didn't know what was going to happen. You're a friend of Mrs. Newman?"

Patrick rested both his elbows on the table and sank his head into his hands, clawing his fingers through his unruly hair. "More a friend of her husband's. We roomed together freshman year. We've been best friends ever since. I was best man at his wedding."

Jesus, thought Tom. *No wonder the boy is ripping himself to shreds.* "I'm sorry for your loss," he said, aware of how pathetically inadequate the words were. "Now, I know this is difficult for you, but I'm sure you want to help us find out whoever did this to your friend, so pull yourself together and think. You're in the dining room, you're doing this routine of yours, mixing Mrs. Newman's drink. Who was watching you? Name them. Sergeant Pursley will write down the names."

Dully, Patrick started reciting. "Edward and Caroline Drew. Charles Caldwell. John MacDonald. Carlos Barreda. José Espronceda y Montalbán. Valerie Powers. Jenny Hancock. Some first years I don't know so well, one of them is named Harry something, another one is Mary or maybe Mary Ann. There was a tall blond woman, stunningly beautiful, who I don't think has anything to do with the University." He was silent for a moment. "That's all I can remember."

"Now, could you just show me, so I can get a clear picture of it, exactly what you were doing when you were mixing this drink?"

Patrick groaned. "Isn't it enough to tell you that I made it utterly clear to everybody there—"

Tom interrupted him. "I'm sorry, Mr. Cunningham, I know you don't want to do this, but it will help us, really it will. So please, go ahead. I assume you were standing up?"

Reluctantly, Patrick dragged himself to his feet and with tremendous self-consciousness gave a lackluster reproduction of the performance in which he had mixed Tracy's black Russian. He used one of the water glasses Mrs. MacDonald had provided but mimed the vodka and Kahlua bottles. When he was finished he sank gratefully back into his chair.

"Thank you, Mr. Cunningham," said Tom, his heart in his boots. It was every bit as bad as Crystal had said, and as the boy himself had said. "Now, when you were actually doing this, I assume you were doing it with, uh, a bit of flair and at fairly high volume? Playing to the crowd, so to speak?"

"I was showing off, yes," Patrick said between clenched teeth.

"So it's fair to say that everybody in the room heard you?"

"They couldn't avoid hearing me, I told you."

"So then, you mixed this drink for Mrs. Newman. Why didn't you take it to her?"

"Because I had an attack of the squits," Patrick spat, still showing all the signs of self-loathing.

"You what?"

"I have a stomach bug, I have an intestinal problem, I have *diarrhea*," he shouted at them as if they were hard of hearing. "It came on me this morning and I've been running to the john all day. But I wasn't about to miss Chacón's lecture or this party. Anyway, I had just finished Tracy's drink when I got another attack, so I backed away from the dining table where I'd been doing my stupid little performance and set the drink down on the sideboard, thinking I'd come back and get it in a minute. Then I ran upstairs to the bathroom. But it was pretty bad, and I was there for, I don't know, seven or eight minutes, maybe even ten. And when I got back

downstairs, Tracy's drink was gone, so I figured somebody else had picked it up and taken it to her. So I went
into the living room to talk to Jamie."

"This would have been not long before Mr. Newman
went out onto the porch and drank Mrs. Newman's
drink?"

Patrick's mouth worked. "Just a few minutes."

"What did you talk about with Mr. Newman, do you
remember?"

"I remember, all right. I was telling him to stop being so
damned obvious when he was talking to Valerie Powers.
He was making a fool of himself. Now, of course . . ."
Patrick's voice trailed off and his eyes filled with tears.

"Mr. Newman was having an affair with Miss Powers?"

"Yes," was the curt reply.

"This is rumor, or something you guessed, or—"

"He told me." Even more curt.

"And you disapproved."

"Yes."

"So you told him to stop being obvious with Miss
Powers and what was his response?"

"He told me to stop being an old woman."

"Ah. And then what happened?"

"He went out onto the porch to talk to his wife."

"And that's the last time you saw him alive?"

Patrick swallowed audibly. "Yes."

"Well, I think that's all for now, Mr. Cunningham. I'm
going to ask you to stay here for a while in case we need
to get back to you—"

Patrick was lifting a hand like a supplicant, a pleading
look on his face. Tom felt sure the boy was about to ask
if he could be released so that he could go over to
Kathryn's and help look after Tracy, but he was wrong.

"Chief—Chief Holder," said Patrick. "Could I be allowed to go to wherever they've taken Jamie? To the morgue, or wherever? To be with him?"

"I'm sorry, son," said the surprised policeman. "We can't allow that. Aside from the fact that there's no place for you at the morgue, we might need you here. Come on now, go back downstairs and be with your friends. You need their support."

Patrick studied him morosely as if trying to decide whether or not to argue this decision. Then he put the heels of his hands into his eyes and rubbed them. "O.K.," he said, emerging red-eyed and resigned. He put his hands on the table, pushed himself heavily to his feet, and walked out of the room, leaving the door open behind him. Pursley got up to close it.

"I don't know who I feel sorrier for," Tom remarked. "Him or us."

"Yeah," Pursley replied, awed out of his usual "yessir." "That's most of our suspects, and ten minutes for one of them to kinda work their way around the table and drop something in that drink. But that would mean they brought the poison to the party ready to use it."

"Oh, yeah, that's obvious. They knew Tracy Newman was going to be here and they came prepared to kill her. They just didn't know the Cunningham boy was going to hand them such a golden opportunity to do it in a way that was going to leave it so wide open. *Damn.*"

"So who do we see next?"

"Edward Drew. He's our best chance for getting the names of all the students who were in the dining room, and we need to complete the list of everybody who was in that room. Once we have that, we work on a list of everybody in the vicinity of the Newmans and Kathryn Koerney and Crystal Montoya when Jamie Newman drank that black Russian and died. When we have those names, we let everybody else go home. And then we spend the rest of the night here."

CHAPTER 15

They indeed spent the rest of the night in the MacDonalds' spare bedroom.

When they got around to interviewing Henrietta Mac-Donald, Tom broached the matter of Crystal Montoya's invitation to the party. She immediately looked about ten times more uncomfortable, if that was humanly possible, than when she had walked in. But Henrietta was made of stern stuff, and she did not fold. She bit her lips, and hesitated a moment, then asked, "You have talked to her already, haven't you?"

"Yes, we have," Tom replied.

"Did she tell you that she called me, and told me that she was a friend of Mason's, and that when the party was scheduled for his house she was invited, and she really wanted to come very badly, and more or less made it impossible for me not to invite her?"

"I'm afraid we can't tell you what other people have told us, Mrs. MacDonald. We ask questions, you answer them. How did Crystal Montoya get invited to this party?"

Mrs. MacDonald bit her lips again. "My husband told me that she would be coming. If anybody asked me why, I was to tell that story. But nobody has asked me until now. And after somebody has been killed in my house, it seems silly to lie to the police about something as small as why somebody else came to the party."

"That's very sensible, Mrs. MacDonald. So what's the real story?"

"I honestly don't know. You'll have to ask my husband. He said something about somebody doing a favor for the Spanish Department, and that we were paying them back. That's all I can tell you."

She was so obviously telling the truth that Tom did not press her any further, but let the Crystal question wait until John MacDonald sat in the witness's chair. After Tom had asked him about Patrick Cunningham's imitation of Professor Witherspoon mixing Tracy's drink, and the movements of everybody else in the room after that (the same questions he had asked Mrs. MacDonald and was of course asking everyone else), he said, "Just one more thing, and I'd appreciate it if you'd be as sensible as your wife and come right out and tell us the truth about this matter."

MacDonald bristled visibly. "I *beg* your pardon?"

"Crystal Montoya. I understand you had some little story cooked up about how she got invited to the party. Now that there's been a murder, little stories won't do. Who did this favor for the Spanish Department, and what was the favor?"

John MacDonald hesitated a second. "I can tell you the favor. It was a donation, a very substantial donation considering that all the donor asked in return was that Miss Montoya be invited to the party. And after all, she was a friend of Mason's, and if the party had been at his house as originally planned, she would have been invited there, as we said in what you call our little story. But I am in an extremely awkward position here. The donor swore me to secrecy. Of course he wasn't expecting—"

"This is a homicide investigation, Mr. MacDonald. Nobody's entitled to privacy."

"I realize that. But this is a man of some standing in the community and I am loath to offend him. I'll tell you what. I will call him tomorrow and tell him what has happened and ask him to reveal his name to the police. He is an honorable man and I believe that he will see that this matter is trivial in the light of a murder investigation and that he will give me that permission. How will that do?"

And from that position Tom could not budge him. Besides, it seemed pretty reasonable, so he let him go. And that was the last they saw of their host until about 1:40 in the morning, when John MacDonald walked back in on them in between interviews and demanded petulantly how much longer his wife was to be kept awake; Tom replied in his mildest voice that Mrs. Mac-Donald could retire to bed at any time she liked, provided she understood that her house was going to remain full of policemen and people they were questioning, not to mention the crime scene team who had laid claim to the porch.

Miraculously, the coffee kept coming, delivered by MacDonald himself, and the quality of it did not deteriorate. At 2:00 A.M. a plate of sandwiches appeared. Tom and his Sergeant fell on them like hungry wolves, and Tom announced that, provided Mrs. MacDonald didn't turn out to be the killer, he had half a mind to marry her himself. Pursley, ignoring the fact that both his boss and Mrs. MacDonald were married already, mumbled his agreement to the spirit of this sentiment through a mouth full of tuna fish.

They finished at 6:20. Tom didn't see any point in going home at that hour, so he went straight back to the station. There he changed into the fresh shirt he always kept there for just such occasions, and got the electric razor out of his desk and ran it over his chin, and figured that would do.

He then set to work trying to make sense of the multitude of testimony he had collected over the past eight hours. He already knew that it did not look good. Six of his original suspects had seen that black Russian mixed and knew whose it was. And although only three of them—Charles Caldwell, Valerie Powers, and Carlos Barreda—seemed to have been on the sideboard side of the dining room at the critical time, at a party like that, with people moving around all the time, you couldn't always trust people's memories. And of course, there was no absolute guarantee that the killer was one of his original suspects, especially if the theory that was currently gnawing at his gut turned out to be true.

But fancy theories aside, police work is ninety-nine percent slog, so Tom slogged. He made charts and diagrams of the movements of all of the people in the dining room at different times according to the testimony of all of the different witnesses there. He breakfasted on six powdered-sugar doughnuts (three times his normal working-at-the-station breakfast, but then he'd been up all night) and another quart of coffee while he plowed through this tedium. Even though he was exhausted, he was meticulous, and determined to make no mistakes; he checked, double-checked, and triple-checked.

At 9:30 his phone rang.

"Yeah?" he managed.

"A Mr. Lincoln Massey. He says it's important."

What the hell was Link Massey bothering him with church business for at work? How could it be important? But he punched the appropriate button.

"Hello, Link? What's up?"

"Hello, Tom. John MacDonald called me this morning. I wanted to tell you myself that I was the one who made the contribution to the Spanish Department so that Crystal could go to that party."

"You did it?"

"Yes. It was no big deal, really, Tom. Crystal is a friend of mine, we know each other from church of course, and she was very disappointed about losing the opportunity to go to the Chacón party when Mason died, and I said I would make it possible for her to go to the party at the MacDonalds'. The money wasn't important to me, it's a tax write-off anyway. I hope that clears up the matter for you?"

"Oh, sure, Link, that's fine. Thanks for calling. See you in church."

Tom hung up the phone.

"Oooooo," he said to himself, "I don't like that. I do not like that one bit." Crystal Montoya was divorced. But Link Massey wasn't. Tom spent no more than twenty seconds in fierce cogitation before calling Manhattan and arranging surveillance on both Crystal and Link from their places of work, because it was obvious that that was where any trysts would be carried out, not here in Harton where it would be far too easy to get caught. Then he went back to his charts and diagrams.

Shortly after 11:30 his phone rang again.

"It's your sister-in-law. From Ohio. She insisted."

Tom sighed. "Oh, fer cryin' out loud. Put her on." There was a pause followed by a click. "Flora, for Christ's sake, I'm in the middle of a double homicide! Why the hell are you—"

"Where the hell is my sister?"

"Come again?"

"You heard me. Where the hell is my sister?"

"Flora, I haven't the slightest idea what you're talking about."

"We always talk on Sundays. It was her turn to call this past Sunday and she didn't. I waited in all afternoon and when she didn't call me I finally called her. She didn't answer. So I called her again on Monday. I called her three times, at nine in the morning and at twelve-thirty and at three-thirty in the afternoon and she didn't answer any of those times. So I called again Tuesday, four times. No answer. So I called again yesterday, all day. I lost count of how many times I called. She still didn't answer. Is she in the hospital? If something's wrong with Louise, Tom, I expect you to tell me. What's going on?"

A hollow feeling had opened in the pit of Tom's stomach. And his mouth had gone dry.

"Flora," he managed to say, "I'm not sure. I, uh, I haven't seen Louise in days, but that's not unusual when I'm working a homicide because I get home at midnight and leave the house at dawn, you know." Suddenly he became aware of how feeble this sounded. "I'll go home right now and check up, see what's uh, happening. I'll give you a call right away and let you know. O.K.?"

"You do that," Flora replied with a snap and banged down the phone.

Tom jumped out of his chair and was out of his office in half a second. "I have to go home," he shouted to his astonished subordinates. "Family emergency. Be right back."

He took one of the squad cars and used the siren, because Flora's phone call had summoned to his conscious mind something that had been sitting buried, unheeded, at the bottom of it.

He had been enjoying his Louise-free days, that was true, but still, he did share a house with her, and he was a trained observer. Although they no longer shared a bedroom, they shared a bathroom. His wife left the bathmat askew; she left the top off the toothpaste; these were the invariable signs of her presence. *And the signs had been missing,* he now realized, *for days.*

He came screeching up to the curb in front of his home, killed the siren, and ran up the walk. He burst into the front door shouting, "Louise! Louise! Are you here?"

Receiving no answer, he looked quickly through the living room, dining room, and kitchen before dashing upstairs to check the two small bedrooms—his and hers—and the bathroom. There was no one there. And the cap was on the toothpaste. He swore at his own stupidity. He looked in the hall closet; Louise owned only two suitcases and they were both there. A nightmarish case of déjà vu came over him; one of his homicide investigations had begun when he had looked in the closet of a missing woman and discovered that none of her luggage was missing. A shiver went up his spine.

Louise's car had been in the garage when he had taken his out the night before. He went pelting down the stairs, through the kitchen, out the back door, and into the garage. There was Louise's car.

Tom went back into the kitchen, wondering what the hell to do next, and that's when he saw Louise's purse sitting on the kitchen table, which was where she always left it. It had been sitting there every night when he'd come in, of course, and every morning when he'd left. He was trying to figure out if he should have noticed if it hadn't changed position in several days when the phone rang and startled him so much, he jumped.

"Hello?"

"Tom? Where is she?"

"Flora, I don't know. She isn't here. Her purse is here, her car's here, but she's nowhere in sight."

"Oh, *great*! My sister's been missing for *four days* and my brother-in-law the cop doesn't even *notice*!"

"Flora, calm down, I'm sure there's a simple explanation for this," said Tom, wondering what on earth it could possibly be.

"Now you listen to me, Tom Holder. If something has happened to my baby sister, I am going to hold you personally responsible. Now you call the police and you *find* her, you hear me?" She hung up.

"I *am* the police, you old bird," Tom grumbled to the dead receiver before placing it back on the hook.

He thought a minute. Sunday afternoon. O.K., assuming Louise wasn't home Sunday afternoon, when had she gone? The last time he'd seen her was at supper on Thursday night, before he'd been called out to look at the body of Mason Blaine. Had Louise been at church Sunday morning? Tom didn't know; he'd been working.

He picked up the phone again and started to punch a number he didn't have to look up. In the middle of it, however, he stopped and put the receiver back on the hook. Who was he going to talk to? Not the Rector, that was for damn sure! Not after that run-in last week. Not the Associate Rector, either, Tom thought. Bob Tucker was all right, but he was unlikely to respond well to a request for an odd favor with no explanation. The Assistant to the Rector, that was who he needed. He picked up the phone, punched the number, greeted the secretary politely and asked for Maggie Nicholas.

"Maggie! Tom Holder. How are you?"

"I'm great, Tom. Missed you on Sunday. I assume you were solving this murder of ours?"

"Trying to. Listen, Maggie, I need a big favor, and it's going to sound really weird, and I'm afraid I haven't got time to explain why I need it. Could you just do something for me and not ask why and I'll explain later?"

"Sounds intriguing. Sure, what is it?"

"Did you see Louise in church on Sunday?"

"Hang on a minute. Yeah. Come to think of it, I administered the chalice to her. Why? Oh, sorry, you said you didn't have time to explain. Is that all?"

"No, I'm afraid not. Can you go around and ask everybody you can find if they saw her, too? It's important, otherwise I wouldn't ask."

"You're right, Tom, that *is* weird, but your wish is my command. I'm going to put you on hold."

About seven minutes later she was back. "O.K., Tom, here's the report. The Rector was deep in conference with Amalie Prescott and God help anybody who interrupted, but Frances and Bob both say they saw Louise for sure, Ginger is almost certain she saw her, and Teddy kind of thinks he saw her. Will that do?"

"That will do fine. Maggie, you're terrific. I'll tell you about it later. Thanks." He hung up.

So his wife had been at church on Sunday morning. Obviously, then, he had been correct in assuming that the reason he'd been enjoying spouse-free days up until then was simply because he'd been leaving the house at six every morning and getting home at midnight after she'd gone to bed. But then Flora had started calling on Sunday afternoon and Louise hadn't been there to pick up the phone, and she should have been. And now the cap was on the toothpaste and the bathmat was straight and they'd been that way for days, and this was Thursday. *Damn.*

He was going to have to file a missing persons report on his own wife. And he was going to have to admit that she had probably been missing since Sunday afternoon. And that he hadn't been aware of it. •

Suddenly his lack of progress on the Mason Blaine homicide looked like a picnic in the park. He could just see Nick Silverman's face, hear the prosecutor's tone of voice: "Now, let me get this straight, Tom: Your wife's been gone for four days and you've just decided to let us know?" A hot wave of embarrassment flooded Tom's face as he contemplated what might prove a major hiccup in his career.

But as soon as he had that thought, it was succeeded by a greater wave of guilt. His first concern should have been for Louise, not for his own humiliation. He knew why it hadn't been: not because there was no love between them, but because there was a peculiar self-sufficiency behind Louise's battiness. He found it hard to believe, despite the fact that she had apparently wandered off without her purse and without any visible means of transportation, that she was in any serious trouble.

He pulled the purse over to him and opened it. Her wallet was still in it, and her car keys. He looked in the wallet and counted the bills. Seventy-three dollars. He had given her one hundred and fifty dollars for groceries and housekeeping money the previous Friday and he knew she'd spent some of it. He got up and looked in the refrigerator. Was that seventy-seven dollars worth of groceries? Or had she taken some cash with her? He sighed. He was putting off the inevitable.

He left the house and drove back to the station and filed a missing persons report on one Louise Buchanan Holder. Just as he expected, this created an uproar that reached Trenton within thirty minutes, and sure enough, here came the expected call from Nick Silverman.

At least he wasn't being sarcastic. Or not the kind of cool, superior sarcasm Tom had been dreading.

"Would you mind telling me how in the (unprintable) hell a police chief loses his wife for four days and doesn't (unprintable) *notice*?"

Tom had decided that the only way to handle it was to jump in the deep end. "One, homicide investigation, you get in at two A.M., you leave at dawn. Two, separate bedrooms. Three, take ten seconds and think about those two things put together before you start yelling again."

There followed a few seconds of silence.

"Oh," said the D.A. more quietly. "Well, I guess under those circumstances it becomes a little more understandable, but listen, Tom, you're going to have to explain about the separate bedrooms to the media, you hear? Now, normally that would be your own private business, but they're going to eat you alive unless you can explain why you didn't notice she was gone, and—"

"Yeah, Nick, I know. I already figured that out. I've been trying to write a statement, but it's, well—"

"That kind of thing can be tricky. Why don't you let my people do it?"

Tom hesitated. "Thanks, Nick. But I think I know somebody at this end who can help me with it."

"Well, O.K., but get on it right away. I want that statement in two hours, so we can have it at the same time we announce Louise's disappearance. This would be big enough news, the wife of a police chief, but it's going to be even bigger because you're the one investigating this double homicide, you understand? The papers are going to have a field day with this, so we've got to do it right."

"Yes, Nick," Tom sighed.

He hung up the phone, scrambled for his St. Margaret's directory, and punched Kathryn's number.

"I'm sorry, Tom," said Mrs. Warburton. "She's not here. She's probably having lunch at the Seminary. Is it important? Would you like her cell number?"

He would.

"Sorry, Tom, could you speak up? It's a madhouse here; I'm in the Seminary dining hall; what, *now*? If it's urgent, of course; anything you say. My house in ten minutes."

Kathryn abandoned her lunch and her colleagues and headed home, agog with curiosity. Tom had previously invited himself over at teatime for conferences, but he had never hauled her away from whatever she was doing and called it a matter of urgency. Maybe he was actually going to tell her something.

"*Missing?*"

"Since Sunday."

"*Sunday?* But she was in church on Sunday morning. I gave her communion myself."

"Oh, yeah, about seventy-five people agree she was in church Sunday morning. It's Sunday afternoon she went missing. Here I am, I'm a cop. My wife's been gone for three and a half days and I didn't know it. And this is why I didn't know it," Tom hastened on, as Kathryn's mouth dropped open in disbelief. "Louise and I have had separate bedrooms for fifteen years now. So we only see each other at breakfast and when I come home from work in the evening. And since Mason Blaine was killed, I've been coming home past midnight and leaving before Louise gets up for breakfast, so you see . . ." He trailed off.

Kathryn saw. She also saw that Tom was acutely embarrassed. At this opportune moment Mrs. Warburton appeared to inform them that if they would seat themselves in the dining room, omelets would shortly arrive. Kathryn thanked her, and bustled Tom into the dining room informing him that he needed to eat and that he also needed to tell her how she could help him.

This brought on another attack of embarrassment. "Well, I need to make a statement to the papers, you see, and it's kind of—"

She came to his rescue instantly. "Oh God, I can imagine! How horrible for you! Would you like me to help? I was an English major, you know, as an undergraduate; I used to be able to write a decent paragraph. Let me just grab some paper—" Here she vanished for a minute in the direction of her study at the back of the house.

"Now, let's see," she said, returning with the requisite tools and seating herself next to him at the table, "first we do the straightforward bits, Tom Holder, Chief of Police of Harton, New Jersey, today announced the disappearance et cetera, et cetera. According to the evidence of Flora—what's Flora's last name?"

"Miller."

"Flora Miller, Mrs. Holder's sister, of—where?"

"Zanesville, Ohio."

"Zanesville, Ohio. Mrs. Holder has not been answering the telephone at her home since Sunday. Chief Holder has not seen her since that date, either. Now, this is where we have to be careful. We have to make separate bedrooms sound normal, not salacious. You should not make this part of the statement, somebody else should. Who's your superior?"

"The D.A. in Trenton. Nick Silverman."

"Good. 'The District Attorney, Nick Silverman, stated, "Chief Holder and his wife have not shared a bedroom for several years due to his wife's ill health and the frequent necessity of a policeman to keep irregular hours. For the past week Chief Holder has returned home past midnight and left home before six each morning pursuing the investigation of the Mason Blaine homicide. Not wishing to disturb his wife's sleep, he did not look into her bedroom. Accordingly, he is not aware at what time Mrs. Holder went missing from their home, and we are only guessing that it may have been Sunday because of the evidence of the unanswered telephone.' "

Tom regarded her with awe. "Kathryn, you're brilliant. That actually makes it sound like I might not be an idiot."

"Well, you're *not* an idiot," she responded crossly, digging into the omelet that was now growing cold on her plate. "What do you think's happened to her?"

"I don't have the faintest idea. I guess she's just wandered off."

"Aren't you worried?"

"Oddly enough, I'm not. Or not much. Maybe if it was the dead of winter and freezing out there I would be, but the weather's not bad. And I guess I've got this notion that she's always been able to take care of herself. Obviously we'll roll out all the usual drill, and we'll find her, but just between you and me I'm not really gonna be worried sick until we do. I don't want you to get the wrong idea, it's not that I don't care what happens to her—"

"It's just that you don't believe anything is *going* to happen to her."

"Yeah, that's it."

Kathryn contemplated what she had observed in Louise Holder and tried to fit it into this picture of eccentric self-reliance that Tom had just drawn for her. It gave her a whole new slant on the lady, who she had always considered to have no strengths whatsoever.

"Oh," Tom said, remembering his manners, "How's Tracy? *Where's* Tracy?" There was a squad car out front, so presumably the girl was somewhere in the house.

"She's upstairs. Sleeping it off under the watchful eye of Patrick Cunningham. Good thing I've got a lot of guest rooms."

"I assume her boss gave her the day off."

"He gave her the *week* off. He's a cupcake."

"Yeah, well, *mine's* not. I've got to get this"—he waved

the statement she had written—"over to the station right away, and do a lot of other stuff. But would it be O.K. if I came back over here this afternoon? I could use your input on some ideas."

"Sure. You know you're always welcome."

He was always welcome. He left feeling a lot better than when he came.

CHAPTER 16

I t was after five, back to their customary teatime con-
sultation. But this time he had to be careful.

"Are Patrick and Tracy here?" The squad car was still
out front.

"Tracy's here; Patrick's gone back to the Graduate
College. Temporarily, anyway."

"Is there somewhere we can talk where we can be
sure she can't overhear us?"

Kathryn was only fleetingly surprised by this question; of course, Tom would want to talk in private, and
the living room was open to the front hall and from
there to the stairs.

She stood, picked up her cup of tea, and gestured for
him to follow her. She led him out into the hall, turned
left toward the back of the house, then opened a door

under the stairs and led him into a small room lined from floor to ceiling with bookshelves.

"Wow," he said.

"No, I haven't read all of them. Here, sit down. That chair's good." She closed the door behind them and seated herself opposite Tom. "Now, talk to me."

Tom settled himself into the huge library chair, took a long swig of his Earl Grey, and considered how to begin. "You remember," he said at last, "when I was talking about Question One and Question Two, why was the body moved and why was it moved to St. Margaret's? And I wouldn't tell you the answers and you were pissed off at me?"

"Well, I shouldn't have been, I was out of line. I had—"

"I'm ready to tell you the answers now."

"Oh." Kathryn's heart started beating faster.

"I have to. Because I need your help. Well, on second thought I guess I don't really *have* to but I'm going to. Because otherwise when I get to what I need to ask you, you might not take me seriously." He took another sip of tea while Kathryn's mind went into spasms of curiosity.

"Questions One and Two go together. If Blaine's body had been left in the place where he was killed, it might not have been discovered for hours. Possibly it might not have been discovered until the next morning. It was moved to St. Margaret's because the killer *knew* that Tracy Newman walked through the St. Margaret's driveway every Thursday night shortly after ten o'clock and that she would find it. That's why Blaine was spread out on his stomach and a knife was stuck in his back, so Tracy would know she was looking at a body, a corpse, not a drunk, so she would come to the station and report it, not walk around it and keep going."

"So the body was moved to St. Margaret's because the killer for some reason or another needed for the body to be discovered that night rather than the following morning."

"No."

"No? I thought you just said—"

"That's what I thought at first. And I was going crazy trying to figure out what kind of advantage it gave the killer to have the body discovered at ten-fifteen instead of the next morning. Then somebody poisoned Tracy Newman's drink and it all got real clear. The murder of Mason Blaine was a blind. Somebody killed him and planted him there so she would find him. Then when she was at the party the following week, a party the killer knew she'd be at, together with everybody who had a motive for killing Blaine, he puts poison in her drink. Everybody's supposed to think that she's seen something in that driveway last Thursday night, and the killer is trying to shut her mouth before she remembers what it is. But I don't buy that. Because it doesn't explain why the body was moved in the first place, why it was moved to St. Margaret's, and why there was a knife put in Blaine's back when he was already dead. And there was another thing. There were tire tracks in the grass just off the driveway around where the body was lying, as if somebody drove around the body. I think what happened was this: The killer drives in the driveway with the body in the backseat of his car. He drives off the driveway to the side so that when he drags the body out of the car, it lands square in the middle of the drive where it's most visible, not over on the side in the bushes where Tracy might miss it. Sure, he could have dragged it to the middle, but driving over to the side saves him a few seconds and when you're moving dead bodies around you want to make a quick getaway. The point is, he *wants* her to see the body. It's a plant."

Kathryn had gone very, very cold. "You're saying—" she began, but her mouth had gone dry and no sound came out. She took a sip of tea. Her hands trembled on her mug. "You're saying that all of this is an elaborate plot *to kill Tracy for her own sake?* Nothing to do with Mason Blaine?"

"It's the only theory that explains all the facts."

Kathryn gulped down the rest of her tea. She remembered thinking at the party that the theory that Tracy had seen something in the St. Margaret's driveway was ridiculous. "This is silly," she said. "Why should I be more upset at the idea that someone wants to kill her for her own sake than that someone wants to kill her because of something to do with the murder of Mason Blaine? But I am." She shook her head. "Never mind. Go on."

"What I need you for," Tom continued, "is to tell me more about her. Everything you can. Beginning with who might have a reason to kill her."

"I can't imagine!" Kathryn cried, in considerable distress. "She is the most harmless creature!"

"O.K. Let's take it from the top. Enemies?"

"Nonsense. The very idea is absurd."

"All right. Who benefits by her death?"

"I don't know, Tom," Kathryn said, irritated by the very idea. "I suppose I could ask her if she has a life insurance policy, but if she does, the beneficiary would most likely be Jamie. Certainly neither one of them has money."

"Why don't you just tell me about them in general? How long have you known Tracy?"

"I met her when she started coming to St. Margaret's at the beginning of last year. That was just after she and Jamie got married. She'd just graduated from Vassar. They met senior year, introduced by friends; I gather it was a bit of a whirlwind romance. Marry in haste, as they say. As I have told you, I believe that Jamie treated her badly, although she never actually came out and told me so point blank. It's just that I recognize the signs. She works as a secretary at Hutcheson Pollard, the insurance brokers, to help put Jamie through the Ph.D. program. He repaid her by having an affair with that platinum-headed slut Valerie Powers."

"How about her, then? As a likely prospect?"

"What, Valerie? Kill Tracy? What for?"

"To get her husband."

"Oh, no, much as I'd love for you to haul Valerie off in irons, the psychology is wrong. Valerie goes through a man a month. She certainly wouldn't kill to get one. Oh, I don't know, she might kill to get José, but he's drop-dead gorgeous and an aristocrat and has more money than God. Jamie was merely very handsome and middle-class and an impoverished grad student. No way she'd kill for him."

"O.K. I'll take your word for it. Mostly because that's the way she strikes me, too. Not enough passion for murder. Much too selfish."

"You are an excellent judge of character, Tom Holder. For that you get another cup of tea."

So they had more tea and discussed possibilities, but Kathryn was unable to offer Tom any ideas on who might have a good reason for doing away with Tracy. In the end he went away unsatisfied, although Kathryn promised she would broach the topic with Tracy herself.

Now isn't that, Kathryn thought, *going to be a jolly conversation?*

Nick Silverman was in Tom's office at 8:30 the next morning, and as District Attorneys do not normally keep those sorts of hours, Tom knew all too well that despite Silverman's wide, oleaginous smile, the man had not come in friendship.

" 'Morning, Tom. Dropped in to see how things were going. Any news of Louise?"

"Not yet."

"Oh, that's rough. You must be worried sick. Has she, uh, ever, uh, wandered off before?"

"No."

The glare that went with this monosyllable would have daunted a lesser man, but Trenton's District Attorney was possessed of a legendary insensitivity, and it bounced off him without making a dent. He pulled out the chair facing Tom's and seated himself as if he'd been invited, throwing out a few sentences of insincere comfort along the lines of: "I'm sure she's all right," and "They're bound to find her in no time," before he settled down to the topic that really interested him.

"O.K., then, Tom, bring me up to speed on our homicides. You need to catch this guy before he kills anybody else, you know! But at least this second one should give you a lot more to go on, surely the guy showed his hand, right? Christ, he did it right in the middle of a party!"

So Tom explained to the District Attorney his theory about the murder of Mason Blaine being a blind for the murder of Tracy Newman. He included all the details he had given Kathryn the previous evening.

When he was finished Nick Silverman looked at him in disbelief and said, "You're kidding, right?"

"Of course I'm not kidding."

"You're going to drop Mason Blaine for some little secretary nobody's ever heard of?"

There was a four-second pause while Tom digested the fact that the D.A. was actually going to let the newsworthiness of the victim dictate his view of the case. "Well, Nick," Tom said, frantically trying to think of an answer that would be both humble and persuasive, when what he really wanted to say was, "You stupid glory hog." "It's a matter of accounting for the facts," he produced in a neutral tone of voice. He was rather pleased with this answer, but Silverman immediately pounced upon the weakness in his new case.

"But you admit yourself that you've traded a victim that half the town wants to kill for a victim that nobody wants to kill. Do you call that progress? I don't."

"I didn't say I'd solved the case, Nick. I just said I think I've figured out something basic about it, namely, who the intended victim was in the first place. Because if we've got that wrong, nothing else is going to go right, is it?"

"Tom, you've got this completely backasswards, and as your superior I am *ordering* you to investigate this case as the murder of Mason Blaine, with the assumption that the attempted murder of the Newman woman, and the accidental murder of her husband, was because she saw something in the grounds of that church last Thursday night that she's forgotten or didn't realize the significance of at the time. I suggest you get her to see a hypnotist."

Tom Holder was famous for keeping his temper, and having lost it spectacularly in this case already with his Rector, of all people, he was not about to lose it with a superior. He drew a very deep breath. "Nick," he said, "you don't mean that. You can't tell me how to investigate my own homicide unless you relieve me of duty, you know that. Now, if it'll settle your mind, I'll ask the Newman girl if she'd be willing to be hypnotized and we'll see what comes of it, but I'll tell you in advance that nothing will, because the killer was long gone before she got there, and why? Because he knew exactly when she was *going* to get there, that's why! He knew she was coming, Nick! I tell you, he knew she was coming—"

But the D.A. was on his feet and heading for the door. "My office will let you know about the hypnotist," he snapped, and was gone.

Tom got up and shut with a bang the door that Silverman had left open behind him. He then cursed soundly. He was scarcely back in his chair again when the phone rang.

"Chief? One of your neighbors, a Mrs. Carter. She says her mother saw your wife on Sunday."

"Well, hot damn. Put her on." Finally something going right for a change.

"Bev?"

"Tom? Is that you? Listen, I've just had a conversation with my mother. She tells me that some policemen came by yesterday asking about Louise, saying she was missing. Is that right?"

"That's right."

"Oh, how terrible! I'm so sorry!"

"Thanks, Bev. But your mother says she saw her on Sunday?"

"Yes. But when the police came around asking about it yesterday, Mama told me she wouldn't tell them anything because she said it was none of their business. At ninety-four you get a little eccentric, I guess, but honestly, Tom, you'd think that after all these years she'd remember that *you're* a policeman. She seems to remember everything else. Anyway, I asked her about it and she said she was watching a movie on television and she looked up and saw a stretch limo pull up to your house, and after a minute Louise came out of the front door and down the walk and got into it and it drove away."

"A *stretch limo*?"

Bev Carter fully understood his incredulity. "That's what Mama said."

CHAPTER 17

Tom felt like eight kinds of a fool. Still, it was the only lead he'd gotten, so what choice did he have?

He was sitting in Bev Carter's living room opposite the formidable Dorabella Mason.

"I don't mind telling *you*, Mr. Holder," she was saying. "She's your wife. It's your business. It wasn't any of *their* business. I wasn't about to talk to *them*."

"I appreciate that, Mrs. Mason. That's very nice of you. Now can you tell me about it? This was on Sunday? You're sure it was Sunday?"

"Of course I'm sure. There's nothing wrong with my brain, young man. It was the day that Beverly works at the hospital for the Candy Stripers, which is the sort of thing that young people ought to do." (Dorabella's youngest daughter, Beverly, was sixty-three.) "That's the way I reared her, to be thoughtful of other people, and I'm proud of her.

I was thinking of that, how proud of her I was, because I was watching a movie on television in which some young people were behaving disgracefully and I was very grateful that my Beverly didn't behave like one of them."

Tom's ears pricked up. "You wouldn't happen to remember the name of the movie, would you?"

"I keep telling you that there's nothing the matter with my brain but I can see that you don't believe me," Mrs. Mason remarked disdainfully. "The movie was called *The Apartment* and it starred Jack Lemmon, Shirley MacLaine, and Fred MacMurray. If you'll check the papers you'll find it was showing on Sunday."

I'll just bet we will, thought Tom, suppressing a sudden urge to kiss the venerable dame. "Yes, Mrs. Mason. So you were watching *The Apartment*. Then what happened?"

"As you can see, the television is there." She gestured. "I sit in this chair here to watch it. That means that if anything really unusual happens outside, it catches my eye. And in this neighborhood even a Cadillac would be unusual. We just don't have limousines around here, do we? And this wasn't an ordinary limousine, this was what they call a stretch limo, one of the extra-long ones. You see, I keep up with the times, I know what you call them because I watch television."

Tom went back to the station with his head in a whirl. He had never talked to a witness who seemed less crazy or more sure of herself than Dorabella Mason. But the idea of Louise running away from home in a stretch limo was the closest thing to pure lunacy he'd ever heard in his life. Well, perhaps she'd finally gone completely around the bend, ordered the car for herself, and ridden away. He'd better check the credit cards. All he'd checked so far (without success) were taxis and public transportation; although

Louise's name was on both the cards, she had never in the history of their marriage used either one of them.

Since he was both the principal cardholder and a policeman, his inquiries were processed instantly. Louise had not hired a limousine—or a car of any kind—on either of their cards. And who on God's green earth would hire a limousine for her? It was preposterous. And yet Dorabella Mason had been utterly believable.

But still—

Tom punched a button on his intercom.

"Yessir?"

"Purze, have somebody get a paper from Sunday and check to see that the movie, *The Apartment*, was showing on television that afternoon around one o'clock."

Pursley had gotten some odd requests from his Chief before but it would be safe to say that this was the oddest. It spoke volumes for his loyalty that it did not cross his mind for so much as a second that the Chief had lost his marbles. "Yessir," he responded enthusiastically, and set forth on the task himself.

Tom's telephone rang. It was Trenton, calling to inform him that an appointment had been arranged for Mrs. Newman to see Dr. Rosenthal at 10:30 that morning at his office in Lawrenceville. Herewith was Dr. Rosenthal's address.

Silverman's not letting any grass grow under his feet, Tom reflected. He began to feel uneasy. Aside from forcing through this hypnosis nonsense, was there anything else Silverman could actually *do? Aside, that is, from dropping in and smiling that nasty smile and making a goddamn nuisance of himself, is there anything he can actually* do *to me?*

Tom began to get worried, which was unusual for him. Normally he didn't worry about his cases, he just ferreted away at them until he got them solved. And he certainly didn't worry about his own position. Now he was actually beginning to feel a bit threatened. He wondered if he ought to pray about it.

Up to this point his private petitionary prayers had always been restricted to his spiritual needs: God, make me more loving, help me to be patient, things like that. But he remembered Kathryn telling the adult Sunday school class at St. Margaret's that in the Lord's Prayer, when Jesus said, "Give us this day our daily bread," he was indicating to us that we ought to ask for everything we needed, not just for spiritual things.

O.K., *then*, Tom thought, *here goes. Dear God, help me to solve this case before that jackass Silverman mucks it up for me. And help me to find Louise before she gets herself into trouble or gets hurt. Not because I love her, Lord, I'm not going to try to pretend, here, you know I don't love her any more than she loves me. But it's my duty. And besides, I don't want her to get hurt. Amen. Oh, and thanks.*

He had just concluded this new venture in personal spirituality when there was a knock on the door. It was Pursley, looking triumphant. "This was still in the lounge from the weekend," he said, waving a newspaper magazine with a colored cover. "It's got the listings for the whole week. Here's Sunday. And here," he announced with immense satisfaction and pointing to the listing, "is *The Apartment.*"

"Well done, Purze. Thanks."

But the Chief looked more troubled than grateful, so Purze went away in turn more puzzled than gratified.

Tom called Kathryn's house to notify Tracy of her appointment, and Tracy promptly called Kathryn on her cell phone to beg for her company. "I could use some moral support. I'm terrified."

Kathryn, however, had a lecture on medieval church history to give and couldn't shake loose. "Tracy, I promise you, Tom is a sweetie pie, he's a darling. Ask him to hold your hand. You'll be fine."

Tracy, unable to avail herself of this advice, was driven to Lawrenceville by the slightly formal Chief of Police, who despite calling her Tracy because they'd gone to church together for a little over a year, didn't offer the kind of emotional support she wanted because she didn't ask for it. Tracy underwent hypnosis, remembered absolutely nothing useful, and was driven back to Harton.

Tom shook hands with her on Kathryn's front doorstep. "Thanks, Tracy. I appreciate that that was difficult for you, and I'm sorry it didn't produce any results. Now, are you working on that list for me?"

"Yes. I'm trying, but honestly, I can't think of anybody . . ."

"Tracy, your husband is dead. Somebody is trying to kill you. We're working on who could have poisoned your drink at that party, but the flat truth of the matter is that there are simply too many people who could have done it, so that angle isn't getting us anywhere. You've got to help us."

Tracy looked so small and frightened that Tom felt like a brute. He deposited her with Mrs. Warburton and departed. The squad car, of course, was back at the curb.

Back at the station he reviewed reports on stretch limos. At least they were rare beasts, so there weren't too many of them to track down.

There was a firm in town, Deluxe Transport, that owned one, but they were able to prove without difficulty that at the crucial time theirs had been cruising out to J.F.K. to pick up somebody with more money than was good for him.

A similar overpriced limo service in Trenton owned two stretch limos but one had been demonstrably engaged at a wedding and the other had been just as demonstrably sitting in their garage getting cleaned and polished. That left the car rental agencies. A diligent search through the Yellow Pages revealed that the only place to rent a stretch limo in North Jersey was one of the major car rental agencies at Newark Airport, either Hertz or Avis. Nobody else had them.

The Hertz office had three stretch limos; only one had been rented on the previous Sunday. A group of Japanese businessmen, fresh in from Tokyo, had taken it to Atlantic City. The Avis office reported that two of its stretch limos had been in service on Sunday. One was rented to a company in Trenton called T.N.K. Public Relations, and the other was in the hands of a rap group from Newark who were celebrating cutting their first CD.

Offhand, Tom couldn't imagine which group was least likely to run off with his wife: Japanese tourists, a public relations firm, or a rap group. He was inclined to think—always assuming that Dorabella Mason had been correct—that a stretch limo had slipped through his net somehow. He was about to dispatch teams to make inquiries of all these people when his phone rang; Sid Garvey wanted to talk to him.

"Sid?"

"Tom! All of the hot-shit experts on the crime scene team want to buy the biggest steak and lobster dinner in Jersey for whoever it was who walked into the MacDonalds' kitchen on Wednesday night and got clingwrap and ice and a plastic bag and wrapped up the god-damn *ice cubes* from that black Russian before they could melt, and packed 'em up surrounded by ice in the plastic bag and put 'em in Mrs. MacDonald's freezer and gave 'em to us when we got there. I bet everybody fifty bucks it was you. Tell me it was you."

"Of course it was me."

"Now tell me why you did it."

"I dunno. I've seen you guys work, you preserve everything at the scene. I got there and there were these tiny little lumps of ice in among the bits of broken glass and I thought, these are gonna be melted by the time Trenton gets here, so I thought I'd preserve them. I thought at the time it was probably stupid."

"Stupid like a fox, my friend. Those little lumps of ice were chock full of cyanide."

"You're shitting me! The poison was in the *ice cubes*?"

"I shit you not, the poison was in the ice cubes. A cute little fact nobody would ever have known if you hadn't decided to show crime scene how it's done. Pick the date for your steak and lobster. Oh, and, uh, Tom. I, uh, heard about Louise. I'm sure she's all right. Don't you worry, they'll find her."

"Thanks, Sid." Tom hung up before it got any more awkward.

The *ice cubes*?

What sort of lunatic would have put the poison in the *ice cubes*?

He called Trenton back, a different department, and asked to speak to the pathologist who was doing the postmortem.

"Don't rush me," she complained. "I'm not finished."

"They found cyanide in the ice cubes in the drink," he responded.

"Oh," she said, deflated. "Well, I guess that rather takes all the fizz out of my report."

"Talk to me about cyanide. Would there be any advantage in putting it in ice cubes?"

"None that I can think of."

"The drink was a black Russian, vodka and Kahlua, pretty strong flavor. Could somebody just drop powdered cyanide in the top of the drink without stirring it, and then a person could pick it up and wouldn't smell it or anything, and they would drink enough of it to kill them in the first sip or two before they tasted it?"

"Absolutely. Cyanide is very deadly. It kills in minutes, and it dissolves easily. The only smell it has is a faint odor of almonds, and the smell of the Kahlua would disguise that. So assuming your killer had the chance to put anything into the glass without being seen, cyanide crystals would have done the trick just fine."

Tom decided against sending other people to chase down renters of stretch limos; he would go himself. He needed a good, long drive, and Harton to Atlantic City to Trenton to wherever the rappers were would do just fine. He did some of his best thinking behind the wheel, and he needed to think about ice cubes.

He put out an A.P.B. on the rappers' limo and set out for Atlantic City. Hertz had been able to furnish him with the name of the casino/hotel at which the Japanese businessmen had planned to become rapidly parted from their cash.

Fortunately Tom knew the way to Atlantic City, so he didn't have to concentrate on the route. He put himself and the car on automatic pilot and tackled the ice cube problem.

First question: How did the killer transport several cyanide-filled ice cubes to the party and keep them frozen, and convenient, until the time he needed them? Tom thought he knew the answer to that. Just surrounding them with ordinary ice wouldn't do it; all the ice would melt, and it would be too bulky. Dry ice. That would do it. Just a bit of dry ice, which was fiercely cold, in his pocket or her purse; that would keep a few normal ice cubes good and frozen.

Second question: Why put the cyanide in ice cubes instead of just bringing along a little packet of crystals and dumping the crystals in the drink?

He was still working on that question when he drove into the subterranean parking garage of the Hotel Palace East. The elevator took him up to the lobby, a garish nightmare of red carpet, crystal chandeliers, and fake-gold slot machines. He walked up to the reception desk, presented his credentials, and asked for the room number of the Japanese businessmen. The manager was summoned. The manager asked what the problem was. Tom explained. The manager asked if he could accompany Tom on his errand in order to maintain cordial hotel-guest relations. Tom acquiesced.

The Japanese businessmen were, needless to say, in one of the penthouse suites. Arriving there, the manager knocked respectfully and he and Tom were admitted by a fully costumed chorus girl who would not have looked out of place in Las Vegas.

"Hello, Louise," said the manager, which made Tom start. "I hope you're behaving yourself?"

"Absolutely within the rules, boss," she assured him

earnestly. "But it doesn't matter. They pour money over you for just being here, really, you don't hardly have to do nothin' for it."

They entered the vast room, which was surprisingly tasteful compared to the lobby. It was furnished entirely in off-white and decoration was at a minimum; in the middle of the room was a beige marble coffee table nine feet square on which the only ornament was the most exquisite orchid plant Tom had ever seen. The Japanese visitors, Tom thought, must have felt right at home.

There were other decorations, so to speak, of a more colorful nature, in the form of more chorus girls, and of course there were room-service carts of wonderful-looking food everywhere and buckets of champagne. Amid these pleasures the happy guests were lounging in kimonos, but as Tom and the manager appeared, all instantly rose and bowed.

The manager went up to one of them and bowed. "Mr. Yakimoto," he said. "May I introduce Chief Holder-san, policeman of Harton, New Jersey, who is so unfortunate as to have lost his wife. He is here to ask you some questions." The manager bowed again and backed away.

Tom bowed to Mr. Yakimoto. "Mr. Yakimoto," he said, hoping to strike the right note, "it is very good of you to let me interrupt your vacation. I appreciate you giving me your time. Please understand that these questions I ask are just a formality. We are asking everyone who has rented a stretch limousine in northern New Jersey in the last few days to tell us where they have been, where they have gone in that car. Now, I understand that you rented your limo from Hertz at Newark Airport last Saturday when you arrived from Tokyo, is that correct?"

It was at that point that Tom discovered what the

manager of the Hotel Palace East had failed to tell him, namely, that Mr. Yakimoto did not speak one word of English. Neither did any of Mr. Yakimoto's friends. There was an awful lot of good-natured smiling and bowing and a positive torrent of what Tom assumed was Japanese.

"But," as Tom said crossly to the manager in the elevator afterwards, "a fat lot of good it did me. Why didn't you tell me they didn't speak English?"

"You didn't *ask*," the manager whined. "Anyway, the driver speaks good old American. He's in three forty-two."

The driver, just as Tom expected, confirmed that he had taken his fares to Atlantic City from Newark without stopping off in Harton to kidnap any dotty middle-aged housewives.

Back in the parking garage, Tom called in to check the whereabouts of the rappers and discovered that they, too, had gone to Atlantic City, to a place called the Atlantic City Viewcrest. Tom's efficient staff had gotten directions.

Another parking garage, another elevator, another garish lobby with another red carpet and more chandeliers and more gold stuff and more slot machines.

My God, Tom thought, *how do people stand this crap?* He couldn't imagine how anybody could have the bad taste to want to come here for a vacation, but he was really thinking more about the people who had to work here. Surely it must be soul-killing to work in such an ugly place?

With these thoughts in his mind, Tom gave his warmest smile to the girl at the desk as he went through the same routine he had before, only this time he was asking for the rap group named—God help him—the Forces of Evil. Again he was escorted up to one of the penthouse suites by the manager.

As they stood before the door they could hear the

awful music. The manager said ruefully, "I make them keep it down, of course, because of the other guests, but I can't make them turn it off completely. Unfortunately."

Tom thought, *This is going to be sheer hell.*

The door opened and they were looking at a fresh-faced boy of about seventeen. "Hey, Mr. Stevenson," he said politely, if somewhat loudly in order to be heard over the music. "Come on in. Are we playin' the music too loud again? We were tryin' to be careful about that."

"No, Freddie, the music's fine. I'm here to introduce Chief Holder of the Harton Police, who's here to—"

Freddie's eyes had gone wide and angry. "Whoa, now! We're clean! We're clean! What the hell's this—"

Tom threw up a hand and made calm-down gestures. "Whoa, yourself, Freddie. I know you're clean. Listen to me. *I know you're clean.* I am here going through some motions, you know what that means? Just going through some motions. In fact, I am here because somebody told me the weirdest story I have ever heard in my entire life and I have to check it out and it has to do with a stretch limo. You want to hear the weirdest story you ever heard in your entire life?"

Tom knew he had him. The light of curiosity had supplanted the light of hostility in Freddie's eye.

"Now where," Tom continued, "are these Forces of Evil I hear so much about?"

Freddie giggled.

This is a nice kid, Tom thought.

"Well, I'm one of 'em," Freddie replied. "C'mon, I'll introduce you to the others."

Mr. Stevenson excused himself, and Freddie took Tom into the penthouse. This was considerably less elegant than the one inhabited by the Japanese businessmen; it was furnished in Ordinary Hotel Modern, and it was cluttered with the paraphernalia of teenagers who had been camped out in it for several days enjoying themselves: shoes, articles of clothing, and various high-tech toys recently acquired were interspersed with pizza boxes and empty soft drink cans.

"This is my brother Harry, my cousin Lawrence, my cousin Martin."

Each boy, not one of whom could have been over nineteen, rose from where he had been lounging spinelessly on a low sofa and greeted Tom with a handshake and "Yo, man," except for Lawrence who actually said, "Pleased to meet you."

Tom said, "My wife is missing."

"Whoa!"

"Holy shit!"

"No, man!"

"Shitfire!"

Freddie said, "I'm gonna get Gee Gee," and galloped over to one of the doors leading off the central living area and banged on it. "Gee Gee!" he called. "Gee Gee! Come out, we need you here!"

There was a short pause and then the door opened to reveal an elderly black woman in an old-fashioned plum-colored dress. "What's all this commotion?" she demanded.

"Gee Gee, we gotta help this man. His wife is missing."

The old lady looked to see who "this man" was and caught sight of Tom. She walked toward him slowly with a care that suggested slight pain, perhaps arthritis. Tom went to meet her. She held out her hand.

"I am Letitia Freeman," she told him. "These are my grandsons. I raised them after their parents were killed in a car crash together when they were babies. Freddie," she said, turning to him, "I know you love your music, but if we are going to talk, you're going to have to turn it off."

"Yes, Gee Gee." Freddie skipped over to a ghetto blaster on a nearby table and snapped it off. The silence was, to Tom, a blessed relief. He introduced himself.

Mrs. Freeman invited Tom to sit and instructed Martin, who was closest to the table with refreshments on it, to get Chief Holder something to drink.

"Some sort of cola would be great," Tom agreed.

"*Martin!*" Mrs. Freeman said sharply. "Don't you pick up those ice cubes with your hands! I bet you haven't washed your hands in a week, I know you boys! You gettin' a drink for somebody else, you use the tongs!"

So Tom got his drink with clean ice cubes, and he told his story, which they all agreed was indeed weird. All four of the Forces of Evil swore solemnly that they had not kidnapped Louise, which of course Tom had no trouble believing, and naturally their grandmother backed them up.

She added, "Now, you're gonna need to talk to our driver, too, to verify our story, aren't you?"

"Mrs. Freeman, I wouldn't dream of wasting my time verifying your story. I never met five more obviously honest people in my whole career as a cop, and besides, as I told Freddie when I first got here, I'm only going through the motions. Why on earth would you people want to run off with my wife?"

"That's true, Mr. Holder. That's true. So you're going through the motions, as you call it, because you have no other information to go on?"

"That's right. No other leads at all. Nothing."

"That must be very hard for you. This must be a very, very trying time. Have you called upon the Lord?"

Only briefly taken aback, Tom replied, "Yes, I have."

"Good. You keep doing that. Once is not enough, you know. You need to keep doing it. Now, I have some advice for you and I hope you'll take it. It's going to surprise you."

"What's that?"

"Take fifteen minutes out of your busy schedule. Take a fifteen-minute break right now and let my grandsons entertain you. I know you think you hate rap music, all people your age think they hate rap music, but my grandsons don't use ugly language and they dance great and the beat is really good once you get used to it. They're really good entertainers. Let 'em entertain you."

From the instant in this speech that she had first made the suggestion, the four boys had been jumping up and down begging for the opportunity. "Oh let us do it! Oh we're terrific! You gotta see us! Oh, please, please, you gotta watch us, we are so, so good!"

Tom looked at those innocent, eager faces and cracked up laughing. "O.K., guys. Strut your stuff. Show me what you got."

Letitia Freeman rose and once more offered Tom her hand. "I'll be keeping you in my prayers."

"Where are you going?"

"Back to my room. I've seen these boys often enough. Besides, if I was here, you probably wouldn't feel free enough to dance."

"You don't think *I'm* gonna dance?"

"Oh, you'd be surprised what my boys can do," she answered with a serene smile, and left him.

Sure enough, her boys had an infectious sense of fun, and after ripping through two numbers in which Tom was astonished to discover that he could not only understand the witty lyrics but sympathize with them (they

were about social injustice, and echoed his own politics), they flew into a comedy number in which Freddie
was lamenting the departure of his girlfriend. Their
dance movements were marvelous and Tom, who had
been no mean dancer in his youth, found his shoulders
twitching. The boys spotted it, and Martin and Harry
dragged him to his feet. Twenty exhausting minutes
later he left the Atlantic City Viewcrest with a rudimen-
tary education in rap dance moves and a gift of bling,
which, it turned out, was what the boys called the gaudy
rhinestone jewelry they wore draped all over themselves. He boldly wore the absurd necklace all the way
down the elevator and through the lobby—*After all*, he
told himself, *this is Atlantic City*—slipping it into his
pocket only when he got back to the car.

One thing's for sure, he decided as he headed back up
the Atlantic City Expressway, *T.N.K. Public Relations is
going to be pretty boring after that.*

Once again driving on automatic pilot, Tom had the
opportunity to crank up his brain. The episode with
Martin and the ice tongs had made him realize that he
had not thought about ordinary, unpoisoned ice cubes in
that dining room. Had Patrick Cunningham added any
regular ice cubes to Tracy's drink? And had they melted
away entirely before he, Tom, had arrived, leaving only
the tiny lumps of poisoned cubes to be cling-wrapped and
preserved and analyzed? Tom frowned very seriously at
the road ahead of him in a fury of attempted recollection,
but he was reasonably sure that Patrick's Witherspoon imitation had not included adding ice cubes to the drink.
Maybe there had already been enough ice in the glass.

Did that mean that *the poisoned ice cubes were in it already?*

Tom nearly drove off the road. They'd been assuming that the crucial time was when Patrick was upstairs in the bathroom. What if it was before that? He'd need to go back and talk to the boy about how he'd gotten the glass from Tracy in the first place, and where it had been before he'd gotten it from her. Suddenly he was very excited; was this the breakthrough he'd been waiting for?

He was tempted not to stop in Trenton, such was his eagerness to get back to Harton to talk to Patrick Cunningham, but he had set out to check on these rented stretch limos, and check on them he would.

T.N.K. Public Relations was housed in an attractive building of glass and brick, not more than ten years old, and furnished with ample parking. *Luxury*, thought Tom.

In the foyer he was greeted by an attractive receptionist who examined his credentials with some consternation but who calmed down considerably when she heard his story.

"I don't see that there should be any trouble about that. If anybody at this firm rented a stretch limo, it would have been to meet some of our clients at the airport and take them around, that's a thing we do frequently. Let me just see. We'll start with Mr. Taylor." She pressed a button on the array before her. "Julie? Can you tell me if Mr. Taylor rented a stretch limo for clients last Sunday? Are you sure? Because there's a policeman here asking, so it's important. Thanks." She pressed the button again and shook her head at Tom. "Not Mr. Taylor. I'll try Mr. Norton now. Sharon? Can you tell me if Mr. Norton had a stretch limo rented for clients last Sunday? Yes? At Newark? Well, there's a policeman here asking about it. Could you come out and talk to him? Thanks."

In about ten seconds a severe-looking woman of about

thirty-five came striding out of a corridor that led from the foyer back into the private recesses of T.N.K.

"What's all this? The police?"

Tom introduced himself, and explained that it was just routine, an attempt to eliminate rented stretch limos from the inquiry.

"Well, then. Mr. Norton rented a stretch limo from Avis at Newark Airport on Sunday to pick up some important clients of ours who were flying in from the West Coast and who needed to be wined and dined, that sort of thing. Apparently they wanted to see Philadelphia. There's no accounting for taste. So that's where Mr. Norton took them. Is that what you needed to know?"

"Yes, thanks. And then they came here?"

"No, as far as I know they're still in Philadelphia."

"And Mr. Norton is with them?"

"No, he's back at work but he's not in the office right now."

"Well, I suppose that's all I need. Thanks very much."

Tom departed in haste for Harton. He wanted to speak to Patrick Cunningham about how he acquired Tracy's glass and when Tracy's glass acquired ice cubes.

Back at T.N.K. Public Relations, a red LeBaron convertible pulled into the space just vacated by Tom's old Ford, and a tall man with tired eyes got out and walked into the building.

"Hello, Joel," said the receptionist. "You just missed a policeman. He was here asking questions about your stretch limo, of all things. The one you rented for those West Coast clients who wanted to go to Philadelphia. But Sharon answered all his questions and he went away."

CHAPTER 18

Tom would not have been able to drive around New Jersey with a mind clear enough to think about ice cubes, nor would he have been able to enjoy the antics of the Forces of Evil, had he had any inkling of the activities of Nick Silverman that Friday.

The District Attorney, upon leaving Tom's office, had returned to his car and used his cell phone to call his office and tell them to make arrangements for the Newman girl to see a hypnotist. He had then left the car and walked to a coffee shop on Main Street, where he had enjoyed a coffee and Danish and a fit of resentment. Something would obviously have to be done about Tom Holder.

He paid his bill and walked back to the police station, intending to have another go at bringing the intransigent Holder into line, but the Chief had gone to interview one of his neighbors who had reported seeing his wife.

"But it's probably nothing," Pursley told the D.A. "The old lady's ninety-four, and she's claiming she saw Mrs. Holder get into a stretch limo and drive off, so obviously the Chief isn't taking it very seriously, I mean, how could he? The old lady's obviously nuts. But he's gone to talk to her because nobody else has reported seeing Mrs. Holder at all, and I guess he's hoping that maybe if he talks to her he can make some sort of sense of what she's saying and figure out what she really did see. If she saw anything at all, that is."

"I see," said Silverman meditatively. "Thank you, Sergeant." Pursley went away. After a moment, the D.A. turned to another officer, one who he had reason to believe would have less personal loyalty to Tom, and asked, "Could you please bring me Chief Holder's personnel file?"

It was an unusual request, but the District Attorney had the authority to make it, so the officer obliged. Silverman took the file out to his car to be assured of privacy and began to look through it. A few minutes later he took it back into the station and returned it to the policeman who had given it to him, and seven minutes after that he was being shown into the office of a surprised Father Mark Randall at St. Margaret's Church.

"How do you do, Mr. Silverman; Mark Randall; very pleased to meet you, sit down, sit down. I would ask what brings you to St. Margaret's but I suspect it must be our unfortunate connection with the murder of Mason Blaine."

"Thank you, Mr. Randall. That's a good guess, but actually it's mistaken. I'm here in connection with the disappearance of Louise Holder."

"Oh, yes, that! Shocking! And so distressing for Tom, of course. How can I help you?"

"Well, as both the Holders are members of this

church, I assume that some of the people in the church are going to be friends of Mrs. Holder, and can talk to me about how she was feeling, where she might have gone, that sort of thing."

There was a long pause.

"Mr. Silverman," Father Mark began tentatively, "I can see that you are not personally acquainted with Louise Holder." There was another pause. "I want to be careful in how I put this. I'm not sure Louise has any friends, *per se*. People are kind to her for Tom's sake, but she is, ah, a bit eccentric."

"Ahhh," Silverman breathed. "I see." He thought for a moment. "Still, I would like to speak to some members of the church about her. Can you suggest a list of church people who would have known her for several years?"

Father Mark considered. "I suppose the easiest thing would be to give you a list of vestry members and mark the ones who've been in the church for more than, say, four years. Would that do?"

"Vestry?"

"Oh, I beg your pardon. The vestry is our governing committee, so to speak. Every three years we elect new members to serve for another three years."

"So the vestry members are the leaders of your church?"

"You could say that."

Nick Silverman agreed that a list of vestry members, marked as suggested, would be perfect for his purposes, and a few minutes later he left St. Margaret's with just such a list in his pocket.

He spent the day hunting these good people down in their homes and places of business and questioning them. Depending upon their personalities and upon the attitude he perceived them to bear toward Tom Holder, his interrogation methods ranged from the sly and insinuating to the brutal and badgering.

The result of this activity was that when Tom arrived back at the station after having stopped for a very late lunch, he found the D.A. in his office waiting for him, trying—and failing—not to look smug.

Tom knew instantly that he was in trouble. The only question was, how much?

"Hello, Nick," he said levelly.

"Hello, Tom. Where've you been?"

"Checking out some things. Doing some thinking about the case. What brings you back here?"

"Sit down, Tom."

Tom circled his desk and sat down. He became aware of his heart beating.

"Tom, I'm really sorry about this, but I'm afraid I'm going to have to suspend you from duty, effective immediately, pending a satisfactory resolution to the investigation of your wife's disappearance. Of course you'll—"

"You son of a bitch! You're out of your mind! You're doing this over *Louise*?"

"Calm down, Tom. I have no choice. The circumstances are just too damning. She's been missing too long. You failed to report her disappearance. You're a police officer in the public eye. I couldn't permit you to run the investigation by yourself; we could be open to the accusation of conflict of interest. So this morning I took a hand myself. I went over to your church and got the names of twelve people who have known you and your wife for more than four years and I talked to them today. Tom, of those twelve people, no less than eight of them—Tom, *no less than eight of them* stated to me that they believed it was possible that you have killed your wife. Tom, these are your *friends*. These are people from your own church. Now, what do you expect me to do under these circumstances?

"As I was trying to say when you interrupted me, you'll be on full pay while we investigate. And Tom, for what it's worth, *I* don't think you killed her. But we have to safeguard the reputation of law enforcement in this county. I'm sure you understand that. So go on home; we'll appoint a replacement to cover for you temporarily."

Tom had turned to stone. His anger at Silverman had evaporated. *Eight people* at St. Margaret's thought he had killed Louise?

Which eight?

Where had Nick Silverman gotten a list of people at St. Margaret's to talk to?

"Tom, you need to go."

Silently, Tom rose and walked out of his office. His feet did not seem to feel the floor.

Nick Silverman traveled happily back to Trenton and set in motion arrangements for somebody to step into Tom's shoes until he, Nick, could solve the Mason Blaine case. Meanwhile Louise Holder would surely be located—not too soon—and there would be a satisfactory ending all around and Tom Holder could go back to his job when he was no longer raining on Nick's parade.

The minute he made the first phone call, of course, the news started ricocheting through the system, and precisely twenty-three minutes later it reached one of the crime scene labs where Sid Garvey happened to be working.

Sid looked at his supervisor and said, "Amanda, I just got a migraine headache. Also, I think I'm gonna throw up. And my knees are shaking, and I can feel an attack of—"

"Go, Sid, take the rest of the day off. And tell him we

all think it's dirty politics and as for me, I've half a mind to drop a cyanide ice cube in Nick Silverman's next martini. Tom Holder's a good man. You tell him that from me. You hear?"

There were several comments of a similar nature from the rest of the people in the room as Sid headed for the door.

"Thanks, Mandy. Thanks, guys. I'll tell him."

On his way to Harton, Sid stopped at a liquor store and bought the most expensive bottle of Scotch they had. It was his firm belief that a man should never drown his sorrows in anything cheap.

Meanwhile, Kathryn's last afternoon seminar had concluded, she had gone home, visited with Tracy, graded some papers, and gotten restless. She wanted to know what was going on with the homicides and with Louise's disappearance. This was the time of day when Tom frequently called and invited himself over for tea and conversation, but the time ticked by and there was no phone call. Finally, unable to contain herself, she called the station and asked to speak to him.

"He's been *what*?"

"Suspended. Pending the investigation into the disappearance of his wife."

"What— wha— wha— Is he under some sort of *suspicion*?"

"Not from anybody here at this station," said the voice at the other end of the line with rather an edge.

"Then who did this?"

"The District Attorney."

"The District Attorney," Kathryn pronounced trenchantly, "has his head up his ass."

"I don't know who you are, lady, but I couldn't agree with you more."

"I'm somebody from Tom's church."

"Well, I'm glad to know that, because it was people from the Chief's church who got him into this. The D.A. said he talked to a lot of people from that church, and eight of them said they thought the Chief had bumped off his wife." (Somebody had been listening at the door, but the woman talking to Kathryn wasn't about to let that bit of information slip.)

"What?"

The woman jerked the phone away from her ear. "I'm glad to hear not everybody feels that way," she said.

"I don't believe he found eight who feel that way," said Kathryn with feeling. "Listen, thanks." She hung up and scrambled in her desk for her St. Margaret's directory and punched Tom's home phone number. She let it ring fifteen times, but there was no answer. This did not convince her, however, that he was not at home. Making a note of the address, she headed out of the house for her car.

She pulled a map of Harton out of the glove compartment, located Tom's street, and set out for his neighborhood. A few minutes later she was driving down the modest road looking at numbers. There was Tom's. It was a white frame house with blue shutters and a neat lawn. There were a couple of trees of the kind that are planted in new subdivisions and designed to grow to great heights quickly; Kathryn didn't know what kind they were. Against the house there were some bushes, trimmed so that they did not obscure the windows. The property was completely unpretentious but well cared for.

There was a car parked at the curb in front of it, a

black SUV; Kathryn parked behind it, got out, went up the walk, and rang the bell.

Sid had arrived approximately three quarters of an hour earlier, and during that time he and Tom had done extensive damage to the bottle that Sid had brought with him. On the principle that a man should not have to drink alone, Sid had phoned his wife, who had encouraged him to stay there and administer medicinal spirits to dear Tom as long as was necessary, up to and including all night, and by no means drive home while alcoholically impaired but rather spend the night on the Holders' sofa.

Thus encouraged, Sid had kept up with Tom glass for glass as they had torn to shreds the character, intelligence, and motives of the District Attorney. When the telephone rang, Tom had announced unequivocally that he didn't want to talk to anybody, but Sid had suggested that it might be Louise, so Tom had risen and stumbled rapidly into the kitchen for the phone.

The caller ID said "Koerney." His heart skipped a beat. She had never called him at home. She must have called the station first. They would have told her the news. Christ, how humiliating! But she would know he didn't deserve it. That's why she was calling. His hand hovered over the receiver. But no. He'd had about a third of a bottle of Scotch. He hesitated through four more rings, then about-faced and returned to the living room.

"Just somebody from church," he told Sid.

"Persistent bastard, isn't he?" Sid remarked, refilling Tom's glass.

It was about eleven minutes later that the doorbell rang, and Tom was even better lubricated by that time.

"Whoever that is, tell 'em to go away."

Sid went, and came back.

"I dunno, Tom. She's gorgeous enough to be therapeutic. Maybe we should let her in. Somebody named Kathryn?"

"Oh Christ! Oh Jesus H. Christ! I can't let her see me like this!"

Sid Garvey was a perceptive man. This anguished cry from his old friend conveyed to him a world of hitherto unguessed-at information. He decided cowardice was not the answer. He grabbed Tom's arm.

"You can sober up faster than any man I know. Get upstairs and splash cold water over your face and drink three glasses of it. I'll put on some coffee and stall her till you get down. Go!"

Tom went.

Sid went back to the door and invited Kathryn to enter. "Tom's gone upstairs for a minute," he explained. "Come on in to the living room and have a seat. I'm about to make some coffee. We were drowning our sorrows, as you can see." He gestured toward the Scotch bottle and glasses, since it would have been foolish to try to pretend they weren't there, as it would have been equally foolish to try to pretend that he himself was sober. "Oh, I'm sorry. Sid Garvey." He stuck out a hand.

Kathryn took it firmly, and gave Sid Garvey a serious looking over. She liked what she saw. He was a small man with a big nose and black hair slicked back over his head and he was never going to win any beauty contests, and besides, it was clear he'd had more Scotch than he needed, but he was looking her square in the eye without apology. And the eyes she was looking into were full of intelligence.

"Kathryn Koerney," she replied, meeting that steady gaze. "I'm so glad Tom has a friend to be with him."

"You're from Tom's church?" Sid asked. Kathryn had

not changed out of her working wardrobe and was therefore still dressed like a priest.

"Yes, but I'm not officially on the staff there. I teach at the Seminary. Look, why don't I come into the kitchen with you? Then we can talk while you make the coffee."

So it was that by the time Tom got back downstairs and came into the kitchen, Sid had filled Kathryn in on the full perfidy of District Attorney Nick Silverman, and Kathryn was so full of righteous indignation on Tom's behalf that she had earned Sid's undying approval.

"Tom! I can't *believe* this! What a snake! Here, have some coffee, this Silverman person I mean, what a loathsome, venomous, idiotic, *asshole*!"

Sid stared at her for a second, then cracked up laughing. Tom, more accustomed to Kathryn's vocabulary and to her forceful expressions of opinion, realized what an impression she must be making on his friend, who had probably never seen a woman priest before and would no doubt be expecting an entirely different standard of behavior. Looking at Sid, roaring with laughter, he too began to laugh, and he laughed until the tears rolled down his cheeks.

Kathryn stared at both of them. "It's not funny," she said crossly.

"Oh, yes it is," Tom disagreed with her as he recovered. "And God, how I needed that." And then, in an act of great boldness, he put down the coffee mug she had just handed him, placed his hands on her shoulders, and kissed her on the cheek. "Thank you," he said.

"Oh, drink your coffee," she said, still cross, sitting down at the table. "Now, what are we going to do about this?"

Both men stared at her blankly for a moment.

"There isn't anything to do," Sid explained. "Silverman has the authority. I told you—"

"I know that." Kathryn interrupted. "I heard you. I mean, what does Tom do now, specifically, about solving the case?"

They stared at her again.

"Tom," she said deliberately, "How drunk are you? Did you drown your brains in that bottle? You are the one who understands what's really going on, right? And the idiot Silverman has it all wrong? Which means if you sit here and do nothing, it will never get solved. So suspension or no suspension, you are going to have to get to work. *Will* the two of you stop staring at me as if I were a freak show? I am making perfect sense."

"You know something? So you are," said Sid. He turned to Tom. "She's right. You can't quit."

"But how can I keep working? I don't have any authority."

"Well, here's what you do have. . . ." Kathryn enumerated, counting assets on her fingers: "You have access to the intended victim because she's living in my house and she will talk to you anytime. You have access to a lot of the people involved in the case because they are friends of mine and will come to my house if I ask them to and they will talk to you. You have money, if any should be required."

"Money?" Sid asked.

"I can afford a little financial investment if necessary," Kathryn said, with spectacular understatement.

"Oh, that's good."

"Kathryn," Tom protested, "I don't want you spending your money on me."

"I'm not spending my money on you, you nitwit, I'm

spending my money defending the life of my good friend Tracy, remember?"

"Oh, yeah, right," Tom replied, abashed.

"So if you could start somewhere, where would you start?" she asked.

"Ice cubes."

So the three of them drank coffee and discussed ice cubes.

Kathryn left a half an hour later, saying she had a mountain of papers to grade before supper.

After she left Sid exploded. "Tom! My old buddy! Why the hell didn't you *tell* me?"

"Tell you what?"

"About *her*!"

"What's to tell?"

"What's to— Are you out of your effing *mind*? A smart, gorgeous woman is in love with you and you don't even bother to tell your old pal Sid about it? I'm hurt, I tell you, I'm hurt!"

"She isn't in love with me."

"Aw, come on, seriously, you don't mean to tell me you haven't *noticed*?"

"No, Sid, you've got it wrong. We're just friends."

"Just friends? Bullshit! She was ready to kill Silverman for you, she's ready to spend money on you, never mind what she says about her friend Tracy, no, the woman was passion all over the place, Tom, and it was all for *you*."

"She's a passionate kind of person."

"Tom, your problem is you're too modest. Why do you find it so hard to believe that a terrific woman could be in love with you?"

"Because I know who she *is* in love with," Tom responded gloomily.

CHAPTER 19

Driving home, Kathryn was trying to ignore the memory of what had happened when Tom had kissed her on the cheek. She should have been merely touched. Instead she had felt an instant's unmistakable *frisson*.

That was absolutely insane. Completely out of the ballpark. She was in love with Kit Mallowan. She had been in love with Kit ever since she'd met him on the train from London to Oxford the previous July. He'd enforced her feelings for him by saving her life at considerable risk to his own a mere five days later. They had then spent the rest of the summer together at his fabulous Tudor mansion in rural Oxfordshire, trying to work out how a marquis and a woman priest could build a happy marriage. They hadn't been very successful. But she was nevertheless deeply in love with him, so she had absolutely *no* business reacting like that to a platonic little peck on the cheek from Tom! She forced herself to think about something else. Like who the hell those stupid eight people could be, and how the District Attorney had gotten hold of them.

When she got home Mrs. Warburton informed her that Tildy Harmon had called. "She sounded upset."

Kathryn went to the telephone and punched call back.

"Tildy? What's up?"

"I'm not sure but I don't like it. The District Attorney from Trenton, a guy named Silverman, came by my office today, grilling me about Louise Holder's disappearance, and it was plain as the nose on your face that he was trying to get me to say that I thought Tom killed her! Can you imagine? Needless to say, I sent him away with a flea in his ear. Now what I want to know is this: Where did the District Attorney get a list of members of St. Margaret's Church who know Tom Holder well? Because I wasn't the only one he was talking to, he said so."

"Oh my God. The Rector."

"I am going to *kill* Mark Randall."

"Not if I get to him first, you're not."

"You go get 'im, sister. Give him one for me."

Kathryn looked at her watch. It was five minutes to five. She called the church.

"Frances, it's Kathryn. Tell me something: By any mad chance did the District Attorney show up to see Father Mark today?"

"Why, yes he did, he was here in the morning. He came about Louise Holder's disappearance."

"And did the Rector give him a list of parishioners to talk to?"

"Yes, Father Mark asked me to Xerox a copy of the vestry members for him," said Frances innocently, little knowing what she had just let her boss in for.

"Is Father Mark there now? I need to speak to him."

"Sure, I'll put you through."

Kathryn told the Rector that she knew it was five o'clock on Friday and she was terribly sorry but she had to talk to him and it was urgent, and would he kindly stick around and she would be there in five minutes. Naturally he had no choice but to say he would be waiting for her. Fortunately, Kathryn reflected, Frances would be gone so she wouldn't hear her employer getting yelled at.

Sure enough, Kathryn passed the secretary at the church door on her way out.

"Hi, Kathryn, he's waiting for you."

"Thanks, Frances. Have a good weekend."

Kathryn walked into Father Mark's office without knocking, slammed the door behind her, marched up to the man's desk, and declared, "I hereby resign from the staff of this church because *you*"—she pointed at the astonished Rector—"are a son of a bitch!"

All parish priests find themselves, from time to time, the targets of hostility in varying degrees from their parishioners and their staff, but it is fair to say that it does not usually come in such a full-frontal verbal assault as this, especially from a heretofore faultlessly civil staff member, and it was only to be expected that it took Father Mark a few seconds before he could do anything but gibber.

"I—I—ah—wha—you—can—I—wha—how—" Finally he managed, "Kathryn, please sit down."

"I don't want to sit down!" she raged. "I'm too angry!"

"Then tell me what I have done to offend you."

"Tom Holder has been suspended from duty, relieved of his command, and it's *your* bloody fault!"

Normally Kathryn was careful to prune the Briticisms from her vocabulary for fear of appearing affected, but she was too furious to care. Besides, Father Mark was pretty affected himself.

"*Suspended?* For God's sake, why?"

"Because, reportedly, eight people from St. Margaret's were prepared to say he just might have killed Louise. Now, to begin with, where might the District Attorney have gotten a list of St. Margaret's vestry members to go talk to?"

The Rector had the grace to blush.

"Well, he got them here, of course. But be reasonable, Kathryn! The D.A. comes around saying he's investigating Louise's disappearance, he wants to talk to some St. Margaret's people, what am I supposed to do? I thought the easiest thing would be to give him a list of the vestry members. What was wrong with that?"

"There wouldn't have been one damn thing wrong with that," Kathryn said, leaning over the desk and glaring at him malevolently, "except for the fact that you had already turned the vestry against him, Mark. Oh, yes. Don't give me that blank look. Tildy Harmon told me all about what happened at that emergency vestry meeting, and Tildy has always been one of your biggest fans. But she said you'd gone off the deep end. Nonstop prayer vigil in the church, *not* until the killer was caught, but until the police were off the property. *Don't you see what you did, Mark?* You made Tom and his men the villains. You were going on about this violation of the sanctity of the church grounds and according to Tildy you were blaming it on the *police*, not the killer. Well, the *'police'* are Tom Holder. So when Louise disappeared, the vestry members, who have all thought of Tom for lo these many years as the salt of the earth, instead of feeling sorry for him, began to feel suspicious of him. At least a few of them did. At least enough of them felt just suspicious enough that the District Attorney, who has his own agenda and wants to remove Tom so he can take over the Mason Blaine case, was able to persuade them to say they thought it was possible he murdered her."

"Nonsense!"

"Eight of them. Eight vestry members, Mark. That's your doing. It would never have happened before that wretched meeting of yours."

The Rector shifted uncomfortably in his seat.

"You're an intelligent man, Mark. Yet I watched you stand toe-to-toe with a Police Chief and order him to clear his officers off of a crime scene as if you had the authority to do it. Would you have *dreamt* of speaking to him that way if he had not been a parishioner of yours?"

Father Mark dropped his head into his hands. "Mea culpa, mea culpa, mea maxima culpa," he groaned. "When I saw those yellow tapes up around the church I went crazy. It was as though my wife had been violated. And there was Tom, in charge of it all. . . . You're right. I blamed him. When I talked to the vestry, I talked about the police, but as you say, they all know that around here Tom *is* the police. My God. You say *eight* vestry members actually told the D.A. they thought he might have killed her? I can't believe it. I wonder which eight? Do you think the D.A. would tell me? I might try talking to them."

"No, Mark, that horse has bolted. You're not going to get it back."

"I can't believe this. What a mess. Do you suppose, now that I've repented and confessed, you might stop berating me and sit down? Maybe together we could figure out a way to minimize the damage."

Kathryn decided this was a reasonable enough request and declared a truce by dropping into the chair facing Father Mark's desk.

She said, "Tom and I and a friend of his from the crime scene team in Trenton are working on getting him reinstated by solving the homicide, which the District Attorney is never going to solve because he's an idiot, and of course if anybody's going to find Louise it's Tom because the D.A. isn't going to bother to look for her."

The Rector nodded. "Good. Then what remains is to reestablish Tom's reputation in the eyes of this congregation, which you tell me I have damaged. Any ideas?"

"Off the top of my head, no. Because the suspicion is so irrational. Granted, nobody in his right mind would *want* to live with Louise, but Tom's put up with her for several decades now, so why should he all of a sudden up and murder her? Why would anybody who's known him forever think for a minute he would do such a thing, even given all these negative feelings you were dishing out about him?"

"Well, Kathryn," said Father Mark, with the merest trace of gentle malice, "there is one new element in Tom's life that hasn't been there for those several decades, and some people around here might suspect that that might make a difference. A very big difference."

"What's that?" Kathryn asked, honestly puzzled.

"Oh, come, come, Kathryn," the Rector chided. "A woman of your perception? Having spent the amount of time you've spent with Tom? Why, you were practically living together at that castle in England last summer! You can't tell me you haven't figured out how he feels about you, when the whole congregation knows it!"

Kathryn did not seem to be able to draw breath; there was a sudden constriction at her heart and a ringing in her ears. Then she felt her entire face flush; even her ears grew hot.

"You *did* know it!" the Rector exulted.

"No. I didn't know until now. But I see it. I should have known it. What an idiot I am."

"So you see, those eight people, whoever they are, much as they may be mistaken about Tom killing Louise, they *would* be able to produce a viable motive if the D.A. asked them for one. Tom wants to marry you."

Kathryn was shaking her head. "He knows he doesn't have a prayer."

The Rector chuckled. "Kathryn, you underestimate the optimism of the male of the species. If we—"

"No. You misunderstand me. Tom knows I'm in love with somebody else. Very seriously in love with somebody else."

"You've told him so? Specifically?"

"In no uncertain terms. Point blank."

"Ah."

There was a brief silence.

"That would be that marquis you met last summer?" the Rector asked.

"Yes."

The Rector thought for another minute. "I have an idea. This marquis—"

"Kit."

"He feels the same way about you?"

"Yes."

"He'd be willing to do you a big favor?"

"Yes."

Father Mark raised an eyebrow. "Those are pretty confident answers."

"He keeps asking me to marry him."

"Keeps asking?"

"So far I haven't said yes. Or at least, I said yes and then changed it to a maybe."

"Why? Not that it's any of my business."

"I am reluctant to be a marchioness. I'm not happy with the idea of living in the middle of nowhere in a mansion in Oxfordshire in a life of rarified privilege. I think it would ruin me. I already have too much money. I'm afraid for my soul." She didn't want to tell Mark about the personal problems, about Kit's possessiveness, about his stubborn refusal to compromise on issues such as how many children they were going to have and whether she was going to get a job in Oxford after they got married or stay at home. She didn't even want to *think* about those problems when she and Kit were an ocean away from each other.

"I'll be damned," the Rector remarked. "I minister to a parish full of rich people and you're the only one I know who doesn't want to get any richer. Congratulations. But let's get back to the point. O.K., if this man keeps asking you to marry him, it's probably safe to assume he might do what I have in mind. Get on the phone and ask him to drop everything and catch the next plane and get here in time for church on Sunday. If you call him this in-stant, he might be able to do it. Then we'll have *Tom*, not you, introduce him to everybody as your boyfriend, with the implication of almost-fiancé, if you don't mind. We will make it clear to everybody that Tom knows all about Kit, accepts Kit, likes Kit, et cetera."

Kathryn frowned. "And how is this going to convince the eight people—and anybody else—that Tom didn't kill Louise?"

"Because it does away with his motive, you see. The only reason anyone at St. Margaret's would suspect Tom of finally being willing to do something violent after all these years would be that he had a temptation, an alternative, namely you. I'm convinced of that. If they see that he knows about Kit, then they'll know that he doesn't have a motive for killing Louise, then these infamous eight people and any other doubters will also come around."

"Mark, you're sure of this?"

"I'm positive. The only reason it sounds strange to you is that you're not accustomed to thinking of Tom being in love with you, and believe me, the rest of the congregation has been whispering about it behind your back for over a year now."

Kathryn could feel herself blushing again, although this time, mercifully, it wasn't so bad.

"So," the Rector continued, "if we have Tom introducing Kit around as if he considers him a fait accompli in your life, there goes Tom's motive, there goes any suspicion of Tom, Tom is reinstated in everybody's eyes, Tom can hold up his head proudly in St. Margaret's, and with any luck we can even find out who these eight people are and get them to reverse what they said to the District Attorney." Father Mark spread his hands in a "nothing to it" gesture.

It seemed to Kathryn that the plan was nowhere near as straightforward and obvious as the Rector suggested, nor the benefits to Tom anywhere near as great as the disadvantages. For there was one huge disadvantage.

"You're going to have to tell Tom that you've told me how he feels about me. Otherwise when you explain the plan to him, how he's supposed to introduce Kit to people, it won't make sense to him."

"Yes, that's true. Well, you were bound to figure it out eventually, weren't you?"

Kathryn hesitated. "I'm considering his embarrassment."

"You ought to be considering his career. I'm telling you, Kathryn, we can get to those eight people and make them change their minds."

"But how do you even have the faintest idea who they might be?"

"Because I annotated that vestry list so Silverman only would have talked to people who've been here more than four years. That shortened it to fifteen names. With a few phone calls we can find out who he actually talked to. And we'll be able to eliminate some of them from the eight because we know they're too loyal to Tom to ever say anything like that to the D.A."

"Like Tildy Harmon."

"Right."

"O.K. You've convinced me." She looked at her watch. "I should call Kit instantly. It's already eleven thirty-five in England."

"Use Maggie's office. She's out on a pastoral call. I'll let you in."

"Thanks, but I'll just go into the nave and use my cell."

The Rector reflected that that was going to cost her a young fortune but that if anyone could afford it Kathryn could.

As she left his office Father Mark asked, "You're not really resigning?"

"No, that was just to get your attention."

"Good. I'd hate to lose our best preacher."

"Shameless flatterer."

Kathryn had a number that rang Kit's own cell phone, not his house; she was thankful for that, as she would have hated to have to ask for Lord Wallwood whenever she rang up her boyfriend. It would have made her feel unbearably pretentious. She was also grateful that he kept that phone with him in his wheelchair at all times during the day and on his bedside table at night.

"Kit?"

"Kathryn! Darling! My God, look at the time! What's happened? Has there been *another* murder? Are you all right?"

"No, no new murder, and I'm fine. I hope I didn't wake you?"

"No, just drifting off. If you're all right, why are you rousing me from my beauty sleep at this hour? Not that I'm not overjoyed to hear from you at any hour of the day or night, my dearest. It's just that these days when I get calls from you at other times than our usual Sunday I tend to expect alarming announcements."

"No alarming announcement. It's just that I am about to ask the most obscenely huge favor of you. There's no excuse for it. I am desperate."

"But darling, whatever you need! Only tell me."

"Tom is in trouble." She told him the story. Kit, who knew Tom from the previous summer, was eloquent in his sympathy.

"But what can I do?" he asked immediately.

"Well, this is the awkward part. I've been talking to the

Rector here at St. Margaret's, Mark Randall." Kathryn took a deep breath. "Mark says Tom is in love with me."

"I could have told you that, sweetheart," Kit said, thoroughly unsurprised.

"Oh. Ah. Why didn't you, then?"

"You didn't seem to want to know."

"Oh, isn't *that* the God's truth! Because now that I do know, I really hate it. Anyway, Mark says that that's the only reason anyone here would ever suspect Tom would kill Louise, that is, because he wants to marry me, so the only way we can convince these eight people or anybody else that Tom *didn't* kill Louise is for you to come over here and have Tom introduce you to everybody as my almost-fiancé, as if he regards you, as the Rector puts it, as a fait accompli in my life."

"Ah, because if I'm a fait accompli he doesn't have a motive."

"Exactly."

"Well, in that case I'd better be on a plane in the morning, hadn't I, in time to be in church on Sunday?"

"Oh, I do love you."

"I am so glad. Will you marry me?"

"You know the answer to that question. Oh, you know you can't stay at my house, don't you? I hate to drag you all the way to New Jersey and then be inhospitable, but my house is utterly and spectacularly wheelchair-unfriendly. I'll find a hotel for you. And I'll phone up an emergency carpenter and see if I can't get a ramp built up my front steps so you can at least see my first floor. Oh, I can't wait for you to meet Mrs. Warburton!"

CHAPTER 20

Kathryn came dancing home to inform Mrs. Warburton and Tracy about the imminent arrival of Kit Mallowan.

"Oh, wait till you meet him! He is the most divine man! He is the most gorgeous, sexy, *witty* man you will ever meet in your entire mortal life and when the sun shines on his red hair and when he wears blue, which he almost always does, ladies, I tell you, no woman in her right mind could resist!"

Mrs. Warburton was smiling indulgently and Tracy was grinning from ear to ear, more amused than she would have believed possible a few hours previous. "I think we get the picture," she told Kathryn. "When does this paragon arrive?"

"Sometime tomorrow afternoon, presumably. He said he would catch a flight in the morning. We need to make a hotel reservation for him, Warby, wheelchair-accessible of course, and we need to find a carpenter, and isn't that going to be fun on a Saturday, to build a ramp so he can get up the steps to the house here."

Mrs. Warburton assured her that the carpenter would be no problem, because if a professional one could not be sufficiently bribed to come out on a weekend, she knew a very nice man at her church (First Presbyterian) who would be more than happy to oblige her.

Kathryn informed Mrs. Warburton that she was a treasure.

"Nonsense, dear. Do we need to go to J.F.K. to pick up this young man?"

"I asked him if that would be necessary, but he said we might be busy sleuthing or guarding Tracy and that he would take a cab."

"I can't say I'm sorry not to have to drive to J.F.K.," Mrs. Warburton said.

"He would never let anyone be inconvenienced for him," Kathryn declared. "He is a darling. He is perfect. I shall go absolutely out of my mind waiting for tomorrow afternoon."

"Mrs. Warburton," Tracy suggested, "I think somebody should throw some cold water on this woman."

But it was Tracy herself who administered the cold water by adding, "By the way, Tom Holder called."

Kathryn came down to earth with a thud.

"Oh," she said. To her overwhelming relief, she did not blush again. Or if she did, at least it wasn't so bad that she could feel it.

If Tracy and Mrs. Warburton detected any pink in Kathryn's cheeks, they attributed it to Tracy's remark about cold water.

"What did he want?" Kathryn asked.

"He wanted Patrick to come over here as soon as possible," Tracy answered, "so he could talk to both of us about what happened *before* that infamous drink got mixed, not after. Seems he wants to start on a whole new idea."

"Fine by me. Have you had any luck getting Patrick?"

"Not yet. I left a message on his phone but he hasn't called back yet."

"Well, girls," said Mrs. Warburton, "I don't think you need me here anymore. I think I'll go see about hotels and carpenters. Kathryn, any preference on hotels? The Harton Inn, perhaps?"

"Oh, yes, I think so. A room overlooking Peller Square, if you can get one on such short notice. But it has to be drop-dead perfect in every respect, you know."

As Mrs. Warburton went downstairs, Kathryn turned to Tracy and asked, "Why did I even bother to add that last sentence? She knows who the room is for. She wouldn't settle for anything less than drop-dead perfect."

"That woman is incredible," Tracy marveled. "Where on earth did you find her?"

"She used to run a bed-and-breakfast in Poughkeepsie and my dates stayed there when I was at Vassar. I was always crazy about her. After her husband died of cancer she was broke from the medical bills because their insurance hadn't been good enough, and she had to sell the house. Rough on her, but I try to pay her enough to make up for it."

"She seems happy here."

"She tells me she is. Actually, she rules me with an iron fist. Are *you* happy here?"

Tracy fetched a huge sigh. "You know I'm not. I am going bananas. But I am physically comfortable, of course. I am slowly making my way through your library thanks to the volumes Mrs. Warburton is bringing up to me. I don't have to worry about my job, because my boss is a sweetheart and he told me to take my time about getting back to work." (Unbeknownst to Tracy, Kathryn was paying said boss to pay the temp who was taking her place.) "I am coming to terms with the fact that I am a widow, which, as you know, is a shock, but it would be ridiculous to pretend to you that my marriage was in great shape and that I am prostrate with grief. Are you asking, would I rather be here than back in my apartment? Yes, I'd rather be here. Despite the claustrophobia, it feels safer."

"Good. Now, excuse me a minute. I'm going to go take off my collar and other priestly attire and change into my Friday night casuals. Then I'll come back and we can plan your future or paint each other's toenails or watch a Pierce Brosnan video or do other girl stuff until supper's ready, how's that?"

"What color do you like your toenails?"

"Fuchsia."

"I'll get out the polish."

They dined at a small table in Tracy's room, as Kathryn still refused to let Tracy out of her luxurious prison. As Tracy tasted the homemade soup that was the first course, she remarked, "I don't care what you're paying her, it's not enough."

Kathryn replied, "I'm sure it's not, but she won't let me give her a raise. I've tried three times."

After supper they climbed onto the bed and propped themselves up on a mountain of pillows and watched the Pierce Brosnan video after pretending for ten seconds to have a spirited debate between Pierce and the fuchsia toenails.

It was almost 10:30 when Patrick called. He apologized for not returning Kathryn's call earlier, but he'd been in the library and of course he'd had the ringer on his phone switched off. Sure, he'd be glad to meet Tom at Kathryn's house the next day. Ten in the morning? Fine. Tell Tracy good-night for him.

"For God's sake, Tracy!" Kathryn exclaimed. "He was in the library! On a Friday night! No wonder they call him The Monk. Have you ever known Patrick to have a date?"

"No."

"Do you think he's gay?"

"Jamie used to talk about it. He said Patrick dated when they were undergraduates but never got serious about any one girl for very long; then after they were graduate students he stopped dating altogether. Jamie thought that's when Patrick might have started to begin figuring out his sexuality. But Jamie never had the nerve to ask him about it."

Kathryn contemplated the now blank television screen.

Tracy said, "He's not, well, you know—"

"Camp? Not in the least. But scads of gay people aren't. They look and act absolutely plumb normal." She turned and looked into Tracy's troubled eyes. "Sweetie," she said, "you're a brand new widow. That's enough trauma for right now. I'd hate to see you get your heart broken."

Tracy turned her head away, but not before Kathryn saw the sudden glint of tears. Kathryn put her arm around her and gave her a quick squeeze. "I'll say good-night now.

You get some sleep. Your session with Tom and Patrick is at ten."

She left the room, closing the door softly behind her. She hoped she was wrong about Patrick's being gay, but he certainly didn't seem much of a ladies' man. And despite the fact that Kathryn had watched him like the proverbial hawk, she had seen no overt signs that he returned the emotions Tracy felt for him. He treated her with unfailing affection, which had sharpened since Jamie's death into a fierce mother-hen-like determination to defend her against all comers, but that was a long way from eros.

She put Patrick and Tracy to the back of her mind and prepared to make the necessary phone call to Tom. She went to her room, sat on her bed, and took several deep breaths. That turned out not to be enough, so she took several more, and said a prayer. She picked up the receiver, noticed that her heart was beating so loud, she was afraid Tom was going to be able to hear it, and put the receiver down again. "Damn, damn, damn, damn, *damn!*" she said. She did some more breathing and some more praying. It took her five minutes before she was finally able to key in the number, and she hadn't stopped either breathing or praying as she waited for the ring.

It only rang once, because Tom had been waiting by the phone chewing his nails.

"Hi, Tom. I'm sorry to be so long getting back to you but we've just now gotten hold of Patrick. Can you be here at ten tomorrow morning?"

"Sure, that's great. What I thought we'd do is—"

"Tom?"

"Yeah?"

"We've both had rather a long day, and it's a bit late . . ."

"Oh, I'm sorry! I'll see you in the morning."

Kathryn hung up in a shuddering confusion of guilt and relief, knowing Tom wasn't going to see her in the morning because she planned to leave the house at 9:45. On second thought, in case he was early, maybe she'd better make that 9:30. Or better yet 9:15.

The next day she informed Tracy she had a lot of work to do, especially since Kit would be coming and taking up a lot of her time over the next few days, so she was off to the Seminary library.

"You're kidding. You don't want to be in on this?"

"I'd love to be in on this, but I've been neglecting my academic work ever since you tripped over Mason Blaine last week, and if I don't get caught up it's gonna be, in that grand old Texas phrase, too wet to plow."

She gathered up a briefcase full of papers to grade and books to read and set off prepared to spend a full day, if necessary, exiled from her own house, during which she tried mightily not to think about either the questions a certain policeman was asking her friends or the feelings a certain policeman entertained for her.

Tom arrived at Kathryn's promptly at 10:00 (Patrick had been there since 9:45) and the first thing that happened was that Tracy got to come downstairs. She achieved this freedom by the simple expedient of asking Tom if he thought it was safe.

"Yeah, I think you're fine as long as you stay in the house. I know Kathryn's been keeping you upstairs but she's just worried about you. In fact, I'm sure you're fine if you go out with your escort out front."

"Hooray for that. I've been humoring Kathryn but it's

beginning to drive me bonkers. So let's sit in the living room, why don't we?"

"Where *is* Kathryn?" Tom asked, looking around.

"She said she had work to do. Sent her regrets."

The stab of disappointment Tom felt at this news was, he told himself, out of all proportion. *Forget her*, he told himself. *You have a woman's life to save here. Not to mention your career to salvage.*

"O.K., Tracy. Mr. Cunningham. Let's—"

"I think it's time you called me Patrick. After all, this is now unofficial, isn't it? Kathryn tells me, quote, the idiot asshole District Attorney has an ego problem with Tom and wants to take over the case so he suspended him, unquote. That about right?"

Tom grinned. "I'd like to think that was it, of course. At any rate, I'm suspended, and you're under no obligation at all to answer any question I ask you. You're here because Kathryn asked you to come."

"That's right, I am. And she has faith in you, and she asked me to answer your questions, so that's what I'm going to do. And so is Tracy, I assume." Patrick looked at her interrogatively.

"Of course." She nodded.

"Good. I appreciate it. Now, as Kathryn may have told you, I've decided I need to start working on a different notion from where I was before because of some new information I got before they chucked me out. You know we were assuming that Tracy's drink was poisoned during the time that you, Patrick, left it on the sideboard and went upstairs to go to the bathroom?"

They both nodded.

"Well, I'm no longer making that assumption. I'm assuming it's possible—not certain, but possible—that the poison was put into the glass at some other time."

Both of them looked at him in deep puzzlement.

"But when?" Patrick asked.

"That's what I'm going to try to find out now. Let's start with the last time you took a sip out of that glass, Tracy, when we know it was healthy. I assume you finished off your drink and decided you wanted another one, right?"

Patrick and Tracy looked at each other, then back at Tom. Both of them looked rather uncomfortable.

"You understand that this is painful, don't you?" Tracy asked.

"Of course, I do," Tom said. "Homicide investigations are always painful. But in this case I'm not only trying to solve a homicide, I'm try to prevent one, so frankly, I'm expecting both of you to put up with the pain."

"Touché," said Patrick. "All right. Tracy finished off her drink. I asked if she wanted a refill. She said she wasn't quite ready for one yet. That was fine with me because I was still working on mine."

"Hang on a minute. Where were you?"

"On the porch. Same place where—where it happened. Tracy didn't move between then and—and later."

"All right. Go on."

"So we talked a bit."

"Who else was there?"

"Oh, let's see, Edward and Caroline Drew. Carlos Barreda. Is that right, Tracy?" She nodded. "So then a few minutes later Edward and Caroline and Carlos all together decide to go get refills and I offer Tracy again and she says O.K. and I say do you want to come along and she says no, she'll stay put."

"So you took the glass directly from Tracy's hand?"

"Yes."

Tom looked at Tracy. "You're sure that after drinking from the glass you didn't put it down anywhere, rest it on a table or anything, before giving it to Patrick to refill?"

"Positive. There weren't any tables on the porch to rest things on. I remember wishing I had a napkin to wrap my drink in because of the condensation: I was definitely holding it all the time."

"Good. That seems pretty clear. So you handed the glass directly to Patrick and you, Patrick, took it straight into the dining room?"

"That's right."

"Now, this is an important question. Tracy, when you gave the glass to Patrick, was there any ice left in it from your last drink?"

"Ice? Why, yes, there was a fair amount. I remember crunching on it when I was talking to the Drews. Why?"

"Never mind. Just something I'm working on. Patrick, when you took Tracy's glass and started doing the Witherspoon thing, did you add any ice along with the vodka and Kahlua?"

Patrick frowned. "I'm trying to remember. As Tracy said, there was a fair amount of ice in the glass already. I might have thought it didn't need any more. And to tell you the truth, I was concentrating more on trying to make people laugh than anything else . . ." He shrugged.

"Thanks a bunch," said Tracy sourly.

"Sorry, kid," he said.

"You take such good care of me."

"Well, there was this really stunning blonde, you see—"

"Do you think," Tom interrupted, "I could get you two to get back to the point?"

"Sorry," they both said.

"So, Patrick, you can't remember if you put any ice into that black Russian?"

"Sorry, no. What's all this about ice, anyway?"

"Never mind. You'll find out later. Just one more thing. Tracy. Kathryn tells me that when she went out to talk to you on the porch, you said you thought you'd had too much to drink, and when Crystal brought you the black Russian Patrick had mixed for you, you didn't drink it. What changed your mind? You send Patrick to get you a drink, you stand around for what, five, eight minutes—without drinking anything, and then you make the statement that you've had too much to drink. I don't get it."

"Oh, that!" Tracy smiled a small, slightly embarrassed smile. "Have you ever suffered a delayed reaction? Well, black Russians are strong little suckers, and I was knocking them back pretty fast. Too fast. I'd had about four of them, which was definitely one too many, and the one I sent Patrick for was my fifth, and while I was waiting for it they all kinda hit me at once. I knew if I started to look drunk in front of the Spanish faculty, Jamie would kill me, so I"—she stopped, realizing what she had just said, and flinched. She resumed, "Figure of speech. I knew I would be in trouble if I started to look drunk in front of the Spanish faculty, so I figured I'd better stop drinking forthwith. I was going to explain that to Patrick when he showed up with my drink, but it turned out to be Crystal who showed up with it, so I didn't explain anything. I just took it and stood there with it and didn't drink it. Then sure enough, here came Jamie to give me hell for drinking too much anyway." She began to tremble.

"Did he often take your drinks from you?"

"He's been known to finish my drinks, yes. We both like black Russians."

"While you were standing there holding the drink but not drinking it, did you happen to notice anything about the ice in the glass? Was there a lot of it? Only a little?"

Tracy shook her head. "Sorry. I didn't look."

Tom ruminated for a minute. He couldn't think of any more questions to ask, and it didn't seem to him that he'd learned anything useful at all. *Damn*, he thought. He simply had to find out more about the ice.

"The ice on the dining table," he said. "The ice the MacDonalds provided for the party; it was in an ice bucket, right?"

Both Patrick and Tracy nodded and said, "Yes."

"What did it look like? Big chunks? Little chunks? Cubes? Crushed?"

Surprised by his previous ice questions, they appeared to suspect that he had perhaps gone around the bend, but Kathryn had asked them to answer his questions, so they humored him.

"It was that crushed ice you buy in bags from convenience stores, wasn't it, Patrick? Irregular size chunks about yea big. At least that's what was in the bucket when I mixed my first two drinks."

"Yeah, that's right. I still don't remember whether I used any in Tracy's black Russian, but that's certainly the kind of ice they were using that night. I know that because I used it other times."

Tom nodded. "O.K. Thanks very much. I appreciate your help." He bid the pair farewell, left the house, acknowledged the sympathetic wave of the man in the squad car, got into his own car, and pulled out his cell phone. He punched Kathryn's cell phone number, which he had taken the precaution of memorizing once he knew he might be needing to get in touch with her anytime, and prayed that she would answer.

She was sitting in the Seminary library and had the ringer off, but fortunately for Tom the phone was in her pocket and she had a vibrate function. Feeling the soft purr, she pulled out the phone and looked at the display: HOLDER. Although she had fled the house to avoid meeting him, she thought she could manage a telephone conversation, so she switched the phone on and whispered, "Just a second."

Grabbing her purse, she stole off into a corner where she thought she might be able to get away with a bit of low-voiced conversation without being on the receiving end of too many dirty looks.

"Hey, Tom," she whispered, "how'd it go with Tracy and Patrick?"

"Not nearly as useful as I'd hoped. Look, this is the only thing I can think of now that will be at all useful." He explained what he wanted her to do.

"Wait. Let me go back to my books and get some paper to write down names."

Fortunately Tom had a good memory, because all his notes were in his files in the police station where he couldn't get to them. When he was through with the list he asked tentatively, "Is there any chance of a cup of Earl Grey this afternoon?"

Again Kathryn was smitten with a paroxysm of guilt and embarrassment. "I'm sorry, Tom. Not this afternoon. Kit's arriving from England."

"*Kit's* arriving?"

"Yes, about four."

There was a brief pause. "Oh. How long will he be in town?"

"I'm not sure."

Another pause. "Well, I guess I'll see him in church."

Oh, brother, will you see him in church. "Yes, of course."

"That'll be nice."

No, it won't. "Sorry about tea."

"Oh, no! Forget tea! Forget I mentioned it. Tell Kit I said hello, welcome to America, all that. See you tomorrow. Bye." He hung up.

Kathryn turned off her phone and folded her arms across her chest in physical pain. After a moment she started to cry and had to retreat to the ladies' room. She was there for half an hour.

Desire, however, is very powerful, and by four o'clock that afternoon there was room in her mind for only one man. She was thanking God that the miraculous weather was still holding, for that meant that she would once more see him with the sun shining on his red-gold hair.

"Please, God, let him be wearing blue. Let him be wearing navy slacks and a royal blue blazer and a pigeon's egg blue shirt the color of his eyes and don't let me be making all this up, don't let me have magnified in my mind how beautiful he was so that it will all be a terrible anticlimax when I see him; above all, don't let it be a complete fiction that electromagnetic field he generates, that palpable energy that comes off him in waves . . ."

She moved from window to window in the living room from 3:30 onward, and as four o'clock approached she moved into the front yard. At five minutes to four she went into the street.

She would have been gratified to know that the passenger of the taxi creeping down Alexander Street at 4:12 looking for the right number was every bit as eager as she was. When she saw the cab, she waved both her arms, and was delighted to see an arm clad in royal blue shoot out of the taxi window and wave back at her.

He had the door open before the cab had rolled to a complete stop, and Kathryn, unwilling to wait until he got in the house, got into the car and fell into his embrace. The cabbie sat patiently while Kathryn completely failed to have any opportunity to evaluate whether Kit was as beautiful as she remembered him, because she was far to close to him to tell.

After a few minutes they emerged breathless from this greeting, looked at each other, and laughingly said hello.

"Shall I pay this good fellow?" asked Kit. "Let him be on his way, instead of making him sit 'round watching us making a disgraceful spectacle of ourselves."

"I've seen worse," said the cabbie laconically.

Kit and Kathryn cracked up. Kit paid the driver, tipping him extra for the comic remark. Kathryn got out, Kit picked up his wheelchair from the seat beside him, unfolded it in two seconds, set it on the ground, and hoisted himself into it with a grace born of twenty years' practice. He wheeled himself up the walk. Kathryn immediately noted that he was wearing exactly what she had hoped he would be wearing. It was what he had worn on the London to Oxford train when she had first met him. Unlike most men, Kit knew what colors best suited him.

She looked around. "Where's your luggage?"

"Dropped it at the hotel first. This is a beautiful house. I see you managed to find somebody to make me a ramp."

Kathryn was enjoying the sunlight on his hair and finding to her delight and relief that her memory had exaggerated his charms not one iota. He was staggeringly attractive. She couldn't wait to make love to him. She knew that some other women might find him too thin, or object to the freckles that dusted his pale face. And she knew, of course, that some women would take one look at the wheelchair and regard him as an object of pity rather than of desire. Some women were idiots.

He negotiated the ramp effortlessly and she opened the front door for him.

"That mirror," Kathryn said as they passed through the front hall, pointing at a gold baroque concoction the size of half a Ping-Pong table, "was sent to me by my mother from France. Everything else here is me."

Kit surveyed the unpretentious living room as he rolled to a halt. "Ah. I begin to see what I'm up against. Well, you could redecorate the entire family wing, you know. I'm not excessively attached to all that Elizabethan stuff, you know."

"You're excessively attached to the title."

"Not attached in that sense," Kit protested.

"Attached in a worse sense. Attached like a Siamese twin. Ah! Mrs. Warburton! You've brought tea. I'd like you to meet Kit, whom I would introduce properly but if I use his title he'd be cross with me for a week so I won't. Kit, this is the magnificent Mrs. Warburton, without whom life in this house would be unthinkable if not impossible."

Mrs. Warburton put the tea tray down on the coffee table and serenely extended a hand saying, "How do you do, Kit. I've been looking forward to meeting you."

Kit took Mrs. Warburton's hand and replied very solemnly, "How do you do, Mrs. Warburton. I hope you'll pardon me if I don't get up."

Mrs. Warburton laughed.

Kit smiled.

Kathryn gawked.

Mrs. Warburton went back to the kitchen, and Kathryn said to Kit, "You made her laugh! She never goes beyond a Mona Lisa smile!"

"That's what you've always told me, so I thought I'd see if I couldn't produce a warmer response. By the way, how did you manage to become more beautiful in the six weeks since I last saw you?"

"I practice a lot."

Kit rolled himself over to the sofa and skillfully flipped himself onto it. "Come here," he ordered.

"The tea will get cold."

"Damn the tea."

Kathryn went to the sofa and sat beside him.

After several minutes she said, "Kit, I don't mean to complain but you seem to have something large and uncomfortable in your left pocket. And that is not a sly reference to a certain Mae West line."

"I do beg your pardon. That's something I've brought for you. It's a loan. For now, anyway." He disentangled himself from her and pulled from the pocket of his blazer, not without difficulty, a parcel wrapped in brown paper tied with string. "In the fullness of time, I hope these will be yours, together with a great many more such baubles from the family vaults. You see, it struck me that if we're going to play out this little charade of ours convincingly tomorrow morning, it might help if you were decked in some of the family paraphernalia, so to speak. It would make our relationship look more serious. By the way, it was a real picnic talking these through customs. I had to swear on the souls of my ancestors that they were going back to England with me."

As he spoke, he was removing the paper and string from a box about twelve inches long, four inches wide, and an inch deep. Out of this unprepossessing packaging emerged a glorious velvet box of faded burgundy trimmed at the corners with what Kathryn suspected was real gold.

Kit opened it and Kathryn gasped.

Inside, on a burgundy silk cushion, was a necklace of gold and emeralds. The stones were rectangular, and they were almost the size of postage stamps. They were set in ornate gold frames, and strung together with clunky gold links. The necklace was so spectacular that it was a moment before Kathryn noticed the matching ring sitting in the middle of the cushion.

When she caught her breath she said, "Well I don't know, Kit. Couldn't you have found something more noticeable?"

Kit laughed until the tears ran down his face, and then he caught her in a firm hug and commanded, "Marry me. You *must* marry me. I cannot live without you. You are the most divine woman I have ever met in my entire life. Please, Kathryn. I promise you, being a marchioness isn't so bad. We can work it out. Whatever you object to, we can get around it."

"Kit, I keep telling you, it's being a marchioness I object to. And a few other things. But let's not have those arguments again now. You just got here. I love you. To tell you the truth, I'd love to marry you, and I'm afraid you're going to wear me down, you know, one of these days, title or no, and—"

"Do you mean it?" Kit's face lit up like a child at Christmas.

"It's just that I can't imagine ever giving you up."

Conversation ceased for a while.

When they had stopped kissing and finished exchanging vows of undying love, Kathryn remembered the burgundy box.

"Kit, about these so-called family baubles of yours. They will certainly accomplish the purpose. If I wear that necklace, everyone will know in an instant it's not mine. How old is it, by the way?"

"Eighteenth century. It belonged to the first marchioness."

"I can believe it. It's a museum piece. Tell you what. How about I just wear the necklace? The ring would imply we're engaged, and that's just too much of a lie."

After a bit of good-natured argument she managed to make Kit agree with her.

Dear God, she thought, closing the box. *This is going to be so hard on Tom.*

CHAPTER 21

Tom was always an early riser, so he was already awake when the phone rang two hours before he would normally have left his house for church. At this unreasonable hour on a Sunday morning, it could only have something to do with either his double homicide or his missing wife, so he pounced on the phone with alacrity.

"Hello?"

"Tom? Mark Randall."

Disappointment mingled with surprise. "Father Mark! Good morning. Is something wrong?"

"No, nothing's wrong. I just wondered if you could come have a talk with me before the eleven o'clock service. It's rather important. Say, ten-thirty?"

"Sure, I could do that."

"Fine. In my office at ten-thirty, then. Thanks, Tom."

Now, what the hell is this going to be about? Tom wondered.

Meanwhile, over on Alexander Street, Kathryn had returned from Kit's hotel and was ransacking her wardrobe for something suitable to wear with the emerald necklace. She certainly wasn't going to wear it with her clergy collar. Finally she decided upon what she called her funeral dress: an unadorned navy wool sheath with long sleeves and a high collar. When she hung the necklace on it she had to admit that the effect was enough to stop traffic.

"Now, what earrings shall I wear with this monstrosity?" she asked herself. "Answer: the smallest ones I own." She opened her jewelry box and took out some modest pearl studs and put them on and surveyed herself in the mirror. She wrinkled her nose in dissatisfaction and took them off. She went into the spare guestroom (the one Tracy wasn't using), opened a drawer in the dresser, took out another jewelry box, and rummaged around in the clutter inside it. Eventually she located the tiny gold studs she had worn for the first two weeks after she had had her ears pierced. She went back to her room, put these on, examined the result, and nodded.

She then went down to breakfast and put on an apron for fear of spilling anything on her finery. She had to take it off again to show Tracy, who nearly swooned.

"Tell me again why you don't want to marry this man?"

"I might have to wear things like this."

"Get serious."

"I *am* serious. Tracy, you don't *like* this thing, do you?"

Tracy opened her mouth, hesitated, then said, "I guess I might like it to hang on my wall and stare at it, but I couldn't wear it. It would wear me."

"Yes, as a piece of personal adornment it has all the subtlety of a Sherman tank. Don't you think so, Warby?"

"I think I have better sense than to offer an opinion on this subject. Orange juice, Tracy?"

When Tom walked into the Rector's office promptly at 10:30 he was a bit on his guard. Father Mark had sounded perfectly friendly, but Tom had not forgotten their last face-to-face encounter.

Father Mark, however, greeted him with an enormous smile and a hearty handshake and a clap on the shoulder. "Tom! Come in, come in. Have a seat." The Rector closed the door and seated himself behind his desk. "Thanks for coming. Now, I know you're wondering what this is all about, so I'll get straight to the point.

"First I want to apologize unreservedly for my behavior the other day. It was inexcusable. You were only doing your job, and I was completely out of line, and I hope you'll forgive me."

This was unexpected and very welcome. Tom felt as though oil had been poured into an open wound. "Why, thank you, Rector. That's nice of you. I appreciate that. Apology accepted. Of course."

"Thank you, Tom. Now that that's out of the way, let's move on to the main reason I called you here. I know that you must have been very wounded by the fact that eight people on the vestry of this church told the District Attorney that they thought it was possible that you killed Louise."

"How'd you know about that?"

"Kathryn told me. She came bursting in here calling

me a son of a bitch and told me it was all my fault because I called an emergency vestry meeting and complained about the police presence on the church grounds. She said I turned the vestry against you. I thought she was going to kill me. That's a very loyal friend you have there, Tom."

Tom's ego, which had been feeling pretty bruised since Kit's arrival, began to take on a warm pink glow. He only hoped it didn't show on his face.

"Anyway," the Rector continued, "the two of us discussed ways we could reverse any damage I might have caused, reestablish your good standing with the congregation, and if possible get you reinstated in your job."

Tom was beginning to feel a lot better. "Why, thanks, Father Mark. Kathryn and a friend of mine are working on the job angle already, but if you have any ideas about reestablishing my good standing in the congregation, as you put it, I'm all ears."

"Well, brace yourself, because parts of it you're not going to like. Did you know that Kathryn's boyfriend, Kit, arrived from England yesterday?"

"Yeah, she told me he was coming."

"You're the reason he's here."

"*I'm* the reason he's here?"

"Kathryn asked him to fly over here to help us. To help you. This is the situation, Tom: You've put up with a loveless marriage to an impossible woman for years. Everybody in the church knows it. Then along comes this young, beautiful, brilliant woman who befriends you and it changes your life. You feel young again. You fall in love with her. It's only natural. You wouldn't be normal if you didn't. Nobody blames you. I think most people are happy for you that you've got Kathryn in your life. But then when Louise went missing, you see, that's where the suspicions came from. People started to wonder if perhaps you'd decided if you got rid of Louise you'd have a chance with Kathryn."

Tom, who had been getting redder in the face throughout this speech, said, "That's crap! I wouldn't have a chance with Kathryn even if Louise dropped dead tomorrow, even if I was younger and better looking and better educated. She's in love with Kit."

"Exactly. She's in love with Kit *and you know it*. And that's the point we're going to make to the people of St. Margaret's this morning. That's why Kit is here. Kathryn is not vesting and sitting up with the clergy this morning, she's sitting in the congregation with Kit. After the service at the coffee hour, she's going to leave Kit to you. He'll be very conspicuous in his wheelchair, everyone will want to know who he is. You are going to take him around and introduce him to everyone as Kathryn's "friend" from England. You will imply that they are almost engaged. Kit is in on this, he knows what to do. Kathryn, on the other side of the parish hall, will be playing the game too, saying things like, "We haven't set the date yet." But the main thing is that you will make it dead clear that *you know all about this*. This is no news to you. Furthermore, you approve of it. You like Kit. You think he's a fine man. Tell people, if you get the chance, that he saved Kathryn's life last summer. Can you do that?"

"Sure I can do it. But you said Kathryn was going to be playing this game, too. And she invited Kit over here to do this. That means—" Tom covered his face with his hands. "Oh shit."

The Rector said uncomfortably, "I have a little

confession to make there. I'm afraid that I'm the one who let the cat out of the bag. She didn't know until I told her."

Tom's hands flew away from his face. "Christ, Mark! You *told* her?" It was the first time he had ever called the Rector "Mark" instead of "Father Mark."

"Well, Tom, it was only a matter of time before she figured it out. She's not stupid, you know. And you *have* been pretty obvious. In fact, I think she suspected it at some level but didn't want it to be true, so she's been in denial about it."

Tom had to know. "How did she react when you told her?"

"First she was embarrassed, then she was distressed for you."

Tom closed his eyes. "Shit."

The Rector tactfully refrained from comment.

After a minute Tom opened his eyes and sighed. "All right, then. So I meet them in the parish hall?"

"You meet Kit in the parish hall. Kathryn plans to be at the other end of it by the time you get there. I think she's too embarrassed to look you in the eye."

"That makes two of us."

Tom left Father Mark's office and went out to the nave to find a pillar to lurk behind as the congregation gathered. He wanted to make sure he didn't wind up sitting anywhere near Kathryn and Kit. Given Kit's wheelchair, there were only a limited number of spaces where they could sit, and he watched those diligently until he saw them arrive.

There they were. Kathryn was taking a place in the back pew, on the outside right seat, and Kit was rolling up beside her. Hang on. What was that thing around her neck? Kathryn never wore flashy jewelry. Tom could only conclude, grimly, that it must be something Kit had given her.

He slipped into a seat on the opposite side of the church and did his very best to concentrate on the service. He didn't succeed very well.

After it was over, he headed in the direction of the parish hall together with the rest of the mob, keeping a careful watch for Kit so that he might begin his introduction game, but an even more careful lookout for Kathryn so that he could avoid her. Since she was doing the same thing to him, for the same reason, they succeeded in eluding each other.

"Good morning, Lord Wallwood," said Tom levelly.

"Don't take it out on me, Tom," Kit said. "I didn't come up with this idea, your Rector did, and he talked Kathryn into it. I hope you're not angry at her, too?"

Tom bit his tongue. "No. I apologize. I shouldn't have said that. You came all the way over here to help me—"

"Don't wallow in it, man! Let's just get the ball rolling. People are beginning to stare. And for God's sake, *please* don't use the title!"

"Right. Laurie! Mike! Good morning! Let me introduce you to Kit Mallowan. Kit is Kathryn Koerney's, how do I put this, Kit? *Very special friend?* From England."

Kit shook hands with Laurie and Mike and exchanged pleasantries while Tom looked around and pulled in another couple. He was especially interested in vestry members, knowing that the notorious eight who had condemned him to Nick Silverman were on the vestry. He told Kit he was going to fetch him some coffee, and used the trip over to the refreshment table to scan the crowd for appropriate prey. As he moved away he heard Kit saying, "Put it this way. I've been trying to convince Kathryn that living in the English climate does wonders for the complexion."

He got back with the coffee for Kit, who thanked him with a dazzling smile and suffered himself to be introduced to the two vestry members Tom had snagged on his excursion.

Laurie stepped out of the general conversation and pulled Tom aside. "Tom, how long has this been going on? Kathryn and this young man?"

"Since last summer. You know, the parish trip to England. Kathryn went over early and she met him on a train. I think it was love at first sight."

"And how long have you known about it?"

"Oh, from the beginning. She told me all about it. And don't tell them this"—he laid a finger on his lips—"but I walked in on them the first time he kissed her. They don't know it, because I backed out again before they saw me." He managed to produce a conspiratorial smile.

Laurie giggled and leaned close to him. "I won't tell," she promised.

But she did tell. Not Kit and Kathryn, but five other women before coffee hour was over. Tom counted on her doing it; that was why he'd told her the story. Otherwise he would never have revisited an incident that had been so intensely painful to him. It was etched in his memory: walking around the corner of Datchworth Castle and seeing them under that tree, Kathryn clasped in Kit's arms.

Well, he knew from the way Laurie bustled off that she was going to tell somebody, so it had worked. So he might as well gird up his loins and use it again. He tapped Kit on the shoulder and said, "I know you're having a good time talking to these folks, but there are some others I'd like you to meet."

Kit said his farewells, asked Tom to hold his coffee, and wheeled himself to the next bunch of persons to be impressed. There they repeated their routine, Tom once more awaiting the opportunity to be cross-examined separately. If none of the people in the group did it now, one of them would do it later. Thus they worked their way around the room. Tom would have been extremely impressed by Kit's performance if only he had been convinced it was a performance. But the thing was, he knew that Kit *did* want to marry Kathryn. So all these hints about impending matrimony were, for Kit, dead serious.

At one point there was a lull. For once, no one was pressing in upon them; there seemed to be space on all sides. Tom suddenly felt very tired. "You know this is killing me, don't you?" he asked.

"I think you're doing valiantly," Kit replied seriously. "And I've always thought bravery should be rewarded, so why don't you and I trundle along the corridor back there as if we were going to the gents and on the way I'll tell you a little something." He began wheeling his chair in that direction and Tom walked beside him.

"Kathryn and I," Kit continued, "talk on the phone every weekend. Naturally we exchange news and of course in that news people get mentioned. Do you know who she talks about more than any other single person? You. I can tell you every single bloody case you've worked on since you got back from England last summer because she's bored me with the details of all of them."

Tom had stopped and was staring at him, open-mouthed.

"Also, you might like to know that I have invited myself over here to visit about twenty-seven times, but it's always, 'I'm terribly sorry, Kit, but I'm frightfully busy with my work, and you'd be such a distraction, you see, I really can't let you come, I'm so sorry, I'll see you over the Christmas holidays.' *But* she snaps her fingers and summons me across the Atlantic on no notice whatsoever with four words: 'Tom is in trouble.' And do you know something? I have a terrible suspicion that the minute Tom is no longer in trouble it's going to be, 'Kit, dear, I'm so sorry to drag you all the way over here and then send you straight back again, but I have *so* much work to do, you know . . .' "

Tom was still gawking at him. "You can't possibly mean—"

"That I'm jealous of you? Just as you're jealous of me? That's exactly what I mean. The feeling's mutual. I know she's in love with me, not you. I know that what she feels for you is just friendship. Or at least, it certainly better be. But it's important to her. It's very strong. And you have this thing you do together, this crime thing, and it leaves me on the outside. Even last summer, when she was falling in love with me, I felt it."

Tom was stunned. "If—if we were ever rude—"

"Tom, you dolt, I am not looking for an apology. I am trying to tell you, because you are a tremendously decent bloke and you deserve to hear it, that I suspect she loves you as much as she loves me, even though it's not the kind of love you wish it was."

Tom swallowed. "Uh, Kit. Speaking of tremendously

decent blokes." He stuck his hand out. Kit took it, and they shook.

Kit suggested, "Shall we return to the party?"

"You do that. I think I'll, uh—" Tom jerked his thumb over his shoulder in the direction of the men's room. "Can you manage on your own for a few minutes?"

"I don't think they'll eat me." He rolled away.

Tom retreated into the men's room, more to collect his composure than anything else. When he came back out into the parish hall, the disaster occurred that he had been trying above all others to avoid: He ran straight into Kathryn.

He was preserved from complete humiliation by two things. One was the conversation he'd just had with Kit, which had fortified his ego ever so slightly; he was far from merry, but at least he was no longer wallowing in the abyss. The other was the necklace she was wearing. One glance confirmed the impression he'd formed in church: this was a gift from Kit. It had to be. He hated it. Kit had hung this godawful thing on Kathryn like staking a claim on her. The reason it saved Tom from embarrassment was that it was so attention-grabbing that it was impossible to think about anything else after he caught sight of it.

"Good grief!" he exclaimed involuntarily.

"Hideous, isn't it?" she said, looking around to see that she wasn't being overheard. "Kit thought our little charade would be more convincing if we had props, so he brought over some of the family jewels. This atrocity has a matching ring, but I drew the line at that. I told Kit a ring would be too much of a lie. What do you think? Isn't it awful?"

Kathryn's condemnation of the necklace instantly

made it possible for Tom to forgive it. "Oh, I don't know," he said mildly. "I'd say its main problem is it's out of place. It's in the wrong century, for one thing. It really needs a hoop skirt and a powdered wig, doesn't it?"

Kathryn was impressed. "Very good, Tom! It's eighteenth century; that's exactly what it needs."

"And the other thing," Tom continued boldly, "is that it's around the wrong neck. You should never wear a thing like that. It doesn't suit you. Besides being inappropriate for a priest."

Kathryn's eyes opened wide. Tom held his breath; had he gone too far? Kathryn sighed.

"Oh, Tom," she said, "would you mind giving *lessons* to Kit? He just doesn't understand."

Tom found this so immensely gratifying, he thought he might actually start to glow. She was telling him he understood her better than Kit!

But Kathryn was reacting differently. Like Tom, she had been spared embarrassment at their encounter by discussion of the necklace. Now she realized she had just asked Tom—poor Tom!—to instruct Kit in how to be a better lover, which was surely thoughtless, heartless, and thoroughly tacky. How could she have been so cruel?

"I need to circulate," she said abruptly, "and you need to get back to Kit." She gave him a little wave and a forced smile and turned and walked away.

Tom blinked at this rapid departure. She had been embarrassed. Surely *he* was the one who should be embarrassed today? Or was she embarrassed because she had paid him too high a compliment? Was she afraid he would take it the wrong way, take it as some sort of encouragement? He shook his head and went looking for Kit. He found him telling Tildy Harmon, among others, that Kathryn would make a splendid marchioness; didn't Tildy agree?

"I'm not sure she would," Tildy answered. "I've heard all about that palace of yours. I think it would drive Kathryn apeshit."

As other members of the groups burst into giggles and guffaws, Tom thought, *Tildy, you marvelous woman, remind me to buy you dozens of roses.*

But Tildy was the only skeptic; everyone else yielded before Kit's undeniable charm. Tom told his story of walking in on Kit and Kathryn's first kiss four more times, and made it transparently clear to everyone that he approved the supposedly upcoming nuptials. Kathryn, for her part, carefully circulating at least twenty feet from the two men at all times, fingered the emeralds while the ladies of the parish swooned over them, and continued, with great effort, to pretend to be looking forward to the day when she could wear them on a regular basis.

Finally it was over. The three players met, by agreement, in the Rector's office.

He beamed at them, and shook Tom warmly by the hand. "Congratulations! It worked. Five people—and don't ask me who they were because it wouldn't be right to tell you—came up to me and said, in effect, that they had told the District Attorney they thought you killed Louise but now they'd changed their minds and they were going to call him tomorrow and say so."

Kathryn gave a little whoop of celebration.

Kit rolled over to Tom and shook his hand. "I'm happy for you, Tom."

"Thanks."

"Well, thank God it worked," said Kathryn with feeling, "because it was bloody *awful.*"

"What, saying you were engaged to me?" Kit asked, ever so slightly offended.

"Oh, the pretense. Letting all the old ladies paw this thing and pretend I loved it when in fact I can't wait to get it off." Kathryn looked at Kit's face and realized how rude she had been. "Oh, I'm sorry, Kit, but it's not my style, you must see that. And it's not at all appropriate for a priest. *Surely* you can see *that*, can't you?"

A little voice inside Tom was chanting, *Thank you God, thank you God, thank you God,* in what can only be described as a very smug tone.

"I brought it," Kit said in a carefully controlled voice, "because it would be appropriate for a woman who was engaged to be married to me."

Kathryn instantly crossed to his wheelchair, dropped to her knees beside it, and with tears springing to her eyes said, "I am so grateful to you for coming to help Tom, and I love you so much."

Kit laid a hand gently on her cheek and kissed her. "Think nothing of it. I love hopping transatlantic flights on eight hours' notice to save the careers of wrongly accused American policemen. I'm thinking of making a hobby of it. It'll keep me from excessive idleness. That's better."

Kathryn was giggling.

Tom's inner voice, however, had changed its tune and was now chanting, *Shit shit shit shit shit.*

CHAPTER 22

It was 2:30 Sunday afternoon. Kit, Kathryn, and Tom had had time to rest from the emotional rigors of that morning, but not, in Kathryn's opinion, nearly time enough. But they had to put it behind them because there was work to be done. The people Tom had asked her to invite were beginning to arrive at her house.

Kathryn had recruited the people she knew personally, namely Carlos and José. With their help they had reached the other students. An appeal had been made to people's public-mindedness: "Come help catch the killer of Jamie Newman." But hints had been dropped about what they were going to be doing, as well, just enough to pique people's curiosity, in case altruism wasn't sufficient to spur them to participate. All told, they had done pretty well; eight out of the eleven people they wanted were now seated in Kathryn's living room drinking coffee and tea and scoffing down Mrs. Warburton's homemade orange pecan coffee cake.

They hadn't seen Tom yet, because he was carefully hidden away in the kitchen. Kathryn had insisted that this thing needed to be stage-managed just right. She had told him to wear drastically casual clothes, preferably a sweatshirt and jeans; he had replied that he didn't own any jeans. Did he have an old pair of pants that he wore to do yard work? Yes. Then those would do fine.

In turn, Tom had done some insisting of his own. Patrick and Tracy were to be absolutely elsewhere, not even in the house. Tracy would be glad of a chance to get out anyway. The squad car could take her back to her apartment and she could fetch some more things for her prolonged stay at Kathryn's, or maybe Rossi would just take Patrick and Tracy for a ride. But the important thing was to keep both of them away from the proceedings because, Tom said, "People will feel inhibited if they're here." Kathryn agreed he was probably right, so Patrick had been summoned for 10:00 to escort Tracy away, much to her delight, and they were given orders not to return before 5:00.

When all of the people had arrived who were expected, Kathryn called them to order and thanked them on Tracy's behalf for coming. "None of you had to be here, this is strictly voluntary. At this point I'd like to explain something. I'm not only a friend of Tracy Newman's, I'm a personal friend of Tom Holder, the Chief of Police. In my opinion he is a card-carrying good guy. What is much more to the point, he is intelligent and competent, more than can be said for the District Attorney, who has serious ego problems." Kathryn told them how Tom had developed his theory that Tracy was the killer's primary target and explained it to the D.A., and then quoted to them Silverman's response. As she expected, they responded with hoots of derision. "Tom stuck to his guns, however," she continued, "and for his pains that consummate asshole of a D.A. has had him suspended from duty. He's using as an excuse the fact that Tom's wife has disappeared, but that's neither here nor there." She waved a placating hand at the shocked and concerned faces. "Tom's wife has a long history of eccentricity and, shall we say, independence of spirit, and he thinks it's quite possible she's just gone off for a while without telling him. We think the real reason the D.A. has suspended Tom is so that he can take over the Mason Blaine homicide case and run it the way he wants to. And we don't think he's going to solve it in a million years because he's got it completely backwards, which is why we've asked you to come here and help us. Tom?"

She turned, as did they all, to see Tom entering from the dining room.

"Hi," he greeted them. "We've met before, but this is different. Last time you had to talk to me, and I was grilling you pretty badly under very unpleasant circumstances. You didn't have any choice. Now you do. You heard what Kathryn said. I've been suspended. I have no authority at all. I'm an ordinary citizen, I'm no longer the Chief of Police, not officially anyway. You don't have to answer any question I ask you. You can tell me to go to hell. But Kathryn asked you to come here to help us catch a killer. Somebody who has already killed two people, Mason Blaine and Jamie Newman, and, more importantly, seems to be trying to kill Tracy Newman, so maybe it would be a good idea if we could catch him before he succeeds. So will you help me?"

There was a subdued chorus of agreement, nods and murmurs of "yes."

Tom thanked them heartily and then explained what he wanted them to do. "You may think this is crazy, but trust me, it will help."

Both Tom and Kathryn could tell from the various expressions on the faces of the eight students that some of them thought that this exercise was going to be a complete waste of time, while others appeared intrigued and willing to give it a try. But even the reluctant dragons had little choice but to go along since they had already committed themselves by showing up. So they all rose and trooped into the dining room.

José, ever the gentleman, volunteered to go first. He wasn't very good. The others offered the comments Tom had asked for, then Carlos, as if to demonstrate that the peasants could outperform the aristocracy, announced that he would go next. One after another the others followed. Kathryn studied all the performances carefully, looking every now and then at Tom to see if he was getting the enlightenment he sought. She couldn't tell.

Finally there was only one student left to go, and fate, or the girl herself, had saved the best for last. She was one Mary Ann Lieberman, and she had been a drama major as an undergraduate. She stepped up to the props Kathryn had set out, picked up the glass and vodka bottle, and magic occurred.

"Now you see here, boys and girls, this object here is a *glass.*" It was perfection. The tilt of the head. The inflection of the voice. Every little unnecessary phrase. At a strategic point halfway through the performance, she put down the glass and the bottle, thrust her hands into the pockets of her floppy denim jacket, rocked back and forth from the balls of her feet to her heels, and shook her head back and forth. She had chin-length curly hair and this produced an admirable effect. Her entire audience burst into spontaneous applause and cries of, "That's it!" and "She's got it!"

Kathryn glanced at Tom. He was standing in the far corner of the room, focusing on Mary Ann with narrowed eyes and with one hand covering his mouth.

Mary Ann pulled her hands out of her pockets and picked up the glass again. She reached into the ice bucket and said, "Now you see, boys and girls, the addition of some ice is necessary in order to chill the drink. You see that, don't you? You see that? So we add the ice—"

And suddenly Kathryn *did* see. She saw what Tom had been looking for. And she knew that Tom himself must have seen it by now, clearly and irrefutably. As Mary Ann rattled on about ice, Kathryn began to feel as though someone were putting ice cubes up her own spine, and she began to feel an acute need to sit down. The nearest chair was six feet away so she had to settle for leaning against the wall. The rest of Mary Ann's routine lasted only a couple of minutes but to Kathryn it seemed interminable. Finally the conclusion arrived, heralded with another round of applause, both manual and verbal, and Tom stepped forward.

"I take it that was accurate in every detail?"

A chorus of agreement.

"Thought so. Thanks, Mary Ann. Thank you all. I know you don't understand what that was about, but trust me, I got what I needed. I hope that some time later when an arrest is made, it'll be clear to you how you've helped. I'm sorry I can't explain now, but I appreciate you coming."

Kathryn stepped in as hostess and also offered thanks, and people began to drift toward the hall. Kathryn wanted to shout at them to hurry up and leave; it was with Herculean effort that she refrained from showing her impatience as they trickled slowly out the front door, Carlos and José lingering as if they had been at a social occasion.

At last they were gone; Kathryn closed the door behind them, stumbled to the sofa, collapsed upon it, and burst into tears.

"Darling! What's the matter?" Kit cried.

"Patrick!" Kathryn wailed. "It was Patrick! Oh, dear God, deliver me, I can't believe it!"

"Your *friend* Patrick?" asked Kit incredulously. "But why would he want to kill Tracy?"

"He didn't," Tom said. "He wanted to kill her husband. Her husband had a habit of picking on her and finishing her drinks at parties. So Patrick told Jamie that Tracy had been drinking too much, and presto, Jamie goes and takes the poisoned drink out of her hand and drinks it himself."

Kathryn looked at Tom. "I was slow. I didn't catch it till Mary Ann did it."

"I saw it when Carlos did it. He was the first one who put his hands in his pockets when he did the routine. You see, when Patrick showed me, the night of the party, how he did it, he didn't include putting ice in the drink. And later when I asked him about it, he said he'd forgotten, but he thought he hadn't put any ice in. I just needed to find out about the ice. That's why I did this thing. When Carlos included pockets in the routine I saw how Patrick could have put the ice cubes in the drink right in front of everybody. But Carlos picked up the vodka bottle afterwards, he got that bit wrong. Mary Ann was the only one who got it dead right."

"I still can't believe it," Kathryn moaned. "He had me completely fooled. Completely. He called her a poor little dab of a thing! Hell, no wonder he stopped dating once he was a graduate student. He'd met Tracy. And here I was thinking maybe he was gay. I'm an idiot. I'm going to turn in my collar."

"Don't be so hard on yourself, Kat," Tom said, unaware that he had used the nickname he had used only once before, the nickname Kathryn's father had called her. It was just so hard for him to see her cry; it brought out tenderness in him he was incapable of reining in, even with Kit sitting right there. "Sometimes we get killers who are amazing actors. Better than Hollywood."

The doorbell rang. Kathryn wiped her eyes. "Oh, God." She raised her voice. "Mrs. Warburton?"

Mrs. Warburton appeared instantly and opened the front door. It was Patrick.

"Hi, Mrs. Warburton, Kathryn! I know I'm early, but— what's wrong?"

Fortunately Kit had wheeled himself over to where Kathryn was sitting so she had a hand to hang on to as she lifted a ravaged face to Patrick and lied, "Migraine."

"Oh, I'm sorry!" And he did look sorry. But he also looked excited. He turned to Tom. "But I'm glad to find you here. I left Tracy over at her apartment with a friend—and her guard, of course—going through Jamie's things." He broke off and flashed a smile at Kit. "I'm sorry, my manners are all to hell and gone. I know who you are, of course; you're Kit. I'm Patrick Cunningham." He held out a hand.

Kit hesitated. He was holding both Kathryn's hands. "I

do apologize," he said, "but both my hands are occupied at present."

Patrick was momentarily taken back, but made a quick recovery. "Oh. Sure, take care of Kathryn. Anyway," he said, turning back to Tom, and letting his excitement show again, Tracy asked me to go over to the library to clear out Jamie's study carrel. I found this behind Jamie's books." He held up a small plastic bag containing about a tablespoon of clear crystals.

Tom stared at him blankly. "You found this in *Jamie's* study carrel?"

"Yes, but the point is that all the study carrels are shared. Two students each. And Jamie shared a carrel with Valerie. Do you know what Jamie was poisoned with?"

"Yes, I do, but I wouldn't be able to tell you if this is it or not. Look, Patrick, I appreciate you bringing this to me, but aside from the information of where you found it, there's nothing I can do with the thing itself. What you need to do is take it to the station right now and give it to them and make a statement. They can send it to the lab in Trenton and analyze it and if it's the same as the poison that killed Jamie, I imagine Valerie will have some questions to answer. Now go fast, because they're gonna want to know why you didn't go straight to them, and you don't want to get in trouble with the D.A."

Patrick went.

Kit said, "Tom's right. The man's an amazing actor."

"I thought Tom did pretty well, too, with that straight-faced response, didn't you?" asked Kathryn, attempting to pull herself out of the emotional pit she had fallen into.

"Indeed I did."

They nodded looks of approval at him and he made them a mock bow.

"The only one," Kathryn said, "who nearly gave the game away, my sweet, was you."

"You didn't really expect me to shake hands with him?" Kit inquired.

"If you had I wouldn't have touched you for a week," replied Kathryn with a set look.

The phone rang. It was Father Mark.

"Kathryn? By any mad chance is Tom Holder with you?"

"Yes, he's here."

"Thank God. May I speak with him, please?"

"Sure. Hang on."

"Tom? Mark Randall."

Tom took the telephone. "Father Mark?"

"Tom, I know you're unofficial right now, but Kathryn says you know more about what's really happening in this investigation than anybody else does and I believe her. That's why I'm asking you. I've just had Shirley Massey on the phone in hysterics. Apparently they've arrested Link for the murder of Mason Blaine. Before I go over there to try to comfort her, it would be really helpful if you would tell me whether he did it or not."

CHAPTER 23

Tom took a deep breath. "Arrested. By the District Attorney?"

"She didn't say."

Tom thought a moment. "It had to be the D.A. He's in charge of the case now. Give me a couple of minutes to try to get hold of him, see if I can find out what's going on. Call you right back." He hung up before the Rector could respond, pulled his cell phone out of his pocket, and punched one of the preprogrammed numbers as he told Kathryn what had happened.

"Nick? Tom Holder. I hear you've arrested Lincoln Massey for the murder of Mason Blaine."

"Tom!" Silverman cried with immense affability. "We're just doing the bookings now. I was going to call you after that, let you know about it before I hold the press conference since you helped me out a bit before you went off the deep end over your little secretary. The people in New York you had tailing Crystal Montoya sent some nice juicy pictures of her having lunch in the Plaza with Lincoln Massey and then getting in an elevator and not reappearing for three hours. We know she and Blaine used to be lovers. Now, get this. Massey lives three doors down from Mason Blaine, did you know that? I figure it this way: Blaine is walking home. Massey is also out for a walk, it's a nice evening. They run into each other. The ex-lover and the current lover get into an argument. Massey kills Blaine. He doesn't want to leave the body there because it's too close to his own house, we'll connect the murder with him. So he puts the body in his car and drives around trying to figure out where to safely dump a body where he won't be seen. Answer, St. Margaret's Church."

"Bookings."

"Huh?"

"You said bookings, plural."

"Oh, yeah. We also arrested Crystal Montoya for the murder of Jamie Newman. I saw in your notes that Massey bought her way into the MacDonalds' party. Obviously they were afraid the girl spotted something in the church that night and Massey sent Montoya to the party with the cyanide all ready to dispose of her."

"Yeah, well I see you got it all worked out. Congratulations."

"Thanks, Tom. I gotta go, now. Bit of a madhouse, here. You understand."

"Oh sure. Bye, Nick." He hung up.

Kathryn instantly shrieked, "He hasn't *really* got it all worked out, has he? What's all this crap about Link Massey?"

Tom smiled beatifically. "All this crap about Link Massey is that our dear District Attorney has just arrested one of the richest and most powerful men in this town on a charge of murder, when all he's guilty of is adultery. He's also arrested his mistress on another charge of murder, which means the rich man's wife's gonna find out all about what he's been up to."

Kathryn smiled with unholy glee. "Which means the rich man is going to be very, *very* unhappy with the District Attorney, and the District Attorney is going to look like a fool. Which of course he is." She got up and began to dance around the room singing the Halleluia Chorus from Handel's Messiah.

"Excuse me," Kit interrupted politely. "Would somebody mind terribly telling me who all these people are?"

"Just as soon as I make a phone call," Tom replied. "Kathryn, can I do a call-back on your phone?"

"Sure."

"Father Mark? Tom. Tell Shirley Link didn't kill Mason Blaine. But listen. The reason he's been arrested is, he's having an affair with Crystal Montoya, and they've arrested Crystal for the murder of Jamie Newman, which is also wrong, she didn't do it. But the business about the affair is probably going to come out because of the two arrests, so I thought I'd better tell you about it. Sure. You're welcome. Bye."

Then Tom explained to Kit who "all these people" were, also filling Kathryn in on Nick Silverman's theory of the double homicide.

When he finished Kathryn frowned. "It's actually pretty good, isn't it, Tom?"

"Oh, yeah. It only leaves out four little details that I can think of, off the top of my head. One, how come

Link was taking a walk with a blunt instrument in his hand ready to clobber Mason Blaine over the head if he happened to run into him? Two, when Link planted Blaine's body in the St. Margaret's driveway, why did he carefully put him in the middle of the driveway instead of just dumping him where he would have naturally come out of the car, on the side? Three, why did he stick a knife in Blaine's back? Was he carrying that on his walk, too? Or did he go back into his house to get the knife after he clonked Blaine over the head with this blunt instrument he was already carrying? And four, assuming Crystal went to the party with cyanide to kill Tracy, why put it in ice cubes?"

Kathryn sighed. "I don't know whether I'm relieved or disappointed. Of course I want you to be right and the idiot asshole District Attorney wrong. But there are other issues here."

"I understand."

"Never mind. What do we do now?"

"We look for the car. Does Patrick own one?"

"No."

"He probably wouldn't have used his own anyway. If you lived in this town and were planning a murder and needed to rent a car to move the body in, where would you go?"

"To one of the car rental agencies at Newark Airport."

"Smart girl. Why?"

"It's out of town. They do a huge volume of business. It's anonymous. Nobody would remember me."

"Right. So we are looking for a needle in a haystack. At least we have a name and a date and there are only so many agencies. The tricky bit is that we haven't got any authority. If we did we could subpoena the records, no problem. But we can't. Instead we're going to somehow have to talk these people into letting us have information that normally they should be keeping private. How are we going to do that?"

"Did they take your badge away from you?"

"No."

"No problem, then. How are these car rental agencies going to know what your status is? You go in, you say, 'I'm looking for a car that was rented by this guy on this date, you show your badge, you say it's in connection with a homicide investigation, you say you can get a court order if necessary, but it'll be so much easier if they'll just check their records, and *if* the guy rented it from them, great, if not you'll move on. And if the car is *there*, you'll rent it and drive off with it and we'll take it down to Trenton and let all the scientists go over it because if it carried Mason Blaine's dead body there'll be traces. And if God *really* loves us, this famous blunt instrument will turn out to be the crowbar."

"You know, that could work. Even though I'm off the case, my buddy Sid knows all those guys and most of them hate Silverman's guts. He could probably get them to take a look at the car."

"If that doesn't work, maybe Sid knows where there are private labs where we could get the work done. Maybe not in Trenton, but perhaps in Newark. Certainly in Manhattan. In fact, that's probably a better idea. We don't want to get Sid and company in trouble. Furthermore, we don't want Silverman stepping in and taking the credit for your solution once the labs in Trenton have produced the evidence. Why don't you get on the horn and ask Sid where we could find a suitable private lab?"

"Kathryn, I might not be able to afford it."

"I told you not to worry about money, remember? I hired you."

"Well, things have changed a bit since then."

"Not that much, they haven't. Call Sid."

Tom called Sid.

When Tom had him on the phone, Kathryn insisted he hand the instrument over to her. Sure enough, Sid knew some private labs, and frabjous day! He had a friend who owned one that occupied a brownstone in lower Manhattan. The frabjous thing about it was that the friend lived in an apartment on the top floor of the brownstone, so if they were lucky enough to find the car that afternoon, they could drive it into the city and leave it with the friend that afternoon and he and his staff would start work on it first thing in the morning.

"But Kathryn," Sid warned. "This guy is expensive."

Kathryn had walked into the kitchen with the telephone, which is why she had taken it away from Tom—in case she needed to discuss money with Sid.

"Am I going to need to take cash, or will he take my American Express gold card?"

"The gold card will do fine, but you should pardon me asking, how much are you willing to spend on Tom?"

"Not much more than a million dollars."

"I'm serious."

"So am I."

"No, really."

"Sid, how shall I put this without being vulgar? I am a very wealthy woman. Tom is my dear friend. I would be willing if necessary to sell the house I live in to get him his job back. The house I live in is a three-story five-bedroom pre-Revolutionary on Alexander Street. I mean every word I have just said. Do I make myself clear?"

Sid whistled. "Very. When do I get to see the house?"

"The minute this is all over."

They hung up.

Sid said to himself, *I don't care what you think, Tom, old friend, the lady's in love with you.*

Kathryn went back to the living room and returned Tom's phone to him and explained to him that they had a lab to take the car to provided they could find it.

"Does this mean you're coming with me to Newark?"

"Try to stop me. But first I should change into clericals. I get a lot more cooperation when I'm in a collar."

Kit, who had for some time been waiting patiently for the other two to remember his existence, at this point ventured, "I don't want to sound insufferable, but if you *really* want to know about cooperation you should try showing up in a wheelchair."

Tom was made slightly uncomfortable by this remark, but Kathryn, who knew Kit better, and knew he was as free of self-pity as it was possible for a man in his situation to be, lit up with pleasure. "You want to go with us?"

"You've just dragged me right way 'cross the Atlantic into the middle of a double homicide investigation; I arrive to find you're about to solve it, and you want to park me in a hotel while you two run off and have all the fun? Not bloody likely!"

"Great! Wait here while I change, I won't be a minute!"

By the time Kathryn got back downstairs sporting a navy wool suit with a light blue shirt and a white dog collar (she owned clerical suits in charcoal and dark rose but she had deliberately chosen the blue to match what Kit was wearing) the men had come up with a strategy. They would travel to Newark in two cars. Tom would take his badge and his official tactics to the likelier agencies, that is, the less expensive ones. Kathryn and Kit would go to Hertz and Avis, the long shots, as ordinary customers with some tale they could concoct along the way.

"He's too polite to tell us in so many words," Kit said to Kathryn, "but basically I think he's afraid we'd cramp his style."

Tom opened his mouth to protest but Kathryn agreed that certainly a cop would look more convincing without a couple of civilians trailing along. She then exchanged cell phone numbers with Tom so they could keep in touch, and announced that she for one was ready to go. "Except, of course, that it's teatime and here we are dashing off without it."

Enter Mrs. Warburton, on cue, from the kitchen. "Tom, this bag's for you. Earl Grey, of course, and sandwiches. Kathryn, this one's for you and Kit, the blue thermos is for you, that's Earl Grey, and the green thermos is for Kit, that's Lapsang Souchong. And Kit, the roast beef is *very* rare."

Mrs. Warburton sailed back into the kitchen, and Kathryn turned to Kit and whispered, "What did I tell you?"

Kit whispered back, "Awesome!"

Kit got himself into Kathryn's car with agility, leaned out, folded up his chair, picked it up, pulled it into the car, passed it over his left shoulder and dropped it into the backseat. Kathryn reflected that as long as you didn't present him with a flight of stairs, he did pretty well for himself. She knew he had tremendous upper-body strength. Not only had she felt the iron muscles in his arms during the nights she'd spent in his bed the previous summer; she'd also seen him in the room in his vast Tudor mansion that he'd had converted to a gym. There he exercised daily every muscle in his body that still worked in order to compensate for his useless legs. He always swore he would never use a motor-driven wheel-chair. "That way lies death. I'll spin my own wheels, thank you."

As they pulled away from the curb, Kathryn said, "You realize, don't you, that our end of this little jaunt is completely useless? Tom's going to be the only one that actually accomplishes something."

"If you think it's that bad then why are we going?"

"I don't know. For the merry hell of it, I guess. And maybe because if we didn't go, Tom might feel like he'd cut me out of it and then maybe he'd feel bad. I'm not really sure. Why did you guys arrange it the way you did? Two separate parties? We could have all driven to-gether, and Tom could have gone into each office alone."

"It was Tom who suggested it. I got the impression he was gallantly allowing us time to be alone together."

"Oh. Well, that was nice of him."

"I thought so."

There was a brief silence while Kathryn threaded her way out of Harton.

"Shall we work on this story of ours, then?" Kit sug-gested.

They did that, and when they were satisfied with it, they dropped it for conversation of a more personal na-ture.

When they approached the vicinity of Newark Air-port, Kathryn followed the signs for car rentals and then for Hertz. As she pulled to a stop outside the office, Kit was already hauling his chair out of the backseat and opening his door; she knew better than to offer him any assistance. She merely lingered a moment to give him time to unfold the chair and get himself into it, but he accomplished this maneuver so rapidly, she didn't have to wait more than a few seconds. She looked at him, and said, "Are you sure you're up for this charade?"

He smiled and shrugged. "What's there to lose? All they can do is say no. Besides, as you pointed out, Tom has the likely places. Let's do it."

So they did it. And, precisely as they expected, they did not get the information they wanted.

Back in the car, Kathryn said to Kit, "I say, you're quite an actor! That was *very* impressive. I didn't know you could do that."

"Oh, I have all sorts of talents you have yet to learn about. You have a lifetime to get acquainted with them."

This was so extraordinarily similar to Patrick's remark on the night of the fateful party that Kathryn's heart skipped a beat.

"What's the matter?" Kit asked, concerned. "Did I say something wrong?"

"No," said Kathryn. "It's all right. A touch of *déjà vu*. Forget it. Let's move on, if you're willing to go through it again."

"I am an Englishman, and therefore nothing if not bloody-minded."

They drove to Avis.

Inside the Avis office, Kathryn did a quick assessment of the people behind the counter. It was instantly clear to her that they must avoid the young black woman with the golden cornrows and the big smile. That one had brains; she would see through them in a second. There was a teenage boy with microscopically short hair and a faint smattering of acne. Much more promising. Kathryn stepped into his line and Kit rolled up beside her.

When they got to the head of the line they launched

into their routine. As rehearsed, Kathryn went first. "Hello, I hope you can help us. A friend of ours who lives in Harton rented a car here on Thursday of last week—"

"Darling," Kit interrupted, "we only *think* he rented it Thursday, he may have rented it a day or so earlier."

"That's right," Kathryn acknowledged. "We know he had it Thursday night because that's when he took us out to dinner."

"The point is, you see," Kit continued, "is that I am missing a ring, a very small gold ring." He held up his hands and with the fingers of his right hand encircled the fourth finger of his left. "I have racked my brain and searched the house and the last time I can be absolutely sure I had it was that Thursday, so the only thing I can think of is that it must have slipped off in that car. We've been to the restaurant and nobody turned it in and we searched all around the booth where we ate and we couldn't find it. So—"

"Would you like to look in our lost and found box, sir?"

"Of course," said Kit promptly.

As the boy disappeared through a door into the back premises, Kathryn opened her purse and extracted a piece of paper. The boy came back with a cardboard box about eighteen inches square and nine inches deep, which he handed over the counter into Kit's outstretched hands.

Kathryn's full attention was on her part, now. "Frankly I think the chances of the ring being in that box are pretty slim because it's a tiny thing and I don't think your clean-up crew will have spotted it. This is what we'd like to do. We want to rent the car our friend rented and go over it ourselves. This is his name and address. Can you look in your records and find which car it was?"

The boy hesitated. Kathryn held her breath.

"I dunno. Maybe I'd better ask the manager."

The boy went over to whisper into the ear of the young black woman. Kathryn was not in the least bit surprised. She turned to see how Kit was doing with his rummage through the lost and found box. In order to facilitate his search for his fictional tiny ring, he had tossed onto the countertop a large, ugly knitted scarf in outdated shades of avocado and orange. Kathryn glanced at it and then executed a classic double take. She stared at it transfixed for a good four seconds, her mouth hanging open, before seizing it to examine it more carefully.

Kit looked up from the lost and found box. "What is it?" he asked.

The young black woman approached them and said, "I'm Loreen Sanchez. I'm the manager. I understand you've lost a ring. Have you found it?"

Kathryn said urgently, "Forget the ring. It's not important. This scarf. Do you keep a record of the cars that lost items come out of?"

Kathryn knew immediately that she had not been wrong in her estimate of Loreen Sanchez's intelligence. In response to Kathryn's intensity, Loreen's eyes narrowed shrewdly. "No. But I remember this one. Now, Charlie here tells me you want to know which car you lost a ring in. Hadn't you people better make up your minds?"

Kathryn took a deep breath. "Ms. Sanchez, I apologize. We weren't really looking for a ring, we were looking for a killer. But we are only the B team. The A team is going to the budget rental agencies, because that's where the killer probably rented the car. Forget the ring, there was never a ring, we made it up. But this scarf is very real, and it belongs to the wife of the Chief of Police of Harton, and she has been missing since Sunday afternoon, and if you'll excuse me for a moment, I'm going to make a phone call." She pulled her cell phone out of her purse, punched in Tom's number, and waited with bated breath for him to answer. "Tom? Drive to Avis. Now. Do not pause for breath. Step on it. No, just come. Now." She hung up.

Loreen Sanchez looked at her. "You're sure about this? You sure you recognize it?"

"Absolutely. I've seen it about eighty times. I go to church with the woman. See this funny stripe here? It's supposed to be her initials, L.H. Are *you* sure you remember what car it came out of? And was it by any mad chance a stretch limo?"

Loreen looked at her with respect. "Indeed it was. But if what you say is true, I should be calling the police."

"Don't bother. I just called them for you. That was the lady's husband, the Police Chief himself, and he is the one who was doing the other car rental agencies looking for this killer I was talking about, so he should be here any second."

Kathryn looked down at Kit and made a little grimace of excitement.

He said with a smile, "I guess we weren't so useless after all."

A few minutes later Tom walked in the door and said to Kathryn, "What's all this about?"

"Look what Kit found in the lost and found box." She held out the scarf.

Tom stood for a moment staring at it, completely dumbfounded. "What the hell—" he said at last, taking the scarf from Kathryn and turning it over in his hands as though he could scarcely believe his eyes.

"It's Louise's, isn't it?" Kathryn asked.

Tom nodded, apparently still too surprised to talk.

"The manager here," Kathryn continued, "says she remembers what car it came out of, and it was a stretch limo. I'm sure if you show her your badge, she'll tell you who rented it."

Tom pulled himself together. He stepped up to the counter and pulled out his credentials and said in his most commanding manner, "My name is Holder, I'm Chief of Police of Harton and I'm investigating the disappearance of my wife last Sunday afternoon. According to witnesses she was seen leaving our home in a stretch limo. If you have any information I'd appreciate hearing it."

Loreen Sanchez said, "I *knew* there was something about that man! I *knew* it! It was the second time he came in here this month. The first time all he wanted was a midsize sedan, nothing special, but I knew the minute I laid eyes on him he was up to no good. He was wired. I don't mean on drugs. On adrenaline. I made notes on him. And I recognized him when he came in again to rent the stretch limo, and when he brought it back in again, I talked to the clean-up crew when they were through with it, and I looked at that scarf. It's not the kind of thing that gets left in a stretch limo, you know what I mean?"

"Yeah," Tom agreed. "It belongs to my wife, and she's not a stretch limo type at all. You made *notes* on the guy? You are my kind of woman. You should be a cop. So you can tell me who he is?"

"Just one second."

Loreen went into the back room and came out again

and handed Tom a photocopied piece of paper on which were some handwritten notes. The photocopy was of a driver's license and insurance card, and the notes described Loreen's impression of the "wired" man who had come into the office in early October to rent a midsize sedan. The man's name was Joel Norton. He lived in Harton.

"Norton," Tom said. "Son of a bitch. Clients in Philadelphia, my ass."

"Come again?" asked Kathryn.

"I was in his office in Trenton," said Tom, disgusted with himself. "T.N.K. Public Relations. His secretary said yeah, he'd rented a stretch limo to pick up some clients who flew in from the West Coast, and the clients wanted to go to Philadelphia for some reason, so that's where the limo took them. And I said fine and walked out and didn't even bother to verify it because I was too damned eager to get back to Harton and talk to Patrick Cunningham about effing ice cubes."

"Well, you can talk to him now. Or at least, you can talk to him as soon as we find Patrick's car."

"Oh. Don't worry about that. I found the car."

"You found the car?"

"Found it, got it, rented it. It's sitting outside the door there."

CHAPTER 24

After a brief round of congratulations they discussed logistics. The original plan had been that if they were successful in finding the car, Tom would drive it to the lab in Manhattan and take a bus back to Newark Airport to pick up his own car. Now, however, it was agreed that Tom really ought to get to Harton to tackle Mr. Joel Norton, whoever he might be, as soon as possible.

"Look, Tom," Kathryn said. "Why don't you drive Kit back to Harton and drop him at his hotel, then go hunt down this Norton guy, and I'll drive the car to New York?"

Kit assumed a highly affronted air and asked, "You assume I'm incapable of traveling by public transportation?"

"It's just that when we say blithely, 'Take a bus back here,' neither of us really knows what we're talking about. It might involve eighty-seven changes, and you *were* on a transatlantic jet all day yesterday. Aren't you the least bit tired?"

"I didn't want to say anything, but since you mention it, I am beginning to feel it a bit."

"Go with Tom, then."

"Gladly."

"Have a little nap, and call me when you wake up."

"Will do."

After a brief stop back at Budget Rent a Car to put Kathryn on the papers as an additional driver, they went their separate ways.

Kathryn had never driven from Newark to New York City and she wasn't looking forward to it. She managed to find a classical music channel on the radio, and she prayed for calm. By some miracle she made all the right turns, took all the right exits. Once in Manhattan she breathed a prayer of thanks. The city streets might be a bit of a headache, but if you missed a turn all you had to do was go around the block; you didn't have to go twenty miles before you could correct your mistake. She managed to find the lab without too much difficulty, rang the night bell, met Sid's friend (who accepted her gold card with complaisance), and explained carefully to him what was required. Then, back out on the street, she considered public transportation for approximately two and a half seconds before she chickened out and hailed a cab.

Tom and Kit, meanwhile, were managing to converse amicably.

Kit said, "I had time to put in a quick phone call to Datchworth before I left, to tell Crumper I was coming. I thought he might want to send you his regards. I was right. He does."

Tom grinned. "Send him mine."

"He also wants to know if you're doing anything about that matter you discussed last summer when you were lying in hospital nursing that concussion."

"Tell him I said to get off my back."

Kit laughed. "You and Crumper have some scheme going?"

"*Crumper* has some scheme going."

"Am I allowed to know what it is?"

"No."

Kit, the perfect gentleman, changed the subject.

Crumper, the butler at Datchworth Castle, had tried in vain to convince a skeptical Tom that he would stand a fighting chance with Kathryn if he would get a college degree.

Soon afterwards, Tom made a remark to which he got no reply, and glancing over at his passenger, saw that he was fast asleep. He wasn't sorry. This way he would be spared about an hour's conversation. Damn Kit Mallowan. He was nice, he was pleasant, he was charming. And that was the whole problem. Tom didn't *want* him to be all those things. Tom wanted to be able to dislike him. Since he knew that this attitude was entirely unworthy of a Christian and a decent guy, he had the grace to be ashamed of it, so he decided to think about something else. That wasn't difficult.

Who the hell was Joel Norton of T.N.K. Public Relations and what on God's green earth did he want with Louise? What kind of scam was this? It certainly wasn't a straightforward kidnapping; no ransom had been demanded. It wasn't an elopement, either. Let alone the fact that Louise had lost all sense of her own sexuality years ago, and now presented herself in such a fashion that no sane man could possibly look at her with desire, Tom had seen the photo on the driver's license. Norton was, as far as he was able to judge, a reasonably good-looking man. No, Norton wasn't eloping with Louise. What *was* he doing with her? And why?

The firm, T.N.K. Public Relations, had looked perfectly respectable. Of course, he'd only seen two of the employees, a receptionist and a secretary. They were the foundation of his impression of the firm's respectability. Mr. Taylor, Mr. Norton, and Mr. K., whatever the *K* stood for, might be crooks, for all he knew, and the women who worked for them might not know it. After all, "public relations" was a vague kind of thing, wasn't it? You could use it for a front for almost anything.

For the first time since Louise had disappeared, Tom began to seriously worry about her. He knew she hadn't been bound and gagged and dragged away; Dorabella Mason said she had walked out of the house and gotten into that car. But obviously somebody had persuaded her to do it. She had been told some sort of tale. She had been duped. And now she was in the hands of a man who, in the words of that clever young woman at the car rental agency, was up to no good. So far that man hadn't made a move, but the move would come sometime.

He had wanted Louise. A batty, middle-aged woman. Suddenly it was appallingly clear to Tom why someone would want Louise. She was the wife of a cop. Worse. She was *his* wife. Was this going to turn out to be some kind of vengeance from somebody he'd put away? He hadn't put away Joel Norton, obviously, but had somebody hired Norton to do the dirty work?

Tom pressed the accelerator a quarter-inch closer to the floor.

Kit came back to life as they slowed coming into the suburbs of Harton and apologized for drifting off; Tom explained what he'd figured out as Kit slept. As they pulled up to the curb in front of the Harton Inn, Kit already had the door open and was unfolding his chair at lightning speed. "Look, I'll go have a brief kip and when I wake up in about two hours I shall expect a full report. Of course you'll have called Kathryn, won't you?" He swung himself expertly into the chair, waved cheerfully at Tom, slammed the car door, and rolled himself up the walk.

Tom headed rapidly off toward the address of Joel Norton.

Norton lived in an affluent neighborhood but not an old one. As Tom drove hurriedly through it looking for the right house, he had time for a few quick impressions. It had rather a naked look about it compared to Mason Blaine's street, he thought. Most of the houses were different takes on fake Colonial with circular driveways, twelve-foot trees that had been bought from nurseries, and lawns that had very obviously been planted in square feet of turf no more than two years previously. Tom realized that his own street looked more honestly homey than this one did, and wasn't sure he would switch if somebody offered him the chance. For all its obvious wealth, this place looked so—what was the word? He'd heard somebody at church use it. Ersatz. That was it.

There was the number. Tom pulled into the drive, got out of his car, went up the front steps, and rang the bell in a fever of impatience. Nobody answered. He rang again. And again. And again. He knocked loudly on the door until his knuckles hurt. No response. There were narrow windows on either side of the door. He peered through one of them, but saw no movement within. He swore.

He went back down the steps, walked across the carefully manicured grass, and looked into a window at what turned out to be the dining room. There was nobody in it. He continued around the corner of the house, looking in windows as he went, until he had circumnavigated the entire house without spying any sign of life. He felt like screaming with frustration.

He walked across the grass to the neighbors' house and rang the bell. Here he was more successful.

The door was answered by a woman whose hairdresser should have told her that it is a mistake to keep one's hair black when one's skin has lost its youth. She looked at Tom sharply, recognizing in an instant that his clothes did not belong in her circle.

"May I help you?" she said in not very friendly tones.

"I'm looking for Joel Norton. Do you know where I can find him?"

"The Nortons are away for the weekend," she said repressively. "You should try tomorrow morning."

"Not tonight?"

"No, tomorrow morning." And she actually shut the door in his face. Tom was now quite positive that he would not trade his comfortable little house for one in this neighborhood. In fact, he was rather surprised the woman had told him when the Nortons were expected home. Maybe it had just been the quickest way to get rid of him. Resisting a childish urge to shoot the finger at the closed door in front of him, he abandoned the premises of the black-haired woman and went back to his car.

He sat behind the wheel for a moment in thought,

then switched on the ignition and drove to the station. Suspended or not, he had a major piece of evidence and a report to make.

At the station he went into his office (nobody made a move to stop him) and called Nick Silverman at home. He told him about the scarf and Loreen Sanchez and Joel Norton and said he wanted a search warrant for Norton's house. He knew that Silverman wouldn't have any choice but to agree with him.

He did. He even managed to congratulate Tom on finding a lead in Louise's disappearance. He allowed as how, under the circumstances, Tom might be allowed to return to duty. He, Nick, would make some calls; Tom could consider himself reinstated. Tom courteously thanked him, then asked guilelessly if Link Massey or Crystal Montoya had confessed yet; Silverman said they hadn't, but he was still working on them. Tom hung up and set out on the uphill task of finding a judge on a Sunday.

It took him two hours. It was fully dark when he returned to the Nortons' charmless neocolonial neighborhood with two squad cars and several officers, among them one who didn't need keys to open locks.

Tom didn't know what he expected to find. He did not expect to find Louise, either wandering around or trussed up in the attic. He had the oddest notion that Louise was in Philadelphia. That secretary had said Norton's clients had wanted to see Philadelphia, so that's where the limo had taken them, and Tom thought the secretary was honest. She was simply repeating what Norton had told her, and he might well have told her where the limo had actually gone because that could be verified.

The searchers spread out all over the house. Tom wandered aimlessly into the living room, which was full of furniture that was beautiful without being intimidating. It was upholstered in blue and yellow and Tom found it quite pleasant. Norton might be a bastard, but Mrs. Norton obviously had taste. Or maybe they just had a good decorator. Just as that thought was passing through Tom's mind, his eye fell on a photograph in a large silver frame sitting on the mantle over the fireplace. He went over to look at it. There was Norton, smiling widely, with his arm around a woman his own age who could only be his wife.

Tom's jaw dropped.

Impossible. Insane.

It was Suzy Norton. Norton, for God's sake! Suzy! Suzy Norton was on the vestry at St. Margaret's! He knew she was married but he'd never met her husband because he never came to church. It happened like that sometimes, you had women whose husbands never darkened the door.

Suzy Norton's husband had kidnapped Louise. The world had gone nuts. Tom walked over to a blue and yellow plaid sofa and sat heavily down on it. Crazy. It made no sense at all.

It still didn't make any sense an hour later when the search team was finished, having found nothing that did not belong in an ordinary, upper-middle-class home. The search team went away and Tom, as he had promised, put in a call to Kathryn.

"Well, we didn't find anything you'd call suspicious. No signs of criminal activity, anything like that. It was just an ordinary house with ordinary stuff in it. Except for one thing."

"What was that?"

"A photograph of Norton and his wife in the living room."

"What was so special about that?"

"You'd recognize his wife."

"Would I?"

"Her name is Suzy."

"You're *shitting* me!"

"No."

"Tom! Our villain is Suzy Norton's *husband*?"

"Yep. I had the same reaction you're having."

There was a short silence. "Kathryn?"

"My mind has seized up. I'm struggling to find speech."

"Well, that's a historical first."

She blew a raspberry at him through the phone and he laughed.

"There's nothing we can do now," he told her, "until they get back, which according to the neighbor is tomorrow morning. Though of course we'll have the house watched to see if they show up sometime during the night."

"Oh, Tom, the suspense must be killing you! To be so close to knowing and have to wait."

She had hit it exactly. That's what was eating him. Now that he knew who had taken Louise, now that he had some hunch where she might be, stashed away in all probability alive and well in order to be used in some plot against him, the thing driving him wild was not concern for his wife, but curiosity. He wanted to know who was behind it all, what they had against him, and what their plan for vengeance was. Thwarting that plan was no longer a problem; after all, he would have not only

Norton but Norton's wife. Norton would hand over Louise in a second.

It was at once both gratifying and painful to have Kathryn understand him so well. "I imagine I'll survive," he said. "By the way, it occurs to me I haven't even thanked you for finding that scarf. If it wasn't for you and Kit, I'd have never found Joel Norton. Tell him I said thanks. And you guys have a nice time tonight."

"Thanks, Tom. I'll tell him."

She turned to Kit, who was sitting next to her on the sofa, fortifying himself after his nap with a strong cup of tea. "Tom thanks us for finding the scarf, and wishes us a pleasant evening."

"That's kind of him. I have every intention of having an *extremely* pleasant evening. Every bit as pleasant as my last evening."

CHAPTER 25

Tom was up at 5:30 on Monday morning, not because he expected anything to happen so early but because dawn rising had become habitual since the murder of Mason Blaine.

He had a terrible headache, almost as if he'd drunk himself stupid the night before, which he hadn't. For a while he couldn't figure out why this should be, then finally decided it was an emotional hangover. How he had gotten through church on Sunday, and coffee hour afterward, God only knew.

It had been the hardest thing he'd ever done.

And then he'd had to show up at her house in the afternoon as if nothing had happened, and watch all those students doing the Witherspoon imitation and try to concentrate on the case. Well, actually, once it had started he hadn't had any difficulty concentrating. Thank God for that. At least his brain still worked.

But then as soon as it was over he had to watch her crying, and of course it was Kit who got to comfort her, not him. It had been kind of her to volunteer to go to Newark with him, but it was so awkward. It was better the way they worked it, better that he went alone.

And now, how was he ever going to face her again? How were they going to go on being friends? That was his greatest terror, that their friendship had been destroyed, that she would never feel comfortable with him again. He had spent the entire remainder of Sunday night in an agony of apprehension about that. Come to think of it, no wonder he had a headache.

But tomorrow, in the immortal words of Scarlett O'Hara, is another day, and headache or no, Monday brought him other things to think about. Joel Norton was supposed to return to Harton on Monday morning. And the lab in New York City (bribed, had he but known it, with a semiastronomical sum) had promised their report for that morning as well. Tom could not have slept past 5:30 if he'd tried, and he didn't try. He took four aspirin, got dressed, went downstairs, and made some coffee.

At 6:00 he made the first call to the unmarked car parked two doors down from the Nortons' house. Not that he expected anything; he just couldn't wait. Needless to say, they had nothing to report. He made himself a substantial breakfast, fetched the paper from the front yard, and tried to concentrate on the front page while he worked his way through his eggs and bacon and toast. Random thoughts about Joel Norton and the lab report kept him from concentrating. Worse, much worse, there were sudden moments when his stomach felt a hollow pain when he remembered Sunday morning. He plodded through the sports section without taking in more than a tenth of it. Finally it was 7:30 and he gave himself permission to do the dishes and leave the house. He drove over to the Nortons' and joined the team in the unmarked car. At least they could all sit and be impatient together.

It was shortly after 9:00 when a late-model Lincoln came down the street and pulled into the Nortons' driveway. The garage door opened to reveal a red LeBaron convertible. The Lincoln pulled in beside it and the garage door closed.

"O.K.," said Tom. "Lucy, Fred. This guy is mine. We have no reason to believe he's armed, and he's with his wife, who goes to my church. I'm gonna go pay a nice social call."

Tom went up to the front door and rang the bell. After a couple of minutes the door was opened by Suzy Norton, slightly travel-weary and very surprised to see him.

"Tom! Hello! Uh, won't you come in? Is this vestry business? I'm sorry, I'm a bit out of it, we just got back from Boston, we were visiting my daughter, she's at Harvard . . ." She stopped talking without actually reaching a period, and looked at him uncertainly.

By this time Tom was standing in the front hall. "Actually, Suzy, I'm here to see your husband."

"My *husband*? I didn't even know that you knew Joel."

"I don't. But I'd like to. Why don't you introduce us?"

"I can't. Not right now. I left him at the airport. We caught the shuttle back from Boston to Newark, you see. He went to rent a limo to go pick up some clients in Philadelphia, and I drove the car back home."

"Tell me about these clients in Philadelphia."

"Tom, I don't understand. Is something wrong? Is Joel in trouble?"

"Don't worry. Suzy, it'll all be fine," he lied. "Just tell me everything you know about the clients in Philadelphia."

"Joel just said they flew in from the West Coast—oh, last week sometime, and they're a big contract so the firm wants to pamper them so they rented them a limo and said, 'Your wish is our command,' so to speak, and they wanted to see Philly, so the limo took them there and they checked into a hotel and they've been sightseeing and now they're ready to come to Trenton to do business so Joel is going to go pick them up. That's all I know."

Tom considered a moment and then pulled out his cell phone. He punched the number for directory assistance and asked for the Avis office at Newark Airport. When he got that number, he keyed it in and asked for Loreen Sanchez.

"Loreen? Tom Holder. I'm the Police—"

"I remember you."

"Did that guy come in again this morning and rent another stretch limo?"

"I came in late today, Chief Holder, because my mother was sick and I had to take her to the doctor. If I'd have seen that man I'd have called you right away. Let me talk to my people here. I'm gonna put you on hold a minute, O.K.?"

She was back in less than three minutes. "Yes, sir, he was here. Stretch limo, same as before, and I have the license plate number."

Tom had used some of his time on hold to pull a small notebook and a pen from his pocket. He said, "Shoot."

Loreen gave him the number. "Listen," she said, "I sure am sorry I didn't know about this the minute it happened. I'd have called you right away."

"No problem, Ms. Sanchez. It's plenty of time. We'll get him. You've been a terrific help. Thanks." He hung up.

"Tom!" Suzy wailed. "What's going on?"

"I'm sorry, Suzy, I can't tell you right now." He patted her sympathetically on the shoulder. "I suggest you have a friend come over and keep you company. This might be a rough day for you. I promise you I'll tell you everything I can as soon as I can." He left the house over her continuing gabble of questions.

Back in his own car he picked up the radio and put out an A.P.B. on the limo. "Don't stop him, just follow him. Make sure he goes to Philadelphia and picks up somebody from a hotel. If he does anything else, *then* you can stop him." He hung up and went to the other car to tell the officers there they were relieved from their vigil.

He then drove to the station and tried to find something to occupy himself with until the report came from the lab in New York. When the phone rang he jumped, and grabbed it with a breathless "hello," but it was only Sid Garvey.

"The little packet of crystals you sent down on Saturday," Sid said. "It was cyanide. It was in a little cubbyhole in the library that Jamie Newman shared with Valerie Powers?"

"Yeah, that's right. Called a study carrel. They're kept locked."

"What fun. And you've called Valerie Powers in for questioning again?"

"No."

"Oh. Any reason why not?"

"I don't like blondes."

"Suit yourself."

They hung up.

The limo was reported to have driven to Philadelphia and parked in a hotel parking garage.

Finally, at 9:47 precisely, came the call that Tom had been waiting for, and as he listened to the report he felt like the Psalmist who wrote, "My cup runneth over." He hung up on the lab and consulted the chart before him, which was a class schedule. He walked out of his office, summoned two uniforms, drove to the University Spanish Department, and made an arrest. Back at the station he went back to his office, sat down, took a nervous breath, and called Kathryn.

"Kathryn, I've made the arrest and I'm calling a press conference here at the station at eleven. I thought maybe you'd like to be here, if you don't have a class?"

"Oh, Tom, congratulations, and no, I don't have a class. I take it the lab came through?"

"In spades. Traces of hair and blood on the crowbar."

"Do you have to warn your buddy the District Attorney what's about to hit him?"

"Unfortunately, yes."

"Too bad. I'll see you at eleven." She hung up. *Dear God*, she thought. *I think I'm going to be sick.*

At a few minutes to eleven she walked across the forecourt of City Hall. She had decided not to bring Kit. This was Tom's moment of triumph; let him enjoy it without competition. A couple of reporters outside the building were doing live shoots into cameras already: "We are hearing reports that yet another arrest has been made in Harton's double homicide . . ." "We'll be going inside shortly to hear a statement from Police Chief Tom Holder . . ."

It was crowded inside. Kathryn wondered, in a brief moment of panic, if someone was going to ask her for her press credentials and throw her out because she didn't have any. But nobody challenged her.

They were all milling around the large lobby. At 11:00 precisely, Tom opened the door in the glass wall that separated the police station from the lobby. He walked over to a bank of microphones under a glare of lights. He looked perfectly at ease, as though he did this sort of thing every day. Kathryn realized she felt intensely proud of him.

He blinked a bit as he was hit by a barrage of flashbulbs going off, but he gave no sign of being discomposed. "Good morning," he said. "We are announcing a new development in the Mason Blaine homicide case. Because of new evidence, Lincoln Massey and Crystal Montoya have been released and all charges against them have been dropped."

He went on to announce the arrest of Patrick Cunningham for the murder of Mason Blaine, adding that Cunningham was suspected of the murder of James Newman but wasn't being charged with it for lack of evidence. He called for questions. He was asked if the police theory was still that Mrs. Newman had been the intended victim at the Alberto Chacón party and her husband had died by mistake, and Tom said no. He said that the theory now (tactfully *not* saying, "I never thought that, that was only the idiot D.A.") was that the murder of Mason Blaine had from the beginning been part of an elaborate plot to kill James Newman. He gave them the barest bones of it, and it threw them into a veritable feeding frenzy.

Kathryn watched the reporters scribbling furiously in their notebooks, and Tom was all but blinded by a renewed battery of flashbulbs. The media instantly perceived that this story was going to be a sensation.

When he finished they pressed him for more details about evidence, trial dates, and such, but when it became obvious that all the beans had been spilled that were going to get spilled, they stampeded for the exits to file their stories. Kathryn got out of the way to keep from getting trampled, and just managed to catch Tom before he got back inside the glass wall of the police station.

"Oh, there you are!" he said, smiling with sudden pleasure. "I wasn't sure you were here or not."

"Tom, I *told* you I would be here," she chided. "You were very good. Very professional. Um, may I come in?"

"Oh, yeah, yeah, come back to my office," he said, torn between pride and self-consciousness, wondering what his subordinates would think.

She refrained from conversation until he ushered her into his well-ordered domain. "You're very neat," she observed approvingly.

"Helps me keep my thoughts straight."

"You certainly kept them straight on this case. I was nowhere."

"You were too close to the people in it."

"I guess that's true. Damn it, Tom! I *hate* this. It's breaking my heart. I have always been terribly fond of Patrick. I've always thought that when he smiled, all the leprechauns in Ireland got up and danced. I've always wished that Tracy would divorce Jamie and that she and Patrick would get together." Tears were beginning to run down her cheeks.

Tom, sitting behind his desk, would have given anything to be able to get up and walk around to her and brush them away. Instead he said simply, "I'm sorry."

Kathryn understood that he was sympathizing, not apologizing, so she said, "Thank you." She got a tissue out of her purse and wiped away the tears.

"And now," she said grimly, "I have the unenviable task of going home and telling Tracy."

Tom looked at her with eyes full of what was unmistakably pity.

"What?" she asked.

"Kathryn, she knows."

"What do you mean, she knows?"

"Think about it. When you went out to her on the porch, she was already saying she'd had too much to drink and she wasn't going to have any more, even though, according to you, she looked quote, 'perfectly sober,' unquote."

Kathryn stared at him for a minute, then closed her eyes, conjuring the scene: Tracy, looking, as Tom said, perfectly sober, saying she'd had enough, saying she wasn't going to have any more, sounding oddly forced, a little awkward about it. Then Crystal showing up with the drink and handing it to her, and Tracy taking it, again awkwardly, standing there, holding it . . .

"Oh!" Kathryn cried. "Oh, *no*!" Her eyes flew open and she looked at Tom. "He told her! He told her not to drink it! When he took the glass to get her a refill, he must have told her, 'Whoever brings this back to you, and it won't be me, for God's sake don't drink it whatever you do, say you've changed your mind, you've had enough.' "

Tom nodded. "He had to have told her. Otherwise—"

"Otherwise only a maniac would poison a cocktail

meant for a woman he loved and leave it sitting around for ten minutes while he went upstairs and let anybody pick it up and take it to her. Oh, God. Oh, God. Oh, *god-damn*." Kathryn had wrapped her arms tightly around her waist and was rocking slightly in her chair. "She knew. She knew. He told her. He told her."

"It's possible that all he told her in advance was not to drink it. She might not have known what he was going to do. He might have said something like, 'Just trust me, I'll explain later.' "

"It's still accomplice after the fact. That's the term, isn't it? You'll notice she hasn't come forward and told you about it."

Tom was silent.

"Are you going to charge her with something?"

"Kathryn, I can't even charge *him* on this murder, remember? I certainly haven't got anything I can charge *her* with. The suspicion that somebody whispered something in her ear when nobody was watching? Forget it. I can't do anything. The question is, what are *you* going to do? She's your friend and she's living in your house."

"I'm going to go home and tell her to g-get the hell out," Kathryn replied, and burst into sobs.

After a minute of watching her cry, Tom couldn't stand it anymore. He got up, walked around his desk, stood behind Kathryn's chair, and rested his hands on her shoulders and gripped them firmly. She turned her head and laid her damp left cheek against his hand. After a moment he lifted his right hand and rested it gently on her hair, hoping desperately that this wasn't too much. But a miracle occurred. After about thirty seconds she stopped crying, blew her nose in a discreet and ladylike fashion, dropped the tissue in her lap, reached up and took his hand from her head, and kissed it. "Thank you, Tom," she whispered. "You are such a good friend."

"I was afraid," he confessed, "that we weren't going to be able to be friends anymore."

Kathryn, who had been fearing precisely the same thing, said, "Nonsense. Our friendship is much too valuable to allow anything to get in the way of it. Agreed?"

"Agreed."

She gave his hand a squeeze, dropped it, and made to rise from her chair. He stepped back reluctantly; it had been both heaven and torture to be that close to her, but there was no doubt that it was pure torture to move away.

"I'll walk you out," he said, but the phone rang. Joel Norton's limo had hit the city limits and appeared to be heading for Tom's neighborhood.

"Sorry, cancel that. I have to go to my house with a welcoming committee for Louise and Joel Norton."

"Oh, Tom, that's excellent! More congratulations! By the way, dare we hope that this snafu on the part of the D.A. means that the idiot asshole is going to lose his job?"

"Kathryn, I am shocked by your unchristian attitude!"

"No, you're not, you are filled with little warm fuzzies inside because your friend loves you." And she went to give him a swift kiss on the cheek. But it was one of those times when the people concerned are unsure which cheek they are supposed to be kissing, and move back and forth, and Kathryn was approaching too fast to draw back. They wound up kissing on the lips.

"Sorry!" Kathryn laughed.

"You're *apologizing*? Do it again!"

"I'd love to, but I don't think Kit would approve." With a smile and a wave she made good her escape.

CHAPTER 26

Tom stood with his heart thudding and his eyes shut, running his tongue over his lips and trying to preserve the moment in his memory forever, certain it would never happen again. He would have been extremely gratified to know that Kathryn was walking across the lobby of City Hall with butterflies playing leapfrog and turning cartwheels in her stomach and her knees feeling uncomfortably wobbly.

"This is ridiculous. It's only because you know he's in love with you," she told herself, conveniently forgetting that she'd had the same reaction when he'd kissed her on the cheek three days previously when she'd had no idea how he felt about her. She turned her mind resolutely to the unpleasant task ahead of her, and the butterflies died instantly.

Tom pulled himself together with difficulty, arranged

for backup, got into his car, and drove home. On the way he checked with the people who were following Joel Norton; yes, Norton was still headed for Tom's house.

Tom was there waiting for him. He was on the phone to the team tailing the limo, so he was at the window when it pulled up. The driver got out and circled the car, but before he could reach his passenger, the back door opened and she got out by herself and started up the walk. Tom went over to the front door and opened it.

"Hello, Louise. Welcome home. Mind telling me where you've been?"

She walked into the house without looking at him and asked in a querulous monotone, "Is there anything to eat?"

"Look in the refrigerator," he replied. He had lost interest in her. The limo driver resumed his place behind the wheel, but another passenger had gotten out of the back and was strolling up the walk. When Joel Norton got to the bottom of the front porch steps, he looked up at Tom and said insolently, "I've brought your wife back to you."

"So I see. Why don't you come in and tell me about it?"

Norton didn't hesitate. That informed Tom immediately that the man hadn't been paid; this was personal.

Like Louise, Norton walked past Tom without looking at him. He went into the modest living room, surveyed it with a curling lip, and sat down without being invited. Tom sat opposite him.

"She's really very stupid, you know," Norton began. "It was easy. I told her I was recruiting contestants for a reality television show called *Runaway*. All you had to do was be willing to walk away from your home leaving everything—family, friends, clothes, belongings, everything—without a word to anyone. You would be taken away in a stretch limo to live in a luxury hotel in Philadelphia and would be provided with everything you needed. You would be paid a thousand dollars a day for every day you could hold out before you broke down and asked to be taken home. She fell for it."

She would, Tom thought. *And she wouldn't care about my feelings.* "Why Philadelphia?"

"Cheaper than New York."

If I could fetch enough distance from this, Tom thought, *that would be funny.* "And the purpose of this was?"

"To make you suffer, of course."

"Well, you succeeded. I got in a lot of trouble. People suspected me of killing her. For a couple of days I was suspended from my job. If it wasn't for a lucky break, I might not have got it back. I hope you're going to tell me why you wanted to make me suffer?"

"Yes, you bastard. Because you're having an affair with my wife."

Tom goggled at him.

Norton went on. "Having seen *your* wife, I don't blame you, but what my wife sees in you I'm damned if I can understand. I'm not a conceited man, or at least I never thought I was, but I can't figure this out. You've let yourself go to hell physically, you're not an educated man; I know, because I had you checked out—"

Tom interrupted this litany of criticism, which was not bothering him a bit because it was beside the point; he had finally recovered from his shock sufficiently to respond. "I am *not* having an affair with your wife!"

"Oh, don't bother to deny it! I know you are!"

"On what evidence?" asked Tom, the cop.

Norton was ready for this question. "I knew she was having an affair when I became aware she was getting love letters. Sometimes they came on Saturday, you see. Blue envelopes. She told unconvincing lies about them and she burned them. And she's out during the day and sometimes during the evening when I don't expect her to be and she always says it's vestry business. Suzy is a very unoriginal liar. When she kept saying it was vestry business, I knew it had to be somebody on the St. Margaret's vestry. Then one day there was a huge bunch of red roses and she said she'd sent them to herself but she looked very nervous, she kept fidgeting with them. While she was cooking supper I found out why. She'd lost the card among the greenery. I found it. It said, 'To my darling Suzy from your loving Tom.' I got out the church directory. You're the only Tom on the vestry."

"Norton, you bastard, I am *not* having an affair with your wife. The only time I ever see your wife is in church or in vestry meetings. Your detective work seems to be accurate up to a point. I'd say your wife *is* having an affair. But it sure as hell ain't with me. Suzy is a nice lady. I like her. But," Tom said, contrasting in his mind's eye that somewhat insipid blonde with the live wire of a brunette who haunted his dreams, "she is absolutely not my type."

"I don't believe you."

"Wait a minute." Tom got up and went to the kitchen, where Louise was sitting at the table eating a sandwich and drinking a glass of milk. She ignored him and he ignored her. He began opening and closing drawers. "I know they're in here somewhere—there they are."

He went back into the living room with a pair of handcuffs.

"What the hell!" Norton exclaimed. "You can't arrest me! I haven't broken any laws!"

"The hell I can't!" Tom snarled, yanking Norton to his

feet, spinning him around, and slapping the cuffs on him with an efficiency born of years of practice. "You'd be surprised what we can do with 'breach of the peace.' Do you realize how many hours of police time you've wasted? And how many dollars of taxpayers' money? You have the right to remain silent. Anything you say may be used against you in a court of law. You have the right to an attorney . . ." And he frog-marched Norton out of the house as he recited to him the rest of his Miranda rights.

The outraged prisoner was still screaming things like, "You can't do this to me!" when Tom turned him over to the backup team. He watched them drive him away, then rubbed his chin in thought for a minute. He went back into the house, found his church directory, and called Suzy Norton.

"Suzy, it's Tom. Look, I found Joel, and I'm sorry to have to tell you this, but he is in trouble. Not life-or-death trouble, but a bit of trouble. I need to come talk to you about it. Can I come now? O.K."

He got in his car and drove over to the Nortons'.

Suzy let him in. She looked paler than ever, and frightened. "What is it, Tom?"

"Suzy, I think you should sit down."

They went into the living room, and Tom saw that Trish O'Malley was there.

"Oh. Hi, Trish."

"Hi, Tom."

"Suzy, I didn't know—"

"It's O.K., Tom. I asked Trish to come over. She's my best friend and she's going to get me through this, whatever it is."

"Suzy, it's *very* personal."

"I don't have any secrets from Trish."

"O.K., then. Here goes. You know that Louise has been missing?"

"Yes, I've been so concerned for you."

"Thank you. Well, she's back now. Joel brought her."

"*Joel* brought her?"

"He's the one that took her." And he told both women everything that Joel Norton had told him.

Toward the end of his recital, Suzy Norton began to cry quietly. Trish got up, fetched her purse, extracted some tissues from it, and handed them to her. After Suzy had used these to some effect, Trish sat down beside her and held her hand.

When Tom stopped talking, Suzy said in a small voice, "Oh, Tom, can you ever forgive me?"

"You didn't do anything to me, Suzy. It was your husband."

"That's kind of you."

He stood up to leave.

"You're not going to ask me who I *am* having an affair with?"

Tom was astonished. "That's none of my business."

The two women walked him to the door. He noticed they were still holding hands.

The scales fell from his eyes.

"Uh, you wouldn't like to tell me," he asked, "if by any chance the note on the flowers signed 'your loving Tom' was capital *T*, capital *O*, capital *M*? Not that it's any of my business!"

Trish O'Malley smiled at him. "You are a clever man, Tom Holder." And for the second time that day, a woman kissed him on the lips.

CHAPTER 27

It was April in Harton. Spring was being hailed, as always in New Jersey, like a long-lost lover.

Patrick Cunningham, confronted with irrefutable evidence that he had rented a car that contained a crowbar on which were hair and blood from the head of Mason Blaine, had confessed on the advice of his lawyer; the lawyer had used the confession in a plea bargain for a lesser sentence. Tracy had left not only Kathryn's house but her own apartment on Merton Street and the fellowship of St. Margaret's Church. No one had heard from her again.

Two days after Patrick's arrest and Louise's return, precisely as Kit had predicted, Kathryn delivered herself of a little speech something to the effect of: "Kit, dear, I'm so sorry to drag you over here and then inhospitably throw you back again, but I'm hideously behind on my work because of all this homicide business, and you are such a distraction you know . . ." Kit sighed and packed his bags.

Tom's and Kathryn's friendship survived the period of initial awkwardness. Kathryn, deliberately looking for ways to spend time with him in neutral situations, started coming to vestry meetings—a thing she had sworn she would never do—and sitting next to him. Then she would grab somebody amenable, like Tildy Harmon, after the meeting, and say, "Why don't we all go have coffee somewhere?" By January they were comfortable again.

Tom even got to the point where he would once more invite himself over for teatime consultations. In February a drunk got into a bar fight with his second cousin; later that night he went over to the cousin's house and shot him. Tom didn't have enough evidence for an arrest; he needed a confession. Kathryn offered him some advice on how to get one; he tried it, and it worked. He wanted to send her a dozen roses, but decided that was too lover-like. He discussed it with the florist and sent the arrangement she recommended. He was rewarded with an ecstatic phone call. "Tom! It's fantastic! Which florist did you use? It doesn't say on the card. I want to know because the next time I need flowers I'm going to use this florist because this is a *gorgeous* arrangement! Thank you!" He didn't touch ground for the rest of the day.

And so he went on loving her, and she went on loving Kit, but at least they were still friends. And he had the comfort of knowing, because he had seen her doing it, that she had worked to make that possible.

One major change had occurred in his life, or was about to. What Louise had done to him with this supposed *Runaway* thing was the last straw. She hadn't given a damn about him, and in not giving a damn she had jeopardized his career and his standing in the church. He went to talk to Tildy Harmon. She was appalled.

"Tom, if you want a divorce, I'll handle it for you, and by God I'll do it pro bono. And I'll get somebody else in my firm to do Louise's part pro bono, too. Do you think she'll accept it uncontested?"

"Cross your fingers and pray to God."

She did.

When Tom had told Kathryn, she had said, "Oh, Tom, congratulations! I'm so happy for you. And proud of you, too."

What Tom didn't know was that Kathryn had instantly gone to Tildy and asked if there were any costs she could help to defray behind Tom's back.

So spring came to Harton, and the events of the autumn, which had been so painful to Kathryn, had been carefully forgotten. Or at least suppressed. So it was when the Assistant to the Rector called her up and made an appointment for a lovely Thursday afternoon, Kathryn didn't have a clue what it was about.

She knocked on the door and two voices called, "Come in!"

She entered to find Maggie Nicholas and Tildy Harmon, both smiling mischievously at her.

"Hi, Maggie, Tildy. What's all this about?"

"Have a seat, Kathryn," invited Maggie, who was looking rather like an elf with a secret. "We have summoned you here in our capacity as chair and cochair of the St. Margaret's scholarship committee. On behalf of the committee, we would like to thank you for presenting us

with the happiest and easiest task we have had in years."
She looked at Tildy and they both giggled like school-
girls.

Kathryn, sinking into a chair, was completely at
sea. "But—"

Tildy rode over her. "We only had two applicants," she
said, "and one of them dropped out because she ceased
to be a member of St. Margaret's. The other applicant
was superlatively qualified, I have to say. This candidate
applied to Harton, Harvard, and Oxford, was accepted
at all three, and has chosen Oxford."

The Assistant to the Rector took up the tale. "Oxford,
I'm informed, is divided into colleges, and applicants are
supposed to list the three of these they would most like
to go to. Our candidate listed Balliol, Magdalen, and
Brasenose, and was again accepted at all three, and has
chosen Brasenose because that's where you went. We
thought you'd like that."

Kathryn's mouth was hanging open. She had forgotten all about the wretched scholarship when Tracy had
vanished from Harton. A second candidate? She had deliberately written the requirements so that only Tracy
could fulfill them.

Tildy was laughing out loud, practically cackling with
glee, enjoying Kathryn's obvious bafflement. "Come on,
Kathryn, don't you want to know who you're sending to
Oxford? Can't you guess?"

Kathryn shook her head.

Maggie mimed opening an envelope and extracting a
card. "And the winner is . . ." She looked at Tildy.

Who announced, with a smile as wide as creation,
"Tom Holder."

ABOUT THE AUTHOR

Cristina Sumners holds a B.A. in English from Vassar, an M.Div. from the General Theological Seminary of the Episcopal Church and an M.Phil. in Medieval English Studies from Oxford University. She has taught English and religious studies and has served churches in Texas and England. Married to a scientist, she lives in Taos, New Mexico.